Ian Wedde is the author of eight nov
two collections of essays, and a numb
monographs. His most recent novel is *The Reed Warbler* (2020), and *The Little Ache – a German notebook,* written while he was in Berlin to research *The Reed Warbler*, was published in July 2021. His memoir, *The Grass Catcher: A Digression About Home*, was published in 2014, and his *Selected Poems* in 2017. *Decentred: Selected Essays 2004–2020* will be published in early 2023.

Ian Wedde is the recipient of numerous awards, fellowships and grants. Among the most recent are the Meridian Energy Katherine Mansfield Memorial Fellowship at Menton in France (2005), a Fulbright New Zealand Travel Award to the USA (2006), an Arts Foundation Laureate Award (2006), a Distinguished Alumni Award from the University of Auckland (2007), an ONZM (2010), and the Landfall Essay Prize (2010). In 2011–13 Wedde was New Zealand's poet laureate. He was awarded the Creative New Zealand Writers' Residency in Berlin 2013–14, and in 2014 the Prime Minister's Award for Literary Achievement (poetry). He lives in Auckland.

The THW Classics collection
celebrates more than half a century of stellar publishing
at Te Herenga Waka—Victoria University of Wellington

The End of the Golden Weather by Bruce Mason *1962*
Ngā Uruora by Geoff Park *1995*
Breakwater by Kate Duignan *2001*
Lifted by Bill Manhire *2005*
Girls High by Barbara Anderson *1990*
Portrait of the Artist's Wife by Barbara Anderson *1992*
Wednesday to Come Trilogy by Renée *1985, 1986, 1991*
In Fifteen Minutes You Can Say a Lot by Greville Texidor *1987*
Eileen Duggan: Selected Poems edited by Peter Whiteford *1994*
Denis Glover: Selected Poems edited by Bill Manhire *1995*
The Vintner's Luck by Elizabeth Knox *1998*
Man Alone by John Mulgan edited by Peter Whiteford *1935*
Six by Six: Short Stories by New Zealand's Best Writers
edited by Bill Manhire *1989*
Wild Dogs Under My Skirt by Tusiata Avia *2004*
A.R.D. Fairburn: Selected Poems edited by Mac Jackson *1995*
R.A.K. Mason: Collected Poems edited by Allen Curnow *1962*
Ursula Bethell: Collected Poems edited by Vincent O'Sullivan *1985*
Dick Seddon's Great Dive and other stories by Ian Wedde *1981*
Lost Possessions by Keri Hulme *1985*
Te Kaihau | The Windeater by Keri Hulme *1986*

DICK SEDDON'S GREAT DIVE

and other stories

Ian Wedde

Te Herenga Waka University Press
Victoria University of Wellington
PO Box 600, Wellington
New Zealand
teherengawakapress.co.nz

First published as *The Shirt Factory and other stories* 1981
This edition published 2022

A catalogue record for this book is available from
the National Library of New Zealand.

ISBN 9781776920204

Printed in Aotearoa New Zealand by Bluestar

Contents

I

II

Acknowledgements

All the Dangerous Animals are in Zoos (ed. John Barnett), *Islands, Landfall, Pilgrims, Radio New Zealand, Spleen, Stand Quarterly.* Most of these stories were published under the editorship of Robin Dudding.

The stories reprinted here were written fifty-odd years ago when I was in my late twenties. Their worlds as descriptions of that time are anachronistic. They don't have cell phones in them. A television set seems to have a single channel. Chuck Berry is touring from the USA in 1974—I went to his Dunedin Town Hall concert attended by the fictional Gringos in my story with that title. There was something called Progressive Rock—King Crimson appear in the story 'The River', in which the voice-character who calls himself Orinoco has a hoard of dexies. In 'The Letter' the central character chain-smokes on the London Underground while going to a drug dealer above a fish and chip bar, passing Rod Argent (The Zombies) posters on the way. Most of the characters are about the age I was when I wrote the stories in a variety of places. The historical worlds they occupy as descriptions of their times seem distant and almost fictional now.

But the characters themselves are still alive and present to me. I think this is because I was trying them out—inventing them and their voices or co-opting fragments of extreme personality traits from people I knew. With the overconfidence of my youth, I was advancing the most out-there options. While the characters' cultures and circumstances may be 'of their times' their natures are less necessarily so. Re-encountering them I find many deliberately unlikeable. Was this perverse? I remember—I confess—that I was wary of the story as a mode of ingratiation, in which the writer sidles up to the reader under cover of a 'compelling' character. Now, I meet these characters as a reader-writer both ruefully complicit in their occasional disagreeability and sympathetic to their hapless plights, and I wish them luck in their encounters with tolerant readers in a changed world.

Ian Wedde
Auckland
26 January 2022

When you wake you may like to reach to a stack of books and with your mind gradually making sense of the prowl of hungry animals, pick up something to help you into the world: short Brecht poem ('Hopeful and responsible/ With good movements, exemplary?'); random lines from long AR Ammons poem ('Take in a lyric information/ totally processed, interpenetrated into/ wholeness . . .'); something so familiar your eye doesn't focus ('Fool who would set a term to love's madness,' Ezra Pound); you lie there in a kind of softoff haze, if you're lucky enough to be permitted sleep past daybreak; then you come to a word that, despite its familiarity, is so new you get out of bed and go to have coffee in the kitchen.

And while you drink it at the kitchen table, you like to prop up something unsententious and tolerant and reflectively observant like Colette's *Break of Day* ('For to dream, and then to return to reality, only means that our scruples suffer a change of place and significance.').

On the cistern lid in the lavatory is a heap: gardening books, comics, thrillers, histories, poetry, and at least three big numbers that the household is 'seriously' engaged with: these have special idiosyncratic bookmarks in them (postcard from Paeroa with snap of The Bottle). But you probably read a thriller, when the last thing you want is to be hassled, or delayed; so it's a good thriller with the wry, well-exercised prose of a Ross McDonald, say, that you can keep on the tank for a couple of days and it's finished.

(You think of fiction as a kind of rhythm beneath the endless obsolescence of fact; a swell beneath the surface chop; oxygen you can't see in the blood whose warmth you can sense under the skin you can touch.)

And so now the day proceeds. You won't have a chance to read again for a while, unless you ride a bus or get chauffeured to town in a limousine, in which case you'll read the newspaper, only that should read 'read': you'll receive a small brainscar of information about eight hundred burning pigs, the corner of your mouth will twitch (you cut yourself shaving with the Singapore Girl's armpit Bic) when you 'read' in tickertape language in the business pages that the spectre of global war going boo! bah! there in the Gulf has driven up gold prices on the Sydney stock exchange, and the minister of defence is suffering bouts of irrational (o)ra(n)ge as a result of exposure to chemical defoliants in Viet Nam via the airconditioning in the Saigon Press Centre (as you get off your bike in the rain and the pre-dawn grey light, the trolleybus wires crack and flash there in the corner of your eye, inside at work there's a jock on the radio yelling pharmaceutical courage, the supervisor walks past smelling of a million cigarettes one-million-and-one now stuck to his smile of a tolerant damaged saint) (someone comes out to the limousine with an umbrella as you carry your newspaper past the world and in at the door).

Then it's lunch, you have time for something more substantial . . . something you are 'having a read of' with commitment and absorption, or with increasing irritation and boredom . . . something at any rate that you 'get down to' for an hour; something you're carrying around. It could be anything, but it's likely to be 'information-intense': eye-popping history of McDonald's fastfood enterprise, the Nineteenth-Century New Zealand *Journal* of Ensign Best, which way was the CIA looking in pre-Aswan Dam Egypt. . . .

(If you're writing, books fly into your hands all day: you follow inexplicable hunches or categorical directives; sped up, your movements would resemble those of a grocer hurrying about his shelves . . . provisions for the semi-familiar faces that come and go, with here and there a regular whose needs you anticipate, 'Here's your bread; your ratpoison . . .'; and here and there a Stranger, 'Don't stock *kimchi* . . .'.)

(You loll at afternoon smoko with your back against a sunny wall; you're reading softporn scifi: *Misty*, 'an adult fantasy'; or the New Testament; or tormenting yourself with Centrefolds; or Studying Form; Marx *Revolutions of 1848*; a car manual; information brochure from State Housing Corporation; *Time* magazine; icy sweating sialorrheal novel by John Le Carre. . .)

(You have your feet on your desk in your large booklined study . . .) (ahem)

(The sherry bottle's empty . . . you come redfaced werewolfly in from the tearose-beds behind the Public Library . . . your eyes water all over something you hauled from the 'Z' shelf in the New Zealand Room. . . .)

You read aloud to children: grotesque mud-creatures that want to be beautiful and loved in Australia, pigs with straight tails in New Zealand, intergalactic warfare in their future not yours.

And now you take your whisky to a good light and a good chair. The moon is up. You have maybe three hours. You, *Go Somewhere*. . . . You're reading this terrific novel, poetry at length, all the stories by someone. . . .

(You snore off beneath broken-glass stars by a pissy bush near Otto's Cabaret at the boat-harbour. . . .)

(You lift the sheet from your Singapore Girl . . . the gold coke-spoon 'drops from her fingers'. . . .)

In bed you again pick up something from that heap . . . yawn, flick pages . . . you fall asleep (or you don't). . . .

And all around the house, the distribution-pattern of the books has changed fractionally: a botany-fad has back-faded into the shelves; there's one more volume of poetry in the dunny than there was yesterday; the Big Fiction has clotted indecisively at the wall-side of the dining-room table; by the telephone are three fresh Childrens' Library books with an emphasis on marine information, but no one's interested, yet. . . . There are veritable palisades of books on your desk, but sit down with them tomorrow, you may find them meaningless. The same goes for those spoor by the bed, the phone, in the kitchen, dining-room table, in the porch, the sofa, on the cistern: viewed over some demographically illuminating timespan, this household fauna of books would be seen to be constantly in motion; and all around it, the slighter agitation of magazines, newspapers, comics, brochures, broadsheets. . . .

This endless migration reveals an ecology. When, from time to time, someone 'cleans up' and shoves *all* the stacks back in the shelves, it's as though they've built a highway through the Amazon.

The rhythm of fiction beneath a daily pattern of reading is not just 'like' a heartbeat; the workings of imagination proper to the language you read in the course of this pattern, are not just 'like' oxygen in the blood; and the larger movements of books in the environment in which you read them, are not 'just' coessential with the living symbiosis and movement of an ecology.

Understanding of character (distinct from that sterile hybrid 'characterisation') begins with the *I* from which your writer's impulse takes off. It may immediately leap out a great urgent distance and haul something back toward the *I*'s scrutiny; or it may extend that scrutiny by degrees until the breaking-strain limit is reached, and there stop and take a look. It is always the primary *character* in any writing, since the drama of its migration, of that risk, is always going to be the primary source of tension. The greatest writers have played on this tension like master musicians; sometimes, you have felt their own excitement and almost disbelief at how far they travelled (Conrad in *Nostromo*), or how minutely, or how fast; how anonymously, or peacefully; sometimes the pain of their struggle.

Even where literary convention demands *character's* self-effacing retraction beneath some carapace of 'style', it's there in the living quality of the language: it *is* the life of the language. Of course, the language is going to be android-bleeps if there's no tension; and it's going to be just as dead if the writer's sent that *I* out too far and has written a story from the point of view of a syphilitic Micronesian pygmy descendant of De Bougainville's plague-landfall at Espiritu Santo in 1768 (say), without admitting that such a leap's going to have to be sustained by the irony of having some of the writer survive in there too.

Such a 'characterisation' may have admirable moral purposes, such as the ritual exorcism of guilt associated with the plague-etiologies of Pacific History, whatever. But its purpose is as nothing without life; and if it's dead, it can't work. And who wants to wake up with something in the morning, hope for a little gentle clarity at breakfast, look forward to a 'good read of' something at lunch, just sail tremendously right into something at night, blink out on a familiar verse in bed—who wants to be disappointed with *all* those chances, all those 'times of day' . . . who wants to come to all those chances in the ecosystem of writing, all those embarkations and migrations, and find they don't work?

It's the excitement and mystery of this risk of *character*, and a sense of vital fictional symbiosis beneath the jostle of facts, that get me going 'as a writer'.

Rereading these stories 'as a book' I find I was putting the spade in deeper than I knew at the time.

They are linked in ways I might not have guessed:
When is 'now'?
Where is 'home'?
What is 'paradise'?
Who's kidding whom?

Ian Wedde
Wellington
May 1981

I

Dick Seddon's Great Dive

1 *Backyard Ocean*

He knelt in the black sand. Each wave sucked trenches beneath his knees. He began to sink and be buried. He lunged under the next one. The wave poured into his nostrils. He came up blind, his balls aching. He'd been turned around. A wave ground him into the dark. He felt his limbs stretched and drawn away. At one moment he saw the night sky and the stars, incredibly clear, but below him. Then they whirled upward and a sound with the mass of an immense wing or horizon slammed against his forehead. He felt the tortoiseshell bracelet torn from his wrist. It was as though his hand had gone.

Moments later he was floating quite gently. He'd passed beyond the fury of the breaking waves and now rose and sank slowly, turning over and over. He no longer had any sensation of struggling. He seemed to have left his body which he now watched calmly as it thrust its limbs out this way and that, jerkily as a child, as though the viscous medium in which it was trying to move had become thin, then a muffled vacuum, finally a space he seemed to pass through . . . through some vanishing point at the back of his neck.

2

'Bring me some *shapely* shells,' she'd once said to him as he left for the beach.

> Because I'm built for comfort
> I ain't . . . built for speed

he was singing. He'd come back with four or five empty ice-cream tubs. 'It's all that's left.'

Wind and more wind. He wanted to gape, to retch. To get out of himself, how could that be done? It was as though he could have hung over the worn railing of the jetty, shoved a finger into his throat, and gasped out the cramped bile of energy which so occupied his time that the world and the friends in it were seen through a kind of veil, that their voices speaking came to him dully, from a distance, and he had to catch at them as they drifted or flew past, bending all his concentration and will to accomplish a simple response to a simple greeting.

'Well, hello . . .'

'Uh . . . (who are you?) . . .'

Though sometimes he heard his own voice, plausible and intense . . . 'That's not what I mean. . . .'

Ah, why did he have to explain so much? Couldn't he settle for anything?

The planks of the jetty were furrowed and scarred down their length. Here and there long splinters had lifted off the surface of the timber, but even these were worn and smooth, soft-looking. The structure was so solid, so resilient, so used! At the end where boats came to fill up with diesel the wood was soaked in dark oil, the broken ends and joints looked to have been charred . . . yet even here, where the jetty had been battered and shaken through years of storms, where the slick poison of the oil had seeped and seeped into the grain of the planks and washed around the greeny standing timbers at the waterline, where the wood had the dead sodden appearance of the slimy apple boxes which washed up from time to time on the beach below the boathouse—even here the boards sprang beneath his weight and gave off a ringing sound when he stamped on them with all the angry force in his body.

Spray from the waves flew into his face. Along the shoreline the water had been stirred up into an ochre broth which matched the scars of slips along the peninsula. But the channel was still blue, like the swept sky, and crowded with speeding whitecaps. He turned his back into the wind, feeling it shove him suddenly towards the lee side of the jetty and almost lift him off his feet, ballooning his coat and trousers, whipping his hair forward around his face. He grunted, turning sideways, catching at the rail. The whole structure was alive, the rail quivered under his hand, the planks bucked against his feet. All at once he laughed, opening his mouth wide. The wind drove sideways between the nerves of his teeth, pushing one cheek out. By opening and closing the apertures of his lips and throat he could alter the pitch of the sound the wind made in him. It yawed and wailed, in his head . . . he wondered if it could be heard *out there* as well: sensational, flashy . . . bringing one hand against his groin, stretching the other out as though to grasp the neck of a guitar, going into a crouch, stamping one foot, miming some crude ferocious chops, opening and closing his lips and throat for the wind to sound in. . . .

He could see her at the shore end of the jetty: white face and dark blue jersey. He strutted towards her along the wet planks, lifting the guitar high, his eyes fixed on the audience, then crouching again over his narrow big-knuckled fingers, one boot sole sliding on to the wahwah pedal, laying that sultry wail over the notes. He kept his eye on her: 'How's the people tonight?' He saw the white flash of her teeth there in the distance. 'Solid,' he answered himself. 'Those chicks gonna leave some wet seats behind. . . .'

Woohah!

. . . lifting the guitar high, eyes fixed on the audience so far down there, the pale mark of her face with the smile just showing, and the wind rushing into him like a giant respirator!

3

She's sitting alone in this room, bent forward over a table on which she's placed paper and pencils . . . done this with sad precision, the neatness of someone who's determined to see something through. Her attitude's that of a woman listening.

It's summer, but cool, here in Port Chalmers, where a breeze from the south is moving the sappy broadleaf outside her window: the only window in the room, which she faces across the table and the blank paper, and which might be the only perspective she has on the world.

Out there the shiny evergreen moves in cool sunlight, also a few ngaio bushes, and some broom which, having been sprayed recently by the council, now has on it a drab olive patina of death. These plants grow from a scruffy clay bank haunted by neighbourhood cats which either doze among the shadows or else stalk blackbirds and thrushes in the undergrowth. Occasionally children slide and scramble down. Above the plants and the bank the chimneys of two houses can be seen. At this time of year there's no smoke. The top half of the window frames telephone wires, cloud, sky. That's her world. From time to time footsteps or a car pass through it. There are changes of light.

She keeps the window closed. It's an old-fashioned sash window. In order to raise it she'd have to bend forward, grasp two handles set at pelvis level in the window frame, and slide the frame upward in its grooves. This action would push her belly forward, arch her back, tip her chin up . . . her hands, at the top of her stretch, would be level with her head . . . the whole action would resemble that of a woman drawing a sweater or nightdress up over her head. Then she'd be standing naked in front of an uncurtained window opening on to a street.

Or else we can imagine her in morning sunlight, stretching naked in front of the same window. It's late morning, she wants to break the last sacs of sleep in her spine and shoulders. It's a gesture to admire. For someone to admire, for example a lover.

When she looks up from the paper on the table her own reflection in the window faces her, its back turned to what she sees through it: the world, her world, its earth, planets, creatures, sky . . . its season, its voyeurs.

The empty paper isn't an invitation, it's an imperative. The attitude of a woman listening changes to that of a woman talking. Soon the pencils are blunt, the paper scattered over the table. In the window the reflection ignores not only the world, it ignores her as well. It never so much as glances at her. The light shifts. When she gets up and goes out she doesn't look at, through, the window, at all . . . she goes out.

Sooner or later she'll almost get up and lift the reflection over her head and stand there as though for the eyes of a lover, in air and sunlight . . .

*

If I reconstruct his life for you it's going to have to be done like this. There's a line in his life which runs from south to north, from north to south, along which he was strung out like one of the strings of his neglected instrument. In the north he was Howlin' Wolf or Willie Dixon . . . out of sight in the ponga grove below Beck's place, twelve-bar blues for the cicadas . . .

> Woo Hoo-oo
> Smokestack lightnin'

In the south it was *He Ain't Give Ya None* . . . 'I got messed up around somewhere . . .': right at the edge. . . .

It always seemed the wrong way around to me until I found myself, in the effort of trying to discover him, stretched tight between those same poles. He'd always had an obsession with the way things got divided along that line: North and South Viet Nam, North and South Korea, North America and Chile, Northern Ireland and the Republic, the silk millionaires of Milan or Como in northern Italy and the destitute south of that country. It was typical of him to bulwark a cheap idea with this kind of data. He collected it. He loved to quote the lines I taught him from a poem by Pablo Neruda, lines which have slipped in already without my even thinking about them: *You come from the destitute south*, and then at the end: *That is why I have singled you out to be my companion*. He'd say that the demarcations were never drawn by the people involved. That I know to be true now. Now that he's dead and I can't go to him and say *Tell me*, now that I have to involve my own imagination in what has the inexplicable (if you don't get it, tough shit) meaning of myth, I find he was often right and I knew it, *then* . . . but I was too proud to admit it.

I have had to learn the simplest things
last. Which made for difficulties.

Stop quoting at me, he'd say. Who are these people, do I know them. It's you I want to hear. It's you.

She stops. There's a commotion outside the window. Her friend Ingrid's coming back from the shops, pushing the baby in a pram. The dog's jumped up and knocked a bag from the end of the pram. Groceries roll into the road . . . Ingrid yelling Fuck off! the baby howling with fright. A neighbour runs out to help. Then the little cavalcade goes out of sight, out of the window space, Ingrid's narrow hands reaching forward to soothe the baby. Kate continues to see the colour of Ingrid's hair in the blond light among the leaves out there . . . everything can be slowed up in that world . . . its visitors linger. . . .

In a way it was as though we never moved, as though he never left, as though I never remained behind . . . except now . . . except that now I understand more about it. He was trying to keep some kind of balance and this had come to have a geographical equivalent. And it also explains why he should be Howlin' Wolf in the harder north, and some kind of paranoid brinksman in the gentler south. His whole life was an elaborate mesh of checks and balances. If he'd found it was necessary to move up and down the country the way he did, then you can imagine the kinds of fantastic migrations he must have been compelled to undertake in his own head.

I know too that among the reasons for his leaving as he did was a desire that I shouldn't be hurt by him. I could always say to myself or to others, 'We had a quarrel, he's pissed off again to cool down.' Well, he tried: 'I'm not dependable,' he said.

I can say more than that. I can say that he loved me. *You come from the destitute south . . . that is why I have singled you out to be my companion. . . .* I remember the occasions he came back into the room where I was after he'd been away, and all I'd say would be, like, 'Oh hello, welcome *home* . . .'. And all the while my heart would be pounding so hard I was afraid he'd see it, and it wouldn't be until we got to bed that I'd let go . . . which he could explain to himself in terms of my being a good fuck. The same thing probably happened to him the length of the country; not a single really open loving embrace, not a single unguarded welcome. He was often a prick. But what's on my mind now, like the sound of him picking out a twelve-bar blues in another room, is the thought that *that* may have been what he was looking for: a home. If I'd welcomed him as my heart now tells me I should have, he mightn't have gone out to Bethells that night and drowned himself, since I know that's what he did.

And so I've got to set out, strung tight as he was, to try to find out if it was so, if I killed him, the only man I ever really loved, much as I must have seemed to resemble the other small cool assassins he knew.

He was right: we are split north from south, and the line isn't drawn by anyone involved. Perhaps if I find out enough about him, I'll find out who draws the lines. That would have been the kind of remark he'd have made. He used to talk of 'Them', until I got mad. I believe in Them now. I'd like to know who they are. Between us, jointly, we killed Chink.

Outside the light's shifted, it's deserted, but she doesn't look up, she goes straight out, leaving the door to bang wide open behind her, rattling the sash window in its frame.

4 *The P.O.W. Snapshot*

His 'Prisoner of War' photograph: that was his name for it. He was what's called a war baby.

'Listen, I'd like to tell you about myself, but I'm only allowed to tell you my name rank and serial number. That's the regulation *you* made, remember?'

Well, well . . .

He said without much bitterness but at the same time without pity, in a strangely flat tone, that the only thing that ever really happened to his father was the war, that the small precious human events which followed became non-events, that his father's youth and the new love for his young wife 'were rendered down into base metal in the furnaces of the war' . . . Kate, hearing these words which seemed rehearsed, wondered if he was putting her on, but he wasn't . . . that by virtue of a strange alchemy, and the catalysis of the R.S.A., the horrors of his father's active service were transformed into a kind of gold standard against which the ordinary currency of his life was measured . . . all those things he'd desperately longed for during the war . . . these, this currency, was propped up by that standard, was found lacking by it. 'That gold was bad metal . . . won, like the South African gold which crutches the present currencies of the West, by slave labour.' . . . Kate again wanting to laugh, not just because she was stoned, but because he was like a parody, accomplished and deliberate . . . ah, but of whom?

'My Dad once said to me: You think you're a bad sort, do you? You think you've been around? Well lemme tell you *I've done worse things than you!*'

The old man was incoherent, shaking, but that was what he wanted to tell his son: he, the old soldier, 'had the edge on him' still, had one or two 'up his sleeve', had done *worse* things than he, for Christ's sake! Chink didn't think of himself as bad. But somehow strength, danger, achievement and badness were mixed up in his father's mind . . . ('*machismo*' . . . 'supercock', Beck would say, allowing his lips to part just far enough to reveal the gap where his left eye tooth had once been . . . a smile he reserved for 'special cases').

The old man thought his son was threatening him, flaunting his shiftless life, making fun of him. It was sad. He was deathly ill, he felt there was no time to lose: he was about to blurt out some confession, some act he'd kept a secret for years and years, to begin with because he was ashamed of it but later because the secret was something which warmed him, something which, like the war, was a grotesquely nostalgic antidote to what seemed to him to be the unremarkableness of his life, which was now about to end. He stood in his woollen dressing-gown, holding the back of the armchair, his face turning purple with the effort to breathe.

'Now listen young feller . . .'

Chink's mother came back into the room. His father's confession sank again to wherever it had lain all those years. The lids dropped a little on his glaring eyes, his head dropped. His wife half carried him back to his bed. He would die with the weight of his secret to take him down among his comrades. Chink couldn't even have held his arm down the passage to the bedroom. There he stood, listening to his father's breath going away. *His shadow before me*. . . .

'A romantic, in a sense. . . . That's it, Kate: sibling rivalry. And for what? For who'd been *worse*, that's what. . . .' He laughed loudly. Ha ha! a demonstration qualitatively less malicious than Beck's 'special case' smile . . . but then, it was Chink's father, and he was dead. . . .

He'd been telling her about the last showdown, the 'terminal quarrel'. She'd only just met him. She wondered if he'd inherited his father's urge to confess. But then, she'd started it. *I've done worse things than you.* That sentence was on his mind: some time he had to do, something he had to see finished. It touched her, in just the right place, at just the right time: she was doing some time of her own, in her own way.

'Is it so funny?'

'Is what so funny?'

'Your father's death.'

'Ah . . . remember the photograph?'

Earlier on he'd produced it, but without rhetorical flourishes and without any apparent irony, from the inside compartment of a battered wallet where he evidently kept it as a talisman of some sort, though not a public one, since he had to grope clumsily with two fingers into this odorous sanctum, finally managing to draw the snapshot out between the forceps of his fingers, handing it across to her: a gesture she was stirred by to recognize as special.

Much later, almost three years later, he gave her the snapshot. He was going away 'again'.

'You might at least give me a photo,' she said. He allowed the sarcasm to sail past, not granting it even the smallest alteration of his expression. For the second time in three years he forcepsed out 'the P.O.W. snapshot' and passed it to her. She still has it: the only surviving likeness.

Battered and yellow, the photograph shows a small boy in shorts, awkward-looking, his feet in closed sandals turned inward at the toes, staring with an expression of mixed worry and distraction at something just to the side of the camera. One imagines his mother standing there saying 'Smile!' while his father aims the lens at the child's head and shouts 'Stand up straight!'

Behind him is a suburban back garden: on his left a dark paling fence, probably creosoted, with what looks like a passion fruit vine at the far end on a wire trellis. Directly behind him the perspective is abruptly halted by the back garden and brick kitchen wall of another house. You know it's the kitchen wall because of the kind of long window which goes above the sink unit. You have the feeling that a neighbour is watching the proceedings from this window.

On the boy's right hand side the photograph stops at a neutral edge broken by the protruding lower half of a deck chair and by the upper branches of a small feathery tree, probably a kōwhai. It's summer: the boy is wearing a short-sleeved shirt, the light is bright and hot and humid, the deck chair is aimed at the sun, its shadow squats invisibly beneath it.

Somehow you know it's the weekend. The little boy looks penned up. He's probably close to tears. His rather thin arms hang at his sides, but stiffly, as though they too have been told to keep still. His fringe of hair has been plastered down and across his forehead, which even at his age (about five, you guess) is high and square and adult-looking, and without a backward slope towards the hair line, so that his eyes look unnaturally large and exposed, though rather lidless, without the protection of a ridge of browbone, as though the sockets are flush with the oddly flat planes of his cheek bones.

His nickname naturally was Chink . . . bestowed, so he claimed, within the first week of primary school, though it sounds too sophisticated for five-year-olds . . . somehow it's not a connexion you'd make without having the nickname there already, though once you had it it seemed obvious. Kate guesses it was probably used by the family.

She can imagine the scene at that first day at school: the

little shy boy answering the teacher's question about his name: 'Chink'. The bright room fills with laughter. *Chink, Chink*! He bursts into tears. Then the young teacher attempts to comfort him.

'We know that's not his real name, now don't we children. . . .'

So not only did he answer the first question wrongly, but the name which stuck was by far the strangest and funniest in the school.

How much do we make of this? Not too much. . . . Kate, face to face with the melancholy, funny image of 'the P.O.W. snapshot', struggles against a procession of associations. But it's real all the same. Because from the very start, possibly even before this first day at school for all Kate knew, he became used to feeling separate.

Instead of retreating, however, his lidless pale eyes learned the habit of staring unblinkingly, sometimes almost without expression, at the person he was talking to, at the countryside, at crowds of people.

She sometimes longed to give him expression. The first time they made love she felt as though her cheeks were puffed out with some kind of pressure coming into her, some kind of breath. Then she looked at him. His face was blank. All at once the mask split slowly. 'Kate!' he shouted. 'Kate, Kate!' The beautiful smile remained there. It was comical. She'll never forget it. And she'll never forget the mask of his face before the smile broke it. It was like a glimpse of a world in which we're able to see the truth behind the cosmetic of gesture . . . ape-skull, dog-skull, sheep-skull . . . some split-second animal reflex just slipping from the face of the person who's been holding our arm or ruffling our hair, who's just kissed us on the lips.

'Listen, I'd like to tell you about myself, but I'm only

allowed to tell you my name rank and serial number. That's the regulation *you* made, remember?'

Before he left school he already had a reputation, based entirely at first on his stare but later, because of the provocations of that stare, earned otherwise, for being tough, unafraid. His neutrality was a taunt. What had once seemed to be shyness came to look like precocious incuriosity. He was punished for insolence. By degrees he began to fit the definition he'd passively caused others to make of him. When he was twenty he spent one bad year at university in Auckland. He got into fights with drunks who thought they detected in his stare some kind of disgust or curiosity.

Yet women liked him. They believed him to be gentler than men did. Perhaps fear was the reason for this also. Kate doesn't really know, and can't stop to think, except of insolence and gentleness: the defined and the natural. Whichever way round it is. Oh, she needed the insolence too, or came to. . . .

'Tell me about yourself, Chink.'

'Listen, I'd like to tell you about myself but I'm only allowed to tell you my name rank and serial number. That's the regulation *you* made, remember?'

'Hey, Chink, this is a party, I only met you today, don't get heavy. I liked the way you told that burglary story. *That's* what I mean. . . .'

'What about what *I* mean? It's easy to be cool, sweetheart.'

His voice had gone flat. He stirred as though to move away. A pang of fear and longing entered her. On impulse she struggled towards him, on her knees, put her arms around his shoulders and kissed him on the side of his neck. He remained still under her mouth and hands. His long hair had a feral smell.

'Ah Chink, I'm sorry. I didn't mean to put you down. Go on, tell me about yourself. I'll *listen*, whatever you mean. . . .'

He sat motionless. Then his face was split by that odd hinged smile. He began to laugh, throwing his head back. His throat was white and stubbly.

'The Story of my Life. First I'll show you a picture of a prisoner of war. . . .'

Chink, the teller of parables, the bullshit artist. . . .

And now she's looking at 'the P.O.W. snapshot' in front of her as though she half expects it to utter something, a cry or words . . . a miracle. . . .

5

It was a dark night, no moon, late autumn. He was cold and tired. He walked up the silent street hoping it wasn't going to rain before he got inside. His shadow passed him. It stretched out as though trying to break free, fell back behind him and then passed him again and again as he walked along beneath the street lamps. The rhythm of its movement and of his own feet drew him forward: the automatic compulsion of a work chant, of a route march, a pit saw. Wearily he amused himself with these imaginings. He decided on the work chant and began inventing African words for it: *Hai hai hai B'wana hai hai hai B'wana.* . . . His shadow advanced like the shadow of the overseer who was approaching him from behind. He awaited the lash. One day he'd rise up, they would rise up, he and his work mates, and chanting rhythmically would break with their mattocks the earth of the overseer's grave. . . .

A strange dim hush of sound filled the street: deep freeze units, people breathing in sleep, his . . . Was he imagining it? There was a morepork and then two cats. The morepork continued for some time, unhurried, monotonous. The cats stopped moaning when they saw him. One of them suddenly ran across the road, its body elongated. The other followed. They disappeared into a dark garden. He strained to hear the breathing of the street but a slight breeze began to move the leaves of evergreens and shrubs. He turned up his collar, more for the sake of the gesture than for shelter, and changed hands on his holdall. He felt a sudden temptation to walk in the middle of the road, and did so. It seemed extraordinarily clean, the pavements too with their rinsed gutters and sharp-edged concrete kerbing. If he chanted his work song the whole street would come alight and alive. Picture windows on the street front would light up, families of two, three or four would stand in the windows looking out at him, like advertisements for pyjamas or oil-fired heating, silent and motionless, smiling. He whistled instead

> If y' see ma
> littl' red rooster
> oh please . . .

The breeze increased, blowing up the street from behind him, parting his hair across the crown of his head, suddenly scattering a few big drops of rain, *smack*, on the asphalt. He turned the corner out of the wind and into the quiet of shelter . . . into his own street.

'His own street' . . . its familiarity, even at night, even after long absence, filled him with an ache of loneliness. As a child he'd never thought of it as going anywhere: it was open-ended but static, and he'd never had any sense of movement until he'd turned out of it. And he'd never returned by way of it. He was 'home' the moment he came round the corner, into the street. At that point all journeys had ceased.

He'd once scraped a charred stick along a neighbour's white-painted paling fence, from one end to the other, *dah dah dah dadadadadad-rrrrrrruuup!* digging that vibration which passed through elbow and shoulder to the shaken cavities of his skull and to his eyes jumping out of focus, the loud machine-gun rattle of the stick over the corrugations of the fence. The irregular charcoal line on the white paint had made a satisfying horizon, a dislocation of the ordered planes of the street. He'd been about to scrape the stick back in the other direction when the neighbour had run out screaming. Under the eyes of both neighbour ('Boys will be boys . . .') and father ('. . . respect for property . . .') he'd had to wash the fence with a cloth and a galvanized bucket of soapy water, on his knees on the pavement, smearing the dish-cloth through his father's shadow on the fence.

Hai hai

The fence was still there, still white. The rain began to bucket down, sluicing along the gutters, but he didn't run the last yards to the door of the house, because he was footsore and tired, because of the old half-remembered inhibition . . . because he didn't know what to say when he got there.

hai hai hai B'wana
if y' see ma
littl' red rooster
oh please . . .

. . . his mind, skidding in weary grooves, was stuck with not much more than that. It made about as much sense as the phrases he'd been rehearsing. Either way, he was going to fuck up.

The rain had soaked his hair and thighs: one of those sudden Auckland squalls. It stopped as immediately as it had come. He stood outside the gate of the dark house, put his bag down carefully and pushed the drenched hair back off his face and over his collar, wringing it behind his neck. Two empty milkbottles stood on the pavement below the letterbox. He picked up the bag and skirting the bottles opened the gate quietly and went up the neat concrete squares of the path. The night was once again still, the silence accentuated by the dripping of wet foliage, earth kisses of sinking wet. He trod carefully on the balls of his feet. It was pitch dark away from the street lamps, but he moved surely, by instinct and memory. Nothing had ever changed, nothing would have changed. There were no obstacles in his father's garden.

He went up the steps to the porch and put his bag down on the mat by the front door. He found he'd stopped breathing, in the effort to be quiet.

'Shit. . . .' He went back down the steps and around the side of the house.

His father's bedroom window was open a few notches. Chink stood beneath it, in the perfume of a lavender bush, listening. This time he had no doubts, didn't have to strain to hear the breathing. His father's breath seemed the loudest thing he'd heard since he'd begun the walk through the neighbourhood. He realized he'd been listening for it from the first moment he'd begun that walk, even from the moment he'd left the south to hitch north.

The old man's sick, the overseer's sick.

Chink stood in the dark beneath the window, head bowed,

in an attitude of submission. Inside the house an old man lay in drenched painful sleep, labouring for breath.

The image of the youthful pyjama advertisement families in their picture windows came to him. They gazed silently, with set smiles, at the dark street. Not a single old man among them to share their intimate and guaranteed comfort, only an old man's son walking alone in the middle of the road. Standing outside his father's window.

His mother's telegram had said 'Father ill'. It hadn't said come, but Chink had assumed that, had assumed the implication of a last chance to see his father. Standing in the damp cool darkness by the lavender bush, listening to his father's breath inside the house, Chink thought 'Why isn't he in hospital?' and realized that it had never occurred to him to wonder whether his father had asked to see him, whether he mightn't be *waiting for that*. . . . Oh Jesus Christ. He stood with his head dipping towards the medicinal odour of lavender. He couldn't believe that, but he should've thought of it. It wasn't impossible. How could he face it, such a scene, at this time? He should've done it himself, long ago, before it came to this . . . some kind of trite tearjerker. A death bed scene, Jesus. And if his father didn't know he was coming, he now thought, that was worse, though it was what he'd assumed all along.

Ah, get on with it. He was helping his father to breathe, keeping to that rhythm. How hard it was.

He was here. Go inside, see him.

But he stood anyway, calming himself. He picked a sprig of lavender and crushed it, to smell. It seemed a violent odour. Rain fell again suddenly, rattling against the stiff karaka leaves above his head. Then it stopped, as suddenly. He heard his father breathing. Go inside, see him, *your Dad*. Fuck your vanity.

As he turned and went back towards the corner of the house

he heard the milk delivery truck clattering further up the street. It must be nearly dawn, a late dawn, being autumn and cloudy. The sound of clashing milk crates opened up his sense of the space he was in. Stepping past the house corner, he stepped clear also of the difficult suffocation of night and his father's breath. He was still holding the lavender in his hand, once again a familiar smell. He stood under the dripping eave of the house, out of sight of the road, not wishing to seem a strange figure, an intruder, in the dim garden. Yes, the first weak light of day showed spaces between shrubs. Beyond the garden, in the grey higher air above the road, the street lamps were now greenish.

How often it was like this, calmness or a decision coming as the sense of a space opening out with dawn: partial, weary, leaving a certain measure to be guessed. How far to the gate? You knew, really. The uncertainty wasn't important. You could walk to the gate in the dark, in any case, without stumbling, if you had to. You had memory and instinct. There were no obstacles. And how often, for him, it happened at this time, literally dawn, a mysterious coincidence. Which way did it work? Was it the dawn, out there, that calmed him? It seemed rather that his action of coming to a decision, that interior part of it—*that* created a new day, drew it up out of the suffocation of darkness and confusion. Then there was light, a large space he inhabited, other people in it also. *He* did that. Nothing was given to him. He had to do it, to make a day for himself to live in, to live. A space, to live. Distance, to pass through. Having not slept all night, he would suddenly be exhausted and would go in and sleep for hours, whether there was a job he should be at or not. After dawn, nothing mattered. Nothing else, that is.

The milk truck reached the gate of his father's house. The milkman was whistling loudly and tunelessly: *a few of my favourite things, these are a few. . . .* Chink stood till the truck had gone, till it had turned the far corner, a long wait.

Then he went to the porch and picked up his bag and walked to the gate. To hell with it. What did it matter. He opened the gate towards himself. Let's go.

The milkman had left the two full bottles right in the centre of the space. The toes of his boots were against them. He'd almost kicked them over. There he stood. Then he bent down and picked the bottles up, awkwardly, with his free hand. He was wet through. What did it matter, after all. Carrying the bottles and his bag, he turned around and went back up the path again to the front door, and rang the bell.

There he stood again, waiting again. He could hear his heart: *hai hai hai B'wana.* Breaking the earth.

6

When he came in that Friday night from Beck's place he was so bent that for a long time he didn't notice anything. It was summer, his father was dead. For some time he'd found he preferred to be alone. But now he wondered why he'd come home, why he was alone, why he should've wished to be alone, how long he *had* been alone.

'Whatta mausoleum, Jesus. . . .'

Then as he was about to go to bed, not even bothering to take his clothes off, he saw a muddy footprint on the sheet, and the window above the bed swinging open.

'Hey . . .'

It was about two in the morning. His watch face spoke out clear and serene. Somehow it seemed impossible at that hour, unravelled as he was, to deduce 'I've been burgled'. Gargled, ogled. Icicle, tricycle, bicycle. It was a *word*, was all it was.

'Someone's *done* this to me!'

Yeah, it was true. Sighing, he checked the flat by rote, counting its contents out under his breath. The furniture lay KO'd upon the carpet. He (she? they?) didn't take the table/ the chairs/ the refrigerator, etcetera.

He zeroed in. Twenty dollars had gone from the cigarette box on the stereo lid, but nothing else (he scrabbled and counted) though there were signs that the thief (the *what*?) had poached himself an egg: the last one of a carton of half-a-dozen had gone, and there were breadcrumbs by the loaf where he remembered having cleared up scrupulously before going out that evening: filth of a forgotten week, dishes socks and bottles. What a time to choose! The pan in which the egg had been cooked lay tidily full of water with floating white bits in the sink. Very cool, he thought. An anal thief.

Then it occurred to him that it must've been a friend ('Yes yes!'). But a friend would've left a note, something ('Yes yes!') especially since twenty dollars wasn't chickenshit. . . .

He sat in the main room of the flat and noticed all at once the mess! Drawers had been opened and left so, the profligate contents of the bookshelves had been pulled out. The wreckage rushed towards him across the carpet. Had he done that or the, ah, thief?

By now it was about three in the morning. Not instinctively, but for some deep reason, though not without hesitation (he closed his eyes to consider) he put his boots on and went out to the road and kicked the bike alive. His head now felt fairly clear. He rode quickly down to the Newmarket police station. He rang the bell. No one came. A cruise car was parked outside, the blue lamp by the front door was on. He rang again, long bursts, holding his finger down.

'Why, Chink . . . !'

'Hello Mum. How's Dad . . . ?'

Still there was no answer. There was a moral in this somewhere.

'Uh . . . 'scuse me. . . .'

He walked around to the back feeling a flutter of panic and laughter in his stomach. His balls ducking for cover. He shook one of the windows.

'What kinda trip is this?'

He went back to the bike and started it. The streets were deserted, there was no traffic, not even through Newmarket. He chugged past a succession of red lights, leaving the bike in top gear and letting the revs drop right down . . . sensing the lights turn to green behind him . . . feeling invisible, insubstantial, adrift. The highest 'vehicular density' in the Southern Hemisphere . . . 'Oh yeah?' . . . Where was everybody? The Stranger rides into town.

Then he thought of the new central police station, the skyscraper! And swung the bike fast up Carlton Gore and towards the centre of town. He was aware that he shouldn't be going fast . . . might ride out of himself . . . sense the signals turning green *back there*, too late . . . but he felt a sudden mad confidence: here's the wronged citizen on his way to redress, yeah!

He opened the bike up along Symonds Street and swooped left down the hill past the Māori Wars memorial statue. *Through War They Won The Peace We Know*. . . . Pax Britannica was lost in the shade of the pōhutukawa. He imagined her: voluptuous, paralytic, one arm locked upward, petrified foliage dripping from her free hand, a breasted *sadhu*. . . .

The traffic lights by the town hall turned green as though for him. 'Thanks.' He had a sense of inhabiting himself again.

He negotiated the island at speed and then cut back and cruised slowly up the hill to the central police station.

It was all lit up, like Christmas, floor after floor, slender and cold. At first he wandered into the garage. There was no sign of anyone ('Whooohooo . . .'). Squad cars were parked in rows under the dim lighting. He walked among them. They were useless, lacklustre, vapid. His boots echoed. There seemed to be no need to tread quietly.

After this he walked straight into the main building through a sprung inside door which sighed and closed behind him. The corridors were fluorescent-lit, deserted, filled with his loud footsteps. He walked past rows of doors towards the vanishing point of a corridor and came to a lift well. He went up floor by floor. It was all deserted. The glaring perspectives of the corridors receded in front of his feet. Vanishing points. He expected at any moment to meet a procession of men with bulging fish-eye-lens faces tramping 'without motion' towards him under the fluorescent tubes. Nothing of the sort happened. He hurried. When he got back to the second floor his vertigo left him.

All at once he saw the night desk off to one side of the main complex. There was a long counter inside a glass room with a swinging glass door. Pushing his unclear reflection aside he walked through to the sergeant behind the counter. There were three or four men in the room, spaced out among the hooded typewriters and the telephones, behind the polished surface of the counter.

'I want to report an icicle.'

The sergeant, a tired man whose head was flat as though moulded by his cap, looked at him from his chair.

'What can we do for you?'

'I've been burgled,' said Chink, looking at the top of the

sergeant's head. He was sure he'd spoken. He'd suddenly thought, 'What the fuck am I doing here?' He wanted to tell the sergeant that the whole station was open, that he'd walked around inside it for twenty minutes, that this seemed weird. He leaned against the counter. The room with the night desk was so bright!

'What time?'

The question skidded past him.

'What time did you notice the offence?' The sergeant repeated the question, a bored mutter, reaching sloppily across his desk for a notepad, not looking at Chink.

'At about two o'clock,' said Chink. He felt suddenly that he'd got it all wrong, that he was about to make an address. He stood up straight, smoothed his hair. The men in the room were looking towards him.

'What address?'

'Birdwood Crescent in Parnell,' said Chink crisply. He gave the number. His mind snapped into focus.

'You were out?'

'Yes.'

'Have you been drinking?'

'No.'

'All right,' said the sergeant. 'Go home and wait. I'll get a car to come round. Don't move anything. There's been a thief working the neighbourhood. You're about the tenth. Was your place locked?'

'He came in through a window.'

'You should know better,' said the sergeant, dialling a number with his pencil. He yawned and massaged his eyes, and rubbed the sad crown of his head. Chink heard him talking to a car: 'Meee maaaa mumm. . . .'

'They'll be there in about ten minutes,' said the sergeant.

'Do you have transport?'

'Yes.'

'Are you all right?'

'I'm fine,' said Chink. 'I'm tired, that's all.'

He'd remembered what was in the flat: some caps of mescaline, some caps of amyl nitrite. They were in a disprin bottle in the living room. Like the debris on the floor of the flat, the bottle rushed towards him. The sergeant still had the telephone in his hand.

'You'd better get back and let the C.I.B. in,' said the sergeant. 'They'll probably be waiting for you.'

'Rightoh,' said Chink. 'Thanks very much.'

He bowed, something like that, ran out. His wild reflection. At first he couldn't find the bike. Then he remembered it was around the other side of the building, at the top of the hill. He forced himself to walk to it. He *knew* he'd left the door of the flat open. He hurtled back across Grafton bridge and through the dark Domain, under an amazing summer night sky, if only he'd known it, pulling up outside the flat at the exact moment the squad car, red light off, stopped on the other side of the crescent. A flashlight probed from the front window of the car at the number on the letter box. Chink bounded across the road.

'This is it, this is the burglary, I'll open the door, just got back from the station, gotta take a leak.'

'Calm down,' an invisible man in the car. 'Don't get excited and don't touch anything, we'll be right in.'

'Fine,' said Chink. 'I'll just take a leak.'

He walked back across the road, taking small steps, then opened the unlocked door, snatched up the disprin bottle, flew through the lit flat to the bathroom. Shove it under the bath? He'd poached an egg, why shouldn't he have a piss? Have had a piss? They might want to look around in here. Ah shit. . . . The mescaline caps floated on the surface of the water when he threw them into the lavatory. He shook the amyls into his palm . . . 'Fuck it!' . . . cracking caps under his nose, snorting hard . . . the reek of cheesy football socks. He heard the Ds come into the main room of the flat. He threw the remaining caps into the dunny and pulled the chain. The objects swirled and disappeared. He opened the window and flapped his arms, then washed under the hot tap, scalding his hands. He dried them and fumbled at the catch of the door. His fingers were shaking. He felt terrific. He put his hands on his knees, bent, and breathed deeply. Blood strutted finely through his body. He opened the door and went into the room where the police were.

'Sorry,' he said. 'I must've got a bit excited.'

There were three plain-clothes men in the room. They were looking at books and things on the floor. Oh, he'd got it wrong, quite wrong.

'Have you been at a party?' said one of the men.

'Yeah,' Chink rubbing his hands, 'but pretty quiet, you know, we were playing chess. Then I got back here, I didn't notice anything at first, then I saw a footprint on the bed, I thought it must've been a friend, he'd poached an egg. But any friend would leave a note, something, so I thought I'd better get on to it quickly otherwise I wouldn't have bothered . . . what's it, nearly four o'clock, hell I seem to've been riding about for hours. . . .'

'Yes,' said the D. 'Could you show us where the entry was made?'

Serious these fellers.

Chink led the procession into the bedroom. The window was swinging open, summer night coming in, the muddy footprint was on the bed *right* next to the pillow. He resisted with difficulty an urge to wave his arm at the ludicrous evidence. The whole thing could have begun again, from the beginning, any number of times: Footprint, the KO, the Egg, Britannica's Paralysis, Fourth-dimensional Christmas in the Cop Shop, nostalgic half-remembered Bikie Heart Stimulant, 'Ah those were the days . . . almost as it used to be. . . .'

But he hadn't got back there, after all. He'd got it wrong. Now he was The Guide. Why had he wished to be alone? Why had . . .

He stood humbly to one side repressing his commentary while one of the men opened a small case and began to dust for fingerprints. In Chink's experience the powder they used was black, but this stuff was white . . . another joke? 'They're planting me.' It lay however like old dust on the cigarette box, the window-sill, the books on the floor. He hadn't got back there at all. . . .

Then the D asked to have Chink's print. A small panic. He almost said, 'You have it already, it's a black one.'

'We have to know what's yours and what isn't.'

'Oh yas. . . .'

'D'you read all this?' Holding up a copy of the *Connoisseur's Handbook of Marijuana*, one of *Cowboy Kate* (black holster a-swing by her creamy buttocks), and one of *Supercock* . . . a quick selection.

'No,' said Chink. 'They belong to a friend, I've just got the loan of the flat until he wants it back, he's from the university. . . .'

'You're not a student?'

'No.' Chink sweating.

'I see.' The D takes details: it all goes in a book. 'But you'll be around for a while? You're not pushing off soon?'

'No.' Chink, meek 'n' mild. *Yes yes yes!* was what he almost said, as though to confess.

'Because we'll need to be able to get in touch with you if we find anything. This man's been working the area, if it's the same one. The prints will tell. Meanwhile, take your boots off before you get into bed, it might avoid confusion especially yours.'

'I did . . . !' Chink, faint and stunned by the possibility that . . .

'It was a joke,' said the D. 'Night-night, sweet dreams.'

Finally they left.

'God. . . .' He waited for an hour, crouched over his tumbling puppy-dog heart, peering past the curtain of the front window from time to time, then rode back round to Beck's place as dawn came up.

The party had finished. Chink made some tea and sat in the cluttered kitchen sifting data. It didn't make much sense. There was a growing racket, half sleepy half quarrelsome, of birds outside in the garden. He opened the curtains and sat drinking the tea from an enamel mug, looking out at the trees in the early daylight.

'Ah me.'

It was still and clear. An occasional car accelerated past the front of the house. He found a packet of cigarettes on top of the refrigerator and sat smoking, sipping the tea without milk or sugar. The house was very quiet. He hoped that someone would wake up soon and come to the kitchen. It was a good story.

'A funny thing happened to me . . .'

Then he yawned till his jaw cracked. There were more cars outside now. His eyelids felt raw. Energy drained suddenly from him. I'll tell someone about it later, he thought, and went out into the garden to piss.

There was some broken glass by the kitchen door. He

remembered why he'd left. No one had been rolled or cut or raped, but that wasn't the point. . . .

What is, *young feller* . . . ?

'Ah. . . .'

His mouth tasted bad. He shook the drops from his prick, yawning, stretching his back till it clicked. Why had he been so long alone? It was now full daylight. The early clamour of the birds had died away. I'll have a sleep, he thought, and went back into the house. He encountered a sour after-party smell as he opened the kitchen door. I should go home. Then he thought, *To that*?

He opened the door to the living-room. Some effort had been made to clear away the mess. Bottles were crowded into a corner, there was a cardboard carton filled with butts and other rubbish in the centre of the floor. The windows were open but the curtains hung motionless across them in the still air. At least the room wasn't stuffy. He went towards the sofa, saw someone on it covered with a tartan blanket, but was by this time too tired to explore further in the house. He took a cushion off a chair, put it in a corner, laid his head on it, and sailed instantly out of himself. The lights changing to green . . . *back there*. . . .

That was how Kate saw him when she woke up later in the morning. . . . And now, looking through her window, she doesn't see light among the leaves, the blond of Ingrid's hair where the leaves are stirring . . . it's another summer altogether, filtered northern sunshine heavy in the corners of the room which is already growing hot, beams of glare shooting through gaps in the motionless curtains, iridescent patches and stripes of heat burning on the walls, a sour night-time exhalation beginning to gather in the silent house, waiting for the moment when the windows and curtains will be flung open. . . . The key ring with the ignition key of the bike is pushed on to the index finger of his right hand, which lies palm-up on the carpet. The hand's large and white, its fingers curled in sleep. There's a tortoiseshell bracelet on his wrist. The other hand's stuck under the waist band of his jeans. His legs are thrown down in front of him, with the scuffed toes of his boots turned out. His head's rolled off the cushion and is hanging to one side, on to his left shoulder, towards her. His nose has been running.

'Oh fuck. . . .'

It was the quiet head who'd sat with Beck most of the night, talking and smoking Beck's shit, who'd left about the time Beck started getting mad. Why was he back? He'd struck her as heavy. But he'd been making Beck laugh.

'He's bad news Kate, but fucking incredible lemme tell you, doesn't need anybody, quite insane, a real survivor. He'll be around for a while. His old man's just died, something shitty was going on there, cut off his power for a while, Chink's I mean. He's got someone's flat in Parnell, and their bike. People treat him like that.'

'Is he gay?'

'I tried him once.' Beck screaming laughter through his nose. 'It was soon after I'd met him, at Jan's place. I really dug him . . . he had nowhere to stay . . . he came back here with me . . . the place was full of the usual creeps . . . he said never mind, he'd find a place to crash somewhere else. I said he could share my bed. He said okay. I went and had a shower, you know, that bridal night feeling. When I got back to the room he was *asleep*, on the bed. I lay awake all night, what was left of it, wondering whether to wake him up and throw him out, or just kill him where he lay. I was so strung out! Finally I jacked off on his head. When he woke up in the morning I ripped into him . . .

said I knew about cockteasers like him . . . that I didn't hold down a fucking awful lucrative job just to keep closets and jerks like him off the street, and he could get out. His expression never changed. He yawned and put a hand up to scratch his head, whereupon of course,' Beck screaming laughter again, 'he felt some glup in his hair. Can you imagine! You've seen him, he's big and strong. He brought his fingers down slowly. His expression still didn't change. Well, I was jumping around the room by this stage expecting to get my face smashed. But what d'you think happened? What d'you think? He just said, "Why weren't you straight with me, man? Why didn't you tell me?" So of course I said I did tell him, but that I didn't think I had to go through the alphabet. I mean, I thought he was *educated.* I mean, I thought he was telling *me*, for that matter. And then I realized what he'd said. I went hot and cold. "So you mean it's all right, you were just tired," I said. "Yeah, I was tired," he said, "but no, it's not all right, it's not my bag, but if you'd been straight with me I wouldn't have stayed with you and strung you out." Then he just got up, had a shower, washed his hair with my shampoo, thanked me for letting him crash, *apologised* again, and left, just like that! I couldn't believe it.' Beck pushed his serious beaky face close to her. It wasn't often he took off his masks. 'Is that naive, or what? Or selfish? Or just very cool? I still don't know what he was doing to me. I can't shake the feeling it was deliberate. Lemme tell you Kate, he's weird. I can't sort him out. I mean, we're good friends now, I see him a lot when he's here, but he's kind of abstract, you know? If I ever made it with Chink I'd feel as though I'd been with something not quite human . . . ugh . . . he doesn't turn me on anymore, but I like his mind, as they say . . . ha ha. . . . Mind you, women really dig him, perhaps if you tried him you'd find a human being, not that I'd recommend it . . . one of these days he's gonna throw the switch, I wouldn't like to be the one he takes along. . . .'

So now she lay there on the sofa staring at this Chink. Beck talked as though she should've known the name. Well, so he was hot shit. He didn't look so good just at the moment. She decided he might be considerate enough, or blocked enough, to rate silent thanks, which was unusual at Beck's place. Beck's boarders were usually long on vanity and short on patience. That night one of them had pinched her sleeping-bag.

Well, let's go. She lay for a while looking at him. Beck was *afraid* of him. She'd never imagined Beck could be afraid of anyone. 'What have I got to lose?' he'd say. 'My *innothenthe*?' Singing, 'Give me your, dir-ty luurve . . .', flashing his eye-tooth gap. Yet Chink robbed him of something, had robbed him. He must be blocked out of his mind to lie like that, she thought. He sprawled there as though he wanted to push his space to its limits. . . . She was sitting with her legs drawn up under the blanket. She thought that most people enter sleep for protection: they draw their space around themselves. They curl themselves over their bellies, their soft parts. But this big pale hood was in occupation. His defencelessness was a kind of contempt.

Then he yelled, a whinny. She was just feeling about on the floor for her dress. *Oh shit.* She pulled the dress over her head. This looked like the time to get out. She struggled with raised arms to get the dress down. When her head pushed clear she saw him staring at her. He'd sat up. She jerked the material over her hips and legs. Too late. His teeth were set and he looked ill, or afraid.

'The Stranger . . .' His lips had barely moved. He's mad, he's really fucked, she thought. Let's go. He was staring and staring. It was like talking to someone who looked at the bridge of your nose. There was a warp somewhere in his perceptions, the matching surfaces failing to come together, sliding out of alignment. C'mon, let's go. She needed to remind herself. Let's go, let's go. Please. She recognized a kind of helplessness immobilizing her. When she moved she would already have admitted defeat.

His stare suddenly fell full upon her, his eyes meeting hers as though for the first time. She saw him slump a little.

'Are you all right?' Well, no point in being original at such moments.

'What's your name?'

'I'm Kate.'

She waited. He was still staring. His gaze retained some insolence.

'Your name's Chink, isn't it?'

'I'm The Guide. . . .' His voice was quiet, rather arch. She was thinking, What a prick.

'Um, Kate. Sorry to bother you. I was having a dream. Last night was pretty weird y'see, I . . .' He stopped, shrugged. It was as though he had something to tell her but couldn't be bothered finding the words. Or was he being polite? She was thinking, What about an apology for the intrusion. For your eyeful of me.

'I thought you were tripping or something,' she said.

'Oh no. . . .'

'I hope it wasn't a bad dream.'

'Familiar enough. And a waking vision to wake to.' He yawned then sat up and blew his nose into a dirty red handkerchief.

A compliment, well. . . . She was even grateful, as he tossed it out.

'Well, see you,' she said. She was going to have a shower.

'Now Kate, be fair. . . .' He'd spoken finally in what she took to be his ordinary voice. She'd almost heard the gears changing somewhere, a shrill whine of effort cut off . . . labouring torque giving way to a disengaged freefall. . . . He stood up and opened the curtains, flung them to either side of himself. It was a beautiful day. Late morning sunshine filled the big room. He stood rattling the keys against his palm, looking out.

'I want to have a shower,' she said.

'Lemme get you breakfast.'

'I want to have a goddamn *shower*.'

He was craning his neck to look out past the corner of the window, towards the street. 'Okay, I'll wait for you here.' He turned around at the same time as she stood up. He was leaning against the window frame, waiting, his eyes calmly meeting hers. She found herself grinning with the puzzled effort of avoiding his quiet insolence.

'But all I need is a cup of tea. . . .' It even *sounded* like a surrender. Why was she giving in when his insistence was so formless, so calm? He was smiling, an odd hinged opening of his face. His eyes simply waited, on her. There seemed to be no gesture she could make to break free of the assumption his manner implied.

'Is that all, a cup of tea?' His smile was beginning to split his head clear in half. She shrugged, flung her hands out.

'Yes, for Christ's sake!'

'Listen Kate, I've got a much better idea than that,' he said. 'Let's go out somewhere. I've got the loan of a bike. Let's go out and have breakfast somewhere. For Chrissake, whatta day! Let's get out of here before . . .'

'Before the rest get up?'

'Yes, yes!'

He was laughing. She'd given in, she didn't know why. It

was a relief. He pushed himself clear of the window frame and cocked his heavy head at her.

'Oh, all right,' she said.

'Okay, Kate . . .'

Somehow he'd sensed her desire to get out of the stale house, right out of it, into the sunlight, out there. For a moment she pondered this package deal. He stood there by the open window, smiling, jiggling the key of the bike. Had he simply passed on his desire to get out? It didn't matter. Yeah, let's go. Saturday mornings at Beck's were usually lazy and bored: records, dope, half-hearted excursions as far as the park or a beach . . . an inertia storing up irritations for the evening and the party.

Remembering this change of heart, she pauses, looks up. In the window her leafy reflection looks back at her. She's smiling. *Let's go. . . .*

'Come on, Kate.'

She had the shower. Chink had splashed water on his face. His long hair, which he fastened with a rubber band for riding, was damp by his ears. He drove quite slowly, heading for the harbour bridge. When they got to Victoria Park he stopped and took off his pea coat. There were games of cricket going on in the middle distance, beyond the dry shade of the trees bordering the park. It was a day of glassy clarity, less humid than usual, small high puffs of cloud appearing and disappearing. Heatwaves rose from the asphalt. Some icecream wrappers had already collected in the dusty gutter along the park, where sparrows were wrangling and fluffing out their wings.

Summer Saturday: hot, blue, and light beating like a pulse against the white concrete of the motorway overpass, against the glaring forecourt of the service station back up the road, out of which cars accelerated towards the North Shore beaches, passing Kate and Chink, filled with children and bright colours

. . . a kind of ferocity of purpose against which, or rather between which and the soporific games of cricket on the other side, Chink's leisurely act of removing his jacket and folding it over the petrol tank of the bike was a perfect cipher of freedom and pleasure: '*This* is our pace, there's as much time as we choose to take.'

They reached the top of the bridge and could see the great yellow crane the Japanese engineers had floated all the way to the Waitemata . . . imagine it in mid-ocean, that absurd beautiful garish machine breaking the horizon, making it finite, whichever way you turned. That was what she imagined, that day. Chink dipped the bike a little towards the centre of the road, a genuflexion . . . 'Moby-Dick,' he said . . . and then they swooped over the vertigo in her stomach and down the long shimmering ramp towards the Shore, the family station wagons still zipping past on their right. Beyond them up the harbour were anarchic clusters of becalmed yachts, and beyond them, islands, olive green and then blue, leading out to an unnatural horizon, slashed, as in a child's drawing, across the whole bright perspective. Below the bridge on their left the houses were also like toys.

Is it 'memory' that plays these tricks? Some sort of current account, where you can make withdrawals so long as you also pay in? She's thinking of value, but not like that. Some memories seem to her like gifts. But others subtract from her when she receives them . . . some kind of negative power, destruction. . . . That Saturday, as she remembers it, is clear and simple, 'childishly' so. To come to her now, it's had to pass through the filters of three confused years. It's emerged brightly, strangely without sound, but full of motion and light and colour, the sense of a body stretching itself in a space which gives it room and time, a dreamlike sense of relaxation, dreamlike transport.

How can there be anything left? Anything which hasn't lodged with the other litter and grit against the interstices of those difficult filters . . . no doubt that's it: what she has, however trashy, is also refined. A defence. It's like the question, 'What else could I have done?' Choices are for the present, or the future: that *now* we keep waiting for . . . or hauling in, like kids fishing, too hopeful to sit out the time until the actual tug of the present on the line tells us we're in luck. . . . The past is litter, pure gold. There's no further reduction to make, except destruction.

In the south once, on a stormy day, Chink had a long discussion with a young poet they'd gone to see. It was at the same house Kate's staying in now, though when she remembers it it seems elsewhere.

It had been raining for days, and blowing from the south. Everyone was on edge. They'd been discussing the problems of a mutual friend, drinking wine. Chink said, after a good deal of wrangling, and with sudden ferocity, that you learned nothing from the past, because there was no such thing, because any decision you made had never been made before. Then Curtis said some lines from one of his poems.

> Last year's emotions
> jack off at the bottom of the garden
> it is better so
> what we go forward on is solid with their solitude

He was drunk, sententious. It had been a boring conversation. The room was stuffy, and stale with coal smoke. The lines sounded crude and easy to her. Yet it seemed that Curtis and Chink agreed. But Chink sat morosely, looking out the window. The rain had stopped and a wash of sunlight flowed over the scrubby expanse of a hill opposite the house.

'That's not what I meant,' Chink said. Then he stood up and asked Kate if she'd like to go for a walk. They went abruptly out, leaving Curtis poking at the fire.

'Why did you put Curtis down?' she asked. They were labouring up a steep hill to the flagstaff above the docks. Chink was leaning forward into the slope. She couldn't see his face.

'Never mind,' he muttered. Then, after a pause, he added, 'I just thought it was a nasty poem—what does he know about such things, sitting in front of his fire?'

'But he's been through some heavy shit.'

'That's what I mean,' said Chink.

He stopped. They'd reached the top of the hill. Below them was the ferrous-red and black asphalt clutter of the little port, the cranes and derricks motionless and deserted, the sea grey. The wind whipped round them.

'That's what I mean,' said Chink again. 'I mean, Curtis just forgets it. He doesn't have any of it with him. Anything that happened once that mattered remains present, right? But he just shovels it all back behind himself. Yeah, you don't learn, you're changed, that's all. Oh, no doubt he's waded through as much shit as the rest of us. But look how clean he is at the end of it! Doesn't look as though he's been through a single change . . . doesn't look as though he's had to change his mind *once* since he was on the tit!' Chink stood, staring down into the cold silent basin of the port. 'I sounded like him then,' he said.

Then he began to walk down the other side of the hill. 'Let's get over to the back beach.'

They scrambled down the muddy path to the road which ran around the perimeter of the township's peninsula, along the channel. Here the sea was a dirty colour, except where the main current was flushing it clear. The tide was running in against the wind, pushing up white horses and spray. She was stumbling after Chink, wanting to say, 'You're wrong about Curtis, if you can think that about him then you can think it about me, and you're wrong . . . it's possible to be born again.' But the wind was driving into her face.

But he'd started running, had leapt out on to a narrow jetty and was flying down it above the turbulent water. She watched in terror. She thought, He's going to jump. . . . It must have been the abandon with which he flung himself along the planks, towards the platform at the end. But when he got there he stood facing up the channel into the wind. Then he turned and started back. She could see how the wind shoved at him. He began to mime a guitar player, dancing towards her, opening and shutting his mouth. When he reached her they grabbed each other. His face was freezing. They hugged tightly, pummelling each other's backs and shoulders, in the lee side of a shed, hearing the water smacking under the jetty, the wind slashing among the trees. She kissed him again and again, pulling his cold face against hers, thinking, You're wrong, oh Chink you're wrong, none of that matters, this is what matters. . . .

But on that summer Saturday in Auckland there was no wind but the warm resistance of the air to the motorbike, and no past either, none that they shared, and no shelter needed, and no more limitation of the time they had than that absurd blue horizon, which would last as long as the day did.

They went and had lunch with some friends of Chink's who lived on the cliff at the end of Stanley Point. It was a familiar neighbourhood for Kate. She'd wished never to see it again. She had the strangest feeling, as it became clear which way Chink was going, that none of this was accidental.

'I used to live round here once,' she said into his ear,

expecting him to turn his head quickly to reply, 'I know.' But he didn't say anything. When he steered into the street she still thought of as 'our street', she found that the bike was sailing her past familiar shop fronts, houses, trees, and it wasn't taking her *back there* at all . . . none of it was worth a pinch of shit!

'Well, well. . . .'

When they got to his friends' house, Chink was welcomed with pleasure ('Hello stranger . . .') as though he'd been expected. She didn't mind. The woman of the house, who was beautiful though no longer young, examined Chink with the proprietary eyes of a lover.

'What've you been up to?'

'Apologising,' he said. For some reason she found this funny. And Kate got her first taste of the legend: the woman's gaze leaving Chink and seeming to break against Kate's young body: 'I name thee. . . .' It was a pleasure of a kind, to be credited with such a role . . . to be credited with the power to play it.

Chink told them about the burglary, making a good story of it. It was the first time she'd heard him speak at any length, having only watched him at Beck's. She could see why Beck appreciated him. But there was no point interrupting him. When he'd told the story he was quiet again, lolling against the wall. It was as though he'd come all the way over to tell his friends the story of the burglary. The woman's eyes flicked at Kate, sorting out the fact that she hadn't been there at the time. They were all a little drunk. Then Chink suddenly said, 'Gotta go.' Kate saw the woman hug Chink goodbye, and quickly bunt her lean pelvis in against him. Then she was waving and smiling as Chink started the bike.

'Come and see us again soon . . . you too. . . .'

They went back to the comical shambles of his borrowed flat and she helped him clear up. She was chattering on about how good it was to be in Auckland again. Then they had a coffee. She realized how tired he looked. It was about four o'clock.

'You look fucked,' she said. 'You'd better crash.'

'Do you want a ride back to Beck's?'

'No, I'll walk.'

'Come and have a meal later, then.'

'All right.'

'I'll meet you in Tony's in Khartoum Place at seven.'

She let herself out. He was wearily dragging off his boots and all at once burst into laughter and threw the boots at the wall.

She didn't go back to Beck's. She walked up to the Domain and wandered around, drank a Fanta. A wedding party was having its photograph taken by the duckpond. Children who didn't belong kept barging in on the scene, trying to get closer to the ducks, to give them bread. Then she sat in the late sun, on the grass, until it was time to set out to meet Chink.

The cars and children were leaving. They were packing up the games of cricket down there. She longed for the place to be deserted. The road which wound through the park was filled with traffic travelling in both directions. It was impossible to imagine where it might all be going, or coming from. It was like blood, a small section of a kind of endless reticulation, a maze, a mystery, within which there was an endless motion, utterly inscrutable . . . yes, and if you tried to make sense of it, you'd go crazy. The lines of traffic were so unbroken that after a while their motion seemed almost to cease: she was looking at a snakelike scintillation, a flicker of stasis. She had the sense of occupying some kind of pivot or fulcrum. The city sounds which reached her seemed to tip past the point of perception where she could hear them. They became a kind of silence. She felt herself poised above a mystery, in a precarious balance.

That woman on the Shore came suddenly to mind. She found herself laughing at the memory of the woman's eyes. How easy appearances were, and deceptions! How much the woman had assumed. All the same it had been pleasant, being cast in that role.

It was getting late. She stood up, brushing dry grass from her clothes. Below her the snake of traffic was once again in motion, and its noise reached her loud and clear. She went down and joined the flow.

She walked downtown across Grafton Bridge. Some Indian couples were going slowly in the same direction. She felt happy, and loose and graceful, like the slender young Indian women in their lovely saris, though beside them, she thought, she must look clumsy and eager. In Albert Park as she went through a few people were still lying about. The sounds of Saturday night traffic in the city rose towards her, muffled by distance and trees, but more it seemed by the warm evening air, filled with the perfumes of hot grass and flowers in the park.

She remembers that she took her sandals off and dipped her feet in the cool fountain, shuffling them dry on the grass, before going on down through the dim, verbena and rosemary scented paths under the trees, towards Khartoum Place.

They had dinner in the small crowded restaurant, then went up to the Kiwi. There was another party at Beck's. The noise and crush in the bar were frightful.

'I'm sick of his cynicism.'

'But it's only a manner. . . .' She wondered whether she should let on that Beck had told her the story about himself and Chink. She found it impossible to guess how he might react . . . and thinking back now, while a cool summer rain storm drenches the green broadleaf outside the window and distorts her reflection in the glass, she finds she can't guess, even now, whether that piece of his past mattered enough to him for him to keep present, in that weird grab-bag of knowledge he contrived to lug around like Bunyan's Christian's burden, like some obscene fleshy encrustment . . . the mask slipping . . . the flicker of animal reflex. . . . And *me:* did he remember *me*, did I matter?

'He loved me, he loved me. . . .'

The words surprise her into looking up: her reflection in the window is sad, its outlines warped by trickling rain: that static glitter of destruction, where time's arrested, where the process goes on and on and on, *there*, without change. Shaking her head, closing her eyes to her reflection.

It was Chink who wanted to go to the party, and in spite of what she'd said, she didn't want to go near it. Chink wasn't being kind to her, as dear Beck had to be, with his lectures on the evils of mandrax and on what he called 'the need to strike the rock with your staff': meaning get on with it . . . have faith. Chink had no advice for her.

The bar was the usual zoo. They left before it closed. Of course they went to Beck's. Hardly anyone had turned up. Beck jogged through the main room with a tape-recorder.

'Had a full day?' He glared at Kate. 'Come with me, I've got a beauty.'

'D'you want to go?' Chink asked, but then went up the stairs anyway. She followed him into Beck's room. Beck was jumping around arranging things.

'This here's an experiment.' He fixed up the machine next to a boy sitting on the bed. 'And this is Julian, he's a poet or should I say another poet.'

They said hello. Beck turned out all the lights but one over his desk. He began to roll some joints there. The rest of them were sitting like a school class on the bed.

'Julian,' said Beck with a magisterial air, 'doesn't believe in rational discourse. He believes that poetry's what comes naturally. So we're gonna have a go.'

The boy was very skinny with long red hair. He had a young white face. He was no match for Beck. They smoked a log. Beck was jumping around the room 'setting up the experiment', chattering away, something about 'Man is not a fly.'

'Everybody relax!' Beck switched on the tape-recorder. 'Now this is gonna come naturally,' he said.

The boy was smashed. He smiled and nodded.

'All right,' said Beck, 'what happens is the first thing you say, the first thing that comes into your head's the first line of a poem. But I'll tell you when you've hit it. Then you go on and say a poem beginning with that first line.'

'I've got a shitty cold,' said the boy.

'Cancel that,' said Beck.

'I've bought a car.'

'Cancel that.'

'It's spring.'

'Cancel that!'

'The broadbeans burst into flower?'

'Cancel that!'

'My lady's pregnant.'

'Uh huh?'

'She's reading Thomas Hardy and others.'

'Not bad. Go on. *Synthesize*, fellah.'

'A pregnant woman discovers the meaning of fiction.'

'Very good. . . .'

The boy suddenly cracked up. He rolled around on the bed laughing.

'All right, here it is:

A pregnant woman discovers the meaning of fiction
for the first time. What incredible
feats of the imagination reveal themselves to her:
e.g. *he* peddles *his* wife in the cattle market
another lovely lady gets around
shooting prize athletes with silver bullets.
She browses over the books in her big blue dress.
She is beautiful. She has never read
this much fiction before.
She has never understood so much.

'Well,' said Beck, and shot smoke from his nose, 'you got a really good first line but you blew the rest. Why couldn't you let the thing follow itself through?'

'Fuck you,' said the boy sleepily. 'You do better.'

'Let's see what you can make of those other shitty lines. What was the first one? Actually "shitty" something . . .'

'I've got a shitty cold?'

'Yes, I've got a shitty cold. Let's see what you can do with that.'

'Okay. I've got a shitty cold.' The boy paused. 'Are you serious?' he said. 'That's not poetry.'

'Not yet it isn't.'

'Let's see,' said the boy dreamily.

I've got a shitty cold. Out at sea
the steamers' smokestacks tootle.
South America's just over there
where the Andes fondle divine nether parts.
You can also blow your nose in them.

They were both rolling around laughing.

'Right, next was . . .'

'I've bought a car,' said the boy.

'Go to it,' Beck looking the other way.

> I've bought a car
> oh no Joplin
> not even Bobby Magee
> history will make no distinction
> let the dealer look at your teeth lady
> this boy's buying older and older cars
> to get Janis back
> time is only consumer goods
> is only as good as the use you make of it
> that's what the man said
> when he sold me this Mercedes Benz

'"O Lord won't you buy me . . . a Mercedes Benz,"' sang Chink in a Janis Joplin falsetto.

'Shut up Chink,' said Beck. 'You can be prima donna some other time. What's the penultimate, "It's spring"? Oh shit, what kind of treatment can you give that?'

> It's spring.
> Prove it.
> O my cock's flowered
> in the sun which
> accompanied her
> down the
> steps.

Then Julian sat back. 'I'm too spaced for this wee exercise,' he said.

Beck's face was white, as white as the boy's, in the dim room.

'Unsatisfactory class of student these days,' said Beck.

'Knock it off, Beck,' said Chink.

'Speak when you're spoken to,' said Beck. 'Buy Kate a ticket for your trip. Meanwhile me and Julian are gonna stay inside, we're conducting an experiment. . . . What's your last chance, Julian?'

'The broadbeans burst into flower.' He really wanted to get out, it was obvious. He jumped to his feet and shouted.

> The broadbeans burst into flower
> Us broads have been thirsting for hours
> Broad inna beam but first by the powers
> The orb's been lost in tough hours . . .

'Oh fuck,' he said. He went out and slammed the door.

'The rest of you can go too, you bore me stiff,' said Beck.

The tape was still revolving on the machine. Chink reached over and turned it off. They went to the door. She looked back. Beck was shaking his head, as though about to cry.

'See you later, old Beck,' she said.

'All right . . . that little shit . . . I should've raped him with my broad-bean.' He began to laugh, still shaking his head.

They descended majestically into the roar of the party. They didn't need Beck anymore, bless him. . . . All at once she felt launched, felt that woman's champagne gaze break like a cool benediction on her skin, which rose in gooseflesh where Chink touched her to turn the corner of the stairs.

She kissed his neck. He told her enough to give them some kind of common past. The day's simplicity was lost. It no longer mattered. The order of things no longer mattered.

'Do you want to come back?'

They smiled at each other. They were transparent. Her heart was banging.

'It might be more peaceful than here.'

'Might be.' His face opened: that smile. 'All right,' he said. 'Let's go, Kate the Kate.'

Beck was shaking his head at her. He drew a thin finger across his throat. She didn't care. She could strike the rock with her staff.

Chink had taken a couple of Beck's joints. They smoked one outside in the garden. The noise of the party came to them like the soundtrack of a cheap film about a war. The sound of John McLaughlin's guitar pitched up from time to time out of the roar of voices, like a general who can't make himself heard. He's babbling retreat, and the army's attacking, or vice versa. Nerve warfare. . . . Near them under the trees two girls were quarrelling. She heard one of them say, '. . . and now you . . .'.

They rode away from it all like survivors. It wasn't even very late, just around midnight. They sailed through the streets. She leaned her cheek on the back of Chink's old coat and sang:

> O Lord won't you buy me
> A Mercedes Benz . . .

. . . and leans her cheek against the back of her hand, in this room where the light's fading again: the familiar coda of these days, a metric which is beginning to wind her up towards some gesture. . . . Though there are days like this one, when she gets up quietly and goes down to the other end of the house, towards the sounds of lives being lived there: the summer light of Ingrid's hair, the baby, Curtis . . . these friends within whose circle she feels adrift, like an empty boat on a calm green lake. . . . But her friends don't know the words.

O Lord won't you buy me
A Mercedes Benz
My friends are all dead
I must make amends

7 *Badedas Bath*

Chink opened the door and went in ahead of her: taking possession. Someone's cleaned up, she thought. The afternoon had backed off. She thought of the people in it as 'him' and 'her'. Their voices had gone flat, the metallic squawk of memory, like Julian's voice on the tape-recorder. Or like the city sounds which tipped past her into silence, in the park. The most vivid surviving fragment was that of the girl's voice saying, bitterly, '. . . and now you . . .'.

The words that came out of her were huge, they filled her mouth, blocking her tongue. She wondered if he could hear them. He was at the far end of the room, turning on the record-player.

Then everything stopped. It had been nothing to do with her. She'd been brought to where she was meant to be . . . as though she were about to emerge, there in Chink's borrowed flat, shedding the last disguise, lifting it from herself. . . . Oh she couldn't even speak. At the same time a vacuum was rising inside her. It seemed to be choking her. She saw Chink turn around. Her arms rose in front of her. Then he disappeared.

Her eyes had closed. Tears were pouring down her cheeks. He'd crossed the room and was holding her. She could feel her arms going around him. He was huge and somehow light. . . .

She was sitting on the sofa and Chink was kneeling in front of her. She began to cry, sobbing and gasping, and fell forward against him, to put her arms around him, her face against his neck. He held her gently, dipping his mouth on to her shoulder.

All at once she saw what she'd done. She saw herself holding out her arms like that: 'Come to me!' How absurd, how fucking stupid!

'Hey c'mon, take it easy, take it easy. . . .'

But it just kept winding out of her, like a siren . . . oh oh oh oh oh. . . . The feeling was *shapely*. . . . She was aware of its limits as she was aware of the limits of her body. She could see her forearm around Chink's shoulder, and she rubbed her lips across it, feeling the small hairs. Then she pressed her mouth back against his neck. She thought that if she let go of him the feeling would go. He was still holding her gently. She found she was trying to say 'Thank you' and the thought of this made her laugh even harder. She wanted to say the shape of her feeling to him. It seemed that almost anything she said would do.

Then Chink pushed her back against the sofa. The instant quiet was like a blow. Chink was kneeling in front of her, his hands on her knees. She heard Howlin' Wolf on the record-player, solid and familiar: '. . . because I'm built for comfort . . . I ain't built for speed . . .'.

'Well,' said Chink. 'You *are* a strange lady. Are you okay?'

'I'm sorry.'

She watched him walk away down the room and into the kitchen. On impulse she got up and began to rearrange things. She pushed some of the chairs around. She was doing this very seriously, with a feeling of sensible purpose. It seemed necessary to bring the room 'up to date'.

Chink came out of the kitchen with two cups.

'For Christ's sake . . .' He stood in the kitchen door holding the cups. She was laughing. For the first time she felt that something depended on her. She sat down.

'D'you wanna go back to Beck's?' She tugged at his hand. Coffee slopped on to the carpet. He leant carefully over her.

'No I don't,' she said. 'I'm a bit stoned and I've had a hard time. That seems over now. I wanted to bring the room up to date, that's all. It's not complicated.'

He slumped down opposite her.

'Listen,' he said as though he'd made a decision, 'don't depend on me too much, that's what I mean. I'm not dependable.'

'I'm gonna have a bath,' she said.

The area he was getting into was unnecessary . . . she refused it. He was still staring at her, with something furious in his expression, drawing pale bones up to the skin. But it was like stepping out of a two-dimensional world into one with depth, a real horizon: Chink in his chair, there. She was glad he wasn't just kind. There seemed to be plenty of time . . . a space as dreamlike as the summer harbour.

'I'm going to have a bath,' she said again, but didn't move: she stared at him, he stared back.

Then Chink suddenly strained his eyes wide. He shot himself with two fingers under his left ear. Then he closed his eyes. He still looked white and weary. He was sitting sprawled in an armchair, his legs stretched out, his chin on his chest, occupying all the space there was.

It was a big old-fashioned bath with lion's-paw legs. The taps had neat porcelain buttons in their tops with 'Hot' and 'Cold'. She decided to fill the bath right up. While it was running she looked into the cupboard above the basin. There was some

Badedas there, so she put it in the water when the bath was full. The water turned green. Then she looked at her face in the mirror. Her eyes were red and there were salty trails on her cheeks. She took her clothes off and looked in the mirror again, from different angles. She thought she'd got thin over the past weeks. But it made her breasts look better. She felt contented and orderly. She picked her clothes up and folded them on a chair. Then she made sure there was soap by the bath. She took a big loofah off a hook on the wall, and dropped it in. She weighed herself. She was a stone less than when Dave had left.

Then she got into the bath and lay flat with just her head out. The water came up almost to the edge. It was deep enough for her to feel suspended in. Her limbs hung, a warped and tender green. Steam had condensed on the white walls of the room, leaving trails, like my face, she thought: skinny, face like a bathroom wall. She ducked her head under and came up rubbing her hair. When she opened her eyes Chink was standing there with a towel.

'What's that green?'

'*Badedas* . . . it was in your cupboard.' She lay still, looking up at him.

'I never thought of it,' he said. He dropped the towel on a chair and left.

Because she was in the bath she began to soap herself, automatically. *Not dependable* . . . she tried the words in her head. Chink had had enough of her after all, 'a neurotic cunt'.

Then the door swung open. There was no one there.

'Goddamn draught.'

But two-thirds of the way up the edge of the door a single finger appeared, creeping around, testing the way as though blind. A second finger appeared, and a whole hand.

'Come in!' she shouted. 'Come in! Little hand, come on in!

Come to Mama! I thought you were never going to come.'

The hand grasped the edge of the door. She was watching it, tense with glee like a child, when some distance below the hand she saw the end of Chink's erect prick creeping slowly into sight like a great cyclamen, an orchid, a corsage being offered shyly at the girl's door. . . . Holy shit! He was mad. . . .

'Bring your vulgar friend too,' she shouted.

Chink walked in, grinning. It was as though he was surfing towards her. She was screaming with laughter. He reached behind her and pulled the plug out. She'd sat with her back against the taps so she could see the door. Put it in lights. She had the feeling she'd been directed in some obscure theatrical game.

When some water had drained Chink put the plug back then gently pushed her head forward and began to soap her back. She rested her forehead on her raised knees.

'What a long back you have, like a real amphibian,' he said. He massaged between her shoulders and neck, then pushed his soapy hands slowly under her arms, passed them over her breasts. She let her weight rest on her forehead and closed her eyes. He held her gently, touching her nipples with the outsides of his thumbs. Then he took his hands away and lifted water with them to pour over her back. She sat up and turned her head. When she opened her eyes his prick was there.

'Hello, "friend" . . .'

His fingers closed her ears . . . she heard sea, Chink's muffled voice: 'Well, now Kate . . .'. She kissed his prick again, touching the side of it with her tongue, and closed her lips over it. It filled her mouth as the words had done earlier. It was as though it was the word she'd needed.

At night, now, she can hear Curtis and Ingrid making love . . . and just at the moment she can hear them all living, *con moto*, there at the other end of the house, and the radio on, as though the sounds of their life have been set to tawdry music, for her benefit. . . . She blocks her ears . . . and closes her eyes, as she closed them then, her mouth at work on this message, her arms reaching awkwardly up out of the bath to hold him. . . .

Then Chink had taken his hands from her ears. He just moved away and got into the bath, his cock breaking surface like some kind of sea snake. They were sitting staring at each other again. She again had the sense of being directed in some game.

'Well,' he said. 'How are you Kate?' He was smiling. She just nodded, reached out to touch his face. He sat with his arms resting along the sides of the bath. 'You look fine to me,' he said. She nodded again. 'Right,' he said.

He soaped himself, whistling, smiling at her.

'You see me now in my element, I'm invulnerable.' Then he got quickly out, dried himself, cleaned his teeth, and left.

When she went into the bedroom she got another shock: the scene was 'set', all the corny paraphernalia . . . a big candle had been lit, and incense, and Chink was sitting grinning on the bed, starting off the last of Beck's joints.

'Why, hello. . . .' She minced towards him, oopedoop. A game two can play, called 'Things happen after a Badedas Bath'. . . .

'Things happen after a Badedas Bath. . . .'

'What a long and lovely girl,' he said, with the same curious inflexion he'd given the words when he first spoke to her, from the living-room floor of Beck's place.

She sat beside him on the bed.

'Nice place you have here.'

'It's comfortable.'

Their bodies touched at thigh and shoulder. They smoked the log in silence, their fingers making the small journey back and forth, smelling each other's breath in the smoke, beginning to turn together until their shoulders no longer touched, until they were almost face to face, until she hooked one leg over one of his . . . and then they did turn together, at last, with a shared groan, the hot roach dropped to the floor, the friend taken into Kate's upstretched fork. . . .

'Things happen after a Badedas Bath. . . .' She had time to whisper it, the name of the game. Then she forgot about it, the whole routine. Ah dear stranger, dear friend. There was that moment of doubt, when depth and time seemed to flatten out, when she saw his face like a mask. Then it broke. His comical smile and shout ('Kate, Kate!') were different from the comedy of the hand, the friend, the anxious lover, the Badedas commercial . . . they weren't part of any game. He lay panting. Hey, strange man, that was lovely. That was a relief.

She was lying looking at him. He was very strongly made, but his body was almost hairless, except for a thin line which grew from his groin to a point just below his chest. His shoulders were broad but rather stooping. This gave him an appearance of menace at such times as he was standing still, in the corner of a room, for instance. *I've missed you, Kate.* His hair was long and black and straight. It was sawn off roughly across his brow, which increased the impression of immobility. All day the summer rain's been tapping at the broadleaf out there. When he smiled his face seemed to split in a straight line. When he laughed it was as though a hinge in his head had dropped: the bottom half of his face fell. His eyes were flat and exposed, set wide apart, grey. He could open them until they seemed to turn red at the edges. When he was angry all that could be seen of them was a wet glint, very bright. His hands were large and quite rough from the work he'd done. But the fingers were long and slender nevertheless. Playing a guitar made his hands look almost feminine, because the bunches of muscle in his palms were drawn inward, so that the whole hand matched the length and slenderness of the fingers. *If you wanna know something you have to ask the right question. It's like you have to know the answer already. So much time gets wasted.* Although his ribs showed, he didn't look skinny, because his arms were heavy and strong, and also because he had a thick waist. He claimed this was from swimming, which he'd done competitively. He kept very clean shaven. His chest and shoulders bore the scars of adolescent acne, as did his cheeks, though you tended not to notice this because of the general heaviness of his face. His feet turned inward ('swimming'), his legs were very long. His feet were ugly, with bunched toes, perhaps because he always wore boots. From behind he looked slender, though heavy across the shoulders. This may have been because, below the muscular waist, his buttocks and legs were skinny. *Hey Kate, tell the boss to blow it out his arse. This offer can't last.* There was a strange disproportion about him, and yet he was 'beautiful': his shapeliness was somehow simple and modest. He once said the same about her. *We were made for each other: watch this. . . .* She guesses it was because she's tall and dark with large breasts, and thin legs which embarrass her into preferring trousers. Lying face to face with their feet stretched out, her toes would come to the beginning of his instep. All day rain and dim humid light. Impossible to tell what time it is. When they placed their faces together his mouth was lower than hers, by the width of a lip, so that he could hold her lower lip between his while she held his upper one. Their eyes were level, though his were further apart. *I've missed you Kate.* His skin was very white, Celtic she thought. He hadn't been in the sun at all that summer.

How much of this she learned that night! She studied him, as though to remember. Anything she learned later, like his hands playing a guitar, was made to fit that first lesson.

Now it seems to her that she studied him because of those precarious moments, during which a brand new certainty was shaken and shaken. Because we're not dependable. In such a short time she'd passed through release, to dependence, to a different equilibrium (she believed) whose balance was maintained by such brief moments as that of Chink's exquisite smile . . . the simple sufficiency of his gentleness. At such moments, she thought, we transcend the inertia that attracts pain as surely as an open wound attracts flies. If only we can remember those moments, and at the same time keep the wound covered with whatever dressing or cosmetic we have, then we'll make it to the next zenith, the next miraculous smile, the next lesson. If it finishes now, she thought, that'll be no more or less than I expected from the start. At any rate I'll remember.

It was as though she heard two voices in the room: Julian saying, 'She has never understood so much', and the weeping girl in the dark garden, '. . . and now you . . .'.

So she turned towards him again. He was lying on his back, his eyelids drooping, looking sideways at her.

'How'd you like to come south with me Kate, the day after tomorrow? We could have a good trip. Let's get out of here. Let's really get out of here.'

At any rate I'll remember. If it finishes now. In hope the mind closes, blinks and closes, like the eyelids of a lover. 'Oh let it happen.' And sometimes you can't open your eyes, even if you want to.

In the morning they put some gear on the train for Dunedin. Chink stored his friend's bike at Beck's place. Beck wasn't home so Kate left a long note: '. . . off to strike the rock . . .'.

The day after, Monday, they began hitching south, in the rain.

It's rained all day, however much day there's been.

It was that simple. The lesson learned and as soon occluded, to be relearned and ('let it happen') obscured, ignored, thrust aside, again and again: *faith's gorgeous frail galleon*, as Beck had said once, sailing his thin hands through an imaginary languid ocean.

'All right,' she said casually, closing her eyes. 'I'll come, I was thinking of heading off soon anyway.'

She'd given in. It was a relief.

And silently, 'Yes, yes, oh Chink, we could have a good trip. Let's really get out of here . . .'.

Let's get the fuck out of here!

8

Choose a date: 1860. Some things have happened, some haven't, and some are in progress. It's incredible how many men have wandered New Zealand keeping meticulous notebooks and sketchbooks. These men are often soldiers, others are surveyors or priests. They travel because they have to. There's no point asking if this compulsion's enforced by powers outside themselves, or by some inner power of their own. Are they functions or causes? Even a century and more later it's impossible to measure the proportions.

But looking at these sketches, the painstaking and oppressive detail of them, the omniscience of the light in which their subjects were seen, we sense the *certainty* of the men who made them. Though the conditions under which they were made must often have been anything but leisurely, they seem nonetheless to be leisurely. They're the products of an expansive faith. They measure time in expansive units. What they conceal are the small units: the time lag between the axe striking the tree and the sound reaching the other side of the valley . . . the man falling, the sound of the musket . . . the crack of the bullock cart's axle and the beasts wrenched to their knees in the river crossing . . . the coughing of a Māori child with measles. They don't so much ignore such a scale as subsume it.

How different this freedom is from Chink's line of need, his exact and claustrophobic dedication. . . . Oh, he knew lots about some things. . . .

At this moment, in her sunny room, Kate's picking her way through a strange assortment of photographs and reproductions Chink had got together.

Delivering stores on the Waipā River near Ngāruawāhia *circa* 1910 . . . for'ard on the flatbottomed steam barge is a large winch. The boat's got almost no freeboard. The wheel's roughly amidships, where sacks of wheat and flour are piled. A plank's been laid from gunwale to bank. In the background are Lombardy poplars whose scale seems incongruous at first: then you realize that they're still young. There are also some macrocarpa, likewise well-established but young. A road runs past a small farmhouse. In the background is dense bush on hills, possibly Taupiri, the sacred mountain.

Here's Dick Seddon's Great Dive. They're waiting for him to come up. 'He stayed under 5 mins. A record!' It's on the Waikato River, at a Ngāruawāhia Regatta. A willow shades a crowd of Māori on the bank. On the river in the distance is a large canoe. Up close are two boats, the steam boat from which Seddon has dived, and a smaller boat with a brass band in it.

Everyone is looking at the calm surface of the river, waiting. . . . In the foreground is a large Māori with a black band on his left arm. On the back of this photograph Chink has scribbled *Te Waiorongo: the tranquil and peaceful waters.*

Ngāruawāhia 1864: here's The Delta, in a lithograph by G Pulman of Auckland. The Key shows King's Palace, King's Tomb, House of Parliament. The note reads: *Most of the natives' huts are back about half-a-mile towards the bush.* To which Chink had added, *Inspection by request.* There are conical military tents. In the background the Waipā River has a wee canoe on it. In the foreground men in military uniform are getting out of a rowboat on the banks of the Waikato. The Delta is like the prow of a canoe, the jutting bows of a galleon. The flagpole, whose power was widely understood, is situated like a mast. Thus the Royal Compound sails faithfully into Kate's present, with Chink aboard. . . .

Here are two early photographs: *The Tomb of Te Wherowhero* and *The Whare of Te Wherowhero.* The tomb is incongruous, built of weatherboard, set among scruffy bracken, on rough clay, the size of a big dog-kennel. . . . Kate remembers a portrait of the King, Pōtatau Te Wherowhero, by George French Angas: a tough kind face, hair fierce and curly as though to suggest energy, impatience, intellect, a large kuru in his left ear, heavy moko, sitting at ease in a blanket, probably on the selfsame Delta. . . . By the tomb stands a soldier: a Guide? The whare's also got soldiers around it, in ill-fitting uniforms . . . some kind of Palace Guard? The proud wretchedness of it strikes her now. She remembers Chink's anger. . . .

In 1910 Simmelhag's Delta Hotel was the same grand building it is now. Then its proprietor was an Irishman, R Ryan. Its spacious upstairs rooms opened on to the impressive balcony. Its chimneys were built in two kinds of brick, for contrast. Its other decorations were solid and on a grand scale. In the photograph Chink kept, Māori sit and lounge in the sun around the downstairs walls. . . .

A man was doing animal imitations at one end of the bar. The room was filled with tuis, dogs, cows. Outside the rain pelted down, the dull sound of a great hidden dynamo. There was a pool table at the far end of the room, and a blackboard with two names chalked up.

'D'you play pool?'

'If Paul Newman was a woman I'd be The Hustler.'

Chink took off his wet pea coat and put it with the bags, then walked down the room and wrote his name on the blackboard: *Chink.* Any questions. Under it he added *Kate the Newman.* He bought a jug at the bar and came back grinning, head falling apart.

A drunk man in a green cardigan caught at his arm. Beer slopped from the jug on to the floor. Chink performed a small arabesque, clutching the jug in both hands. He bent over the man. They appeared to be conferring together. Then Chink filled the man's glass.

'Rightoh mate.'

Because of the rain the room was about half full. Many of the drinkers were off the road repair gang. The animal man made a farting sound with his mouth: 'That was a student.' Chink took no notice, pulling his hair back and wringing at it.

'Gesundheit, Kate.'

'Sweet dreams, Chink.'

Clink: to Faith's Galleon. . . .

Every mile south he gets higher and quieter and crazier. His head's ripping right round. That's not a smile, it's . . .

'D'you know how I feel?' she said.

'Like two big tits on a pole.'

'No, listen. The other day I was walking up Queen Street. One of those Christian revivalists stopped me. He was outside John Courts, really weedy, wearing a suit and one of those Texan string ties. Behind him was a display window full of undressed mannikins like a lot of scalded naked women in body stockings. He was really insistent. Young lady, young lady! The setting was so weird that I stopped. Then he asked if I'd been born again. He was staring at me like you do sometimes. . . .'

'Yeah . . .'

'No, shut up. It was obvious he didn't care that I was a woman. He hadn't noticed all those obscene mannikins behind him. I mean he'd chosen a piss-poor spot for his pitch. He stared at me and asked if I'd been *born* again. Usually I'd have said something smart, or walked on. But this time it was different. I was taller than him, but he was really intense. I heard myself saying, Yes, yes, I've been born again. His face lit up like a beacon. God bless you! he said. God bless you! God bless you!—about six times. Then I walked away. It really knocked me out. I really felt as though I *had* been born again. I even felt grateful to him. He really had power . . . when I looked back, he'd gone.'

'Yes?'

'Don't things ever happen to you like that, Chink? You wonder if they were real. Yet they had this terrific feeling of purpose. It's as though you needed to invent them, as a kind of lever, to get yourself over. . . .'

Now why didn't that story get across. . . .

'Do you want to travel, Kate?'

'You mean overseas?'

'I mean Lake Chad, the Atlas Mountains, ultimately other

universes. . . . There's plenty of time. . . .'

'I've never had the bread. I almost got to Wales once. . . .'

'Wales?'

'. . . But I've been tied down this way and that.'

'That's not what I mean. Like the feeling you're getting somewhere. Like right now, ah . . . I'm in Marrakesh! I'm in Xanadu!'

'Can I come?'

She'd been rehearsing her story about the revivalist. It's unlikely that considerations of trust occurred to him. To be straight, *no more name rank and serial number*, and to announce that you're *not dependable*, to crow like that: *I'm in Xanadu*! . . . what kind of vanity was at work here? She felt her heart sink.

'I'm talking about dreams, Kate. That's a habit of mine. Didn't you say Sweet dreams just now? I even met you in one, right? Here we are. It's Xanadu, it's amazing. . . .'

But the magic had gone: the room with its loud creatures, the sanctuary. She was going south, a direction she'd only recently escaped. Why? It was no part of any plan she had. It had nothing to do with her. She remembered Beck slicing a finger across his jugular. She thought, Go back to Auckland, Kate. It was as though Chink had addressed her, as though this was his first serious advice: You want to trust me? Okay: fuck off. . . .

His neutral face dips to his glass. He's stitched his comic head together. He puts a cigarette in his mouth. He watches her in silence: another staring session. Who are you. That's not a question.

She was going to stand up . . . 'I'm sorry' . . . walk back on to the road north. He wouldn't dream of her, even for the time it would take him to step out the door and continue in the opposite direction. He'd left everything. She could feel her legs preparing to stand. Goodbye lay like a morning-after taste on her tongue. . . .

Then Chink's eyes flicked right past her.

'Our names are up, Kate Hustler Newman.'

'Hey whatsyername. . . .'

'That's us.' He lofted one arm in the air. 'Come on Kate.' He stood up and leaned over the table and kissed her. 'We'll clean them up. We're quits now, no more name rank and serial number, okay?'

It was a kind of trial: paws running, running to charge his generator . . . a maze to thread for her reward: Chink. She had the choice. She'd been given it.

Meanwhile he'd walked to the other end of the room where the pool table was.

You arrogant shit. . . .

He was chalking the end of a cue: efficient flicks of his wrist. The other two men watched her walk over. Hey, lookit this. . . .

'This is Kate Newman,' said Chink, 'the best pool player in the Pacific.'

'Chink, couldn't we . . .'

'C'mon now Kate, you can't back out. We can beat them.'

The men were watching. They were drunk, friendly, scornful. One of them was the man in the green cardigan. Chink whistled and looked along his cue. She didn't want to play this fucking game.

'Right.' Chink wasn't going to break his stride. He rested the butt of his cue on the floor and grinned at the two men.

'What d'you want on?' asked green cardigan.

'A dollar?'

'Shee-it!'

'Rightoh,' said green cardigan.

Chink bought a jug. His head was dropping open again. He

padded around the table between shots, whistling between his teeth. 'Distraction!' shouted someone. He played with panache, shooting quickly, filling the glasses. 'We're pretty good Kate . . . gotta look after the brass. . . .'

They cleaned the men up. They played two more games and won. The opposition earnestly sliced shots round the table.

'Double or quits,' said green cardigan. His companion was playing not paying.

'You're mad,' he said. 'This bloke's a cracker.'

'This time,' said green cardigan. He spat on his hands. There were four dollars up, counting the original one Chink had put in.

'Nothing in,' said Chink. 'Just double or quits on this, I'll make this a kitty, fair enough?'

'Fair enough,' said green cardigan. 'Who wants to be rich?'

But they won again. Green cardigan handed over another four dollars. Chink took his own out, put another on the bar, held the remaining six in his hand.

'Anyone going south?'

'Smart bugger aren't you,' said the barman. 'There's more like you in the other bar. They look as though they could do with a few bob.'

Chink pulled his coat on in the shelter of the porch, flicking the collar up round his hyena grin.

'Hang on,' he said. 'I'll see what I can do with these people in here.'

'I'm not coming, Chink. You treat me as if I were just tagging along. What kind of stuff was that you were putting on in there? You were laughing at that guy in the green cardigan. You could see how pissed he was, and you kept tipping it into him.'

'I could've lost.'

'You didn't.'

'*We* didn't. Anyway it looks as though I have.'

'Chink stop playing games with me. No more name rank and serial number, remember?'

'So you'll come?'

'I don't know what to do. I never know whether you're playing a game with me or what. Even that night at your place.'

He was very pale. She saw his eyes, like that, wet glints.

'Why should I wish to prove anything to *you*, dear lady? What makes you think I'd want to turn it on for you? "That night at my place" . . . what night? I'm not the boy next door. I'm not fucking Santa Claus either. . . .'

'All right then you bastard, just fuck off! You're full of shit. . . .' She was shouting in his face, crying with rage. The road behind him was slick with rain.

'Suit yourself. . . .'

Chink, love. . . . Just who are we always putting down? *Visionaries?* I sometimes hear my own voice, bitchy, like the woman who lived over the road when I was married to Dave. She used to abuse her kids, on and on. All they were doing was building some kind of secret place in the macrocarpa hedge.

Chink was a dreamer. Do we call him a visionary? Here we are, surrounded by the sea. The horizons are so endless we can almost meet ourselves setting out: endless possibility. . . . What is there to talk over?

It was Chink who showed me the horizon out from Seacliff or Karitane, in the south. I'd looked at it before, often enough. But never *seen* it. When the day was hot with haze gathering in the distance, the line between sea and sky disappeared, so that the planes of the horizontal perspective curved upward into the vertical, into the milky blue dome of the sky, and back to horizontal, and over your head: a glaring wave of space and distance, within which you felt exhilarated, robbed of the simplest certainties: what was up and what was down, how to balance, how to *keep on* in a straight line. . . .

That day Chink demonstrated it: a swooping motion of his arms in front of himself and upward, plunging them finally over his head, and down to cradle it and clasp the back of his neck, his forearms and elbows pressed to the sides of his skull and sticking up like wings.

'The vanishing point is the back of your neck, or else within you,' he said mockingly from between the wings of his elbows, standing on the high cliff edge as though to chuck himself out like a dark ugly bird above the rocks and foam of the shoreline. 'So why kid yourself that physical motion's the most important part of journeying?'

He gave a flap with his elbows and began to walk backwards from the cliff across the paddock.

'I'm not moving,' he shouted. 'But *it* is!'

Then he tripped and fell on his arse, laughing and laughing.

I suppose I became irritated with Chink and put him down as I continue to even now because in my heart I was sure he'd never in fact move gracefully out and away, leaving *us*.

Yet I suppose I had some kind of intuition early on of what his wandering up and down the country meant, and saw that those barely perceived migrations of mind and spirit which were the real, the massive correlative of the main trunk road—saw that those almost invisible migrations were substituting for something.

To the casual observer his life must have seemed an endless series of repetitive grubby excursions, campings, borrowings, ripoffs, bad deals, specious survival techniques. To those who subscribed to the cult of Chink, he was 'on the road': free and spaced, a gypsy freak. But those closest to him could see that Ngāruawāhia was Marrakesh. Xanadu.

I could see that. Or I suppose I could. But it made me angry. I sensed how exclusive it was: *Can I come?* I sensed that you didn't get invited . . . but that you had to 'make a decision', as the revivalists say, all the same.

That woman over the road knew what her kids were up to. She knew that the macrocarpa hedge was Xanadu, for example: the city of endless possibility. Yet she screeched at the kids. Of course there were also practical reasons: perhaps she longed for peace. . . .

But why couldn't I accept the endless possibility of Chink's vision? I stood there as he turned and went casually into the lounge bar. I had no real intention of leaving. Perhaps he guessed that . . . he was vain enough.

I signed up for the trip by default. I didn't make any decision. It just wasn't within my power, at the time. I was in some kind of current. From time to time I'd get my head up, every few months, and then I'd be swept on.

Well, pick up on the company. A few ghosts here.

'Goodness me . . . why hello. . . .'

It was Andrew who'd worked as a model: Vance Vivian slacks, grainy advertisements on the dull newsprint of the daily newspapers, a shit-eating smile on glossy Jaegger swimwear handouts, end-of-season specials at Keans Jeans. . . . His likeness arrived unsolicited in your letter box. Years ago he'd collected rent from a house in Mount Eden left to him by his mother. Kate had had a room there when she was at training college and university. They all said Andrew was a bit of a dealer.

A month after moving in she'd got her *entrée* to that world. The narcs who busted the place pretended to be surprised to find her there.

'What are *you* doing here, sweetie?'

A really straight little arrow . . . but that didn't prevent them from tipping her drawers out on the bed, pulling the carpet up, riffling through her Stage One textbooks. While the Ds did the house she sat with her flatmates in the kitchen. Sure enough there was a little stash of acid under the stairs. None of them knew anything about it.

'Now what about visitors . . . who comes here?'

'There's nobody, just us.'

'Now Kate, surely you realize how important this is. There must be someone you remember. We need your help. . . . These people must be taught a lesson. You don't have anything to be afraid of. We know it's nothing to do with you. . . .'

'Nobody, there's nobody. . . .'

It was all true. But when Andrew got off the charge she felt as though she'd contributed. Some of the others moved out. She stayed.

'Now Kate here, she's not just a pretty face. . . .' Andrew's sarcasm was wary. She was on the inside. Thank you, officer: it's a whole new world, all right.

'. . . what about it, Kate? You'd really dig Sydney. . . .'

'Pick up for Andrew? For fuck's sake!' It was her new friend, 'Auntie Beck'. 'Listen, that bastard would've planted his own old mother. Four days in King's Cross . . . far out. . . . What'll you do there? You don't think Andrew's connexion's gonna show you around, do you? Ah Katie, I can just see you, eating another bag of prawns, going to the zoo, going to the pictures, and all you want to do really is take the deal back and say you want to forget it and go home . . . only you don't know where to take it, because it was a girl you met by arrangement somewhere, and you haven't seen her again and you're not likely to. . . . So you carry your stash back through.

'Purpose of visit?'

'Holiday.'

'Four-day return concession?'

'Yes.'

'Have a good time?'

'Yes . . . a good break before finals. . . .'

'I dunno, students these days . . . your parents shouted you, did they?'

'Ah. . . . For Christ's sake Kate! And then here you are back again, say, you've been scared shitless, only you pretend it was "really far out", and you see Andrew getting around in a brand new van. . . . You know what he calls you? "Suzy Creamcheese" . . . yeah, that's right. . . .'

And now here he was again. He was wearing a black stetson with a peacock feather, white billowy trousers . . . she forgets.

'If it isn't Kate!'

'How are you, Andrew . . . it's been a long time.'

'Certainly has. . . .' He lifts his hat: his hair's cropped close. 'Three years . . . yes they finally did it.' The Sportswear Smile, that wincing of the lips, his eyes avoiding something, or waiting for the glare of the studio lights. . . .

The other two she'd never seen before. One of them was older than the rest, about forty. She didn't catch his name. She got the impression he'd just chucked his job, and perhaps more than that. She lingers over the memory of him, wanting to sort him into some special category, but he won't keep still . . . there's something about his resolute loneliness. . . .

Then there was the third, 'Californian John'. How did his hair get so blond, his denims so clean?

'Has this much time passed?'

Then, she thought back to herself as a student in Andrew's house . . . 'Jesus . . .'. Now she struggles to recognize herself at the Ngāruawāhia pub. Is she that much wiser? 'I don't suppose I learned the simplest things last, or first.'

John was marching off up the road towards the bridge over the Waikato.

'I saw something, man. . . .'

They followed, in the rain. He was leaning over the bridge, looking at the ceremonial canoes moored there by the bank a little way up river, where the Tūrangawaewae marae was. He whistled in admiration.

'Lookit that,' he said. 'Look at *those*, those are Māori canoes, man.'

He held a hand out above the water: some kind of obscure salutation. The rain was pissing down and he had no coat on. There he stood, his shirt turning pink and transparent with wet, reverently shaking his head, one hand stuck out above the parapet of the bridge.

'Ah shit. . . .' Andrew sprinted back to the pub. The silent teacher followed him. Chink flashed Kate an enormous grin of derision. Then he began a lengthy address to John: the Huntly Line . . . Bishop Hadfield . . . the King Movement . . . Waitangi. He was holding the American by the arm.

'Is that right, man, is that right?'

Chink frogmarched him across to the other side of the bridge and pointed downstream.

'It used to be there, on the Delta. There used to be a flagpole. The Delta sailed into the heart of this country. Now there's a fucking band rotunda, see?'

He frogmarched him back, John's tippytoeing feet trying to manage some sort of resistance. But he didn't stand a chance.

'. . . the first King was Pōtatau Te Wherowhero, he was a good man. His descendant Te Puea Hērangi died not so long ago. The pallbearers represented all the ancestral canoes, *canoes*, right?—all except the Host Canoe, Tainui. They carried the coffin out of the gates, there. . . . When Te Wherowhero died his tomb was a little wooden hutch: that's what you *saw*, like you're seeing those canoes. But there was more to it than that, buddy . . . now listen. . . .'

Chink was holding him by the upper arm: Kate could see John beginning to try and pull away. 'The night when the spirit leaves this world's called Te Pō-kumea, the vertiginous night, and it's carried off on Te Au terena, the steady current, which joins Te Au kumea, the dragging current at the beginning of Te Pō tē kitea, the hidden night . . .'

'Hey, man . . .'

'. . . shut up and fucking well listen, you might learn something. . . . When the soul's been prepared in Tiritiri o Matangi it's ready to go on the last stage of its journey. . . .'

John now listened sadly, rain running off his beard. Some men had come down to the canoes and seemed to be preparing to move them. They were wearing bright yellow oilskins. Their shouts came downstream through the sound of the rain. Back up the road outside the pub Andrew began honking the horn of the kombie.

'. . . the spirit's conducted to Te Wai-o-Rongo, the tranquil and peaceful waters, where purification rites're performed before admittance to the temple of Rangiātea, the splendour of the heavens. . . .'

Chink had let go of the American's arm. Obviously he was putting the American on. Obviously he was serious. Kate couldn't measure the proportions. The rain was so heavy it was splashing from the road back up on to their legs. Upstream the men were shouting as they baled the canoes out with bright ice-cream buckets. She looked back down the river. What had been the Delta, that prow with its flagpole mast, was obscured by rain. Chink's voice droned on and on. She heard the American say, 'Okay man, now that's it, all right . . .' and Chink, 'One more thing, mister.' He quoted the inscription on the Māori Wars memorial, corner Wakefield and Symonds Streets in Auckland: something about 'the friendly Maoris who gave their lives for the country during the New Zealand Wars 1845–1872: Through War They Won The Peace We Know.'

'How about *that*,' said Chink. He was hanging on to the American's arm again. John was about to hit him.

'Rightoh friend, school's out now,' Chink said, and the American ran back up the road, his back showing pink through his shirt.

Chink was doubled up with laughter. 'Ain't he a one,' imitating John's accent.

'You're a bastard. Where did you get all that stuff from? Was it for real?'

'Ah, I know what I'm talking about!' He was screaming with laughter. There they stood, laughing into each other's faces, under the rain which was pelting steadily down on them, the marae, the men with the canoes, the cars hissing by on the highway—a kind of difficult benediction.

'We've crossed the Huntly Line!' shouted Chink. 'We're out of range! Let's go, let's get it on! Fuck you all, white trash!'

And he went hopping up the side of the road, big dark awkward spider man, towards Andrew's kombie.

'Hai hai hai!'

*

There was Chink in the front seat with Andrew.

'The ten o'clock ferry. . . .'

'Awright. . . .'

Officers' quarters. . . . The back of Chink's bluc pea jacket was turned towards her. Rain drove against the windscreen. In the back of the van there were only mattresses, too low to see out the windows.

It was what's called O.P.: Officer Potential, the ability to make decisions in spite of others. John kept jamming cassettes into a player and turning the volume up. The officers had their heads together, they were making decisions. John took his wet shirt off. His skin was crawling with gooseflesh.

From time to time he'd pop up and look out the window: the barn, the town, the geese, the forest. Mezzanine sections of the landscape flicked past.

The quiet one closed his sad eyes. Ah, memories. . . .

A fun trip. . . .

'Hey, captain!'

Outside was the gloomy pine forest south of Tokoroa. It was dark in the van. Chink's face when he turned to answer was indistinct.

'Do you want to stop for a pee?'

She mouthed at him, *I'm sick of this.*

'Can't hear. . . .'

She waved him away. The din in the decrepit van as it wound through steep sections was shaking her vision to a blur. Andrew tossed over a bag with a chillum and hash. Ah yes . . . the whole routine. Yeah yeah. Keep them quiet. Up front the quarter-deck was doing speed, little pills. She'd just as soon have stopped right there. The back of that dark blue pea coat was beginning to tremble with velocity, laughter. . . .

Well, fuck it. . . .

At least John was quiet, chills racing over his immaculate Californian skin. She thought that he wore his origins like a Diners' Club seal of recommendation. That was one to tell Chink when she got the chance.

The Doors, over and over: 'This is the end, Beautiful Friend, I hate to set you free . . .'. Nah nah nah. Dave had dug it. This had always struck her as a joke . . . if you believed that custom and passion overlapped too rarely in a life already made short by the conventions of the times. . . . Claustrophobia! That was it. That was it again and again! A joke. 'I'll ne-ver, look-in, to-your, eyes, a-gain. . . .' And that life: little Jane, *Jane Mortimer Hamden* it said on the forms, which made it easier because the full name was so much one of those conventions. All that.

But he smells like the bin. The lino on the corridors, overheated wards, the folding chairs, the needle, the green wraparound smock bending over, 'There she goes now . . .'. All those smells: the lingering horrible formaldehyde smell of dissection, the smell of those little wads of cotton wool they dab you with before and after injections. It's like her friend Marie, a Czech Jewess who survived the Nazi camps and came here. She's a specialist teacher for deaf kids. One day an assistant mixed instant pudding for the kids to finger-paint with. They found Marie retching in the corridor. *You can't use food like that.*

The place where they taught the simplest things. It was . . .

But all at once it was as though her memory tore free somewhere. Some kind of gap opened up. She was thinking of Marie roasting a marinated leg of lamb: the good astringencies of rosemary and garlic, and hot potato pancakes. Somehow Chink had stepped between her and that other memory.

The van was grinding through the dark stretches of highway approaching Taupō. Kate lay back staring at Chink's head where he sat up front rapping with Andrew.

'Marrakesh . . . Xanadu. . . .'

Ah, it was good at last! She struggled up to the front on her knees and leaned over the seat. The van was accelerating slowly on to the highway over the hill into Taupō. The rain had stopped. Clear of the forest, you could see how a steady wind was sweeping clouds from the sky. As the top of the hill crept towards them they all craned their necks. Then they were over.

The lake stretched into the distance in the pearly light of approaching dusk. At the southern end, hard-edged in that clear glow, the volcano was sending a plume of steam or snow-spume skywards from its cone. As they descended, the exhaust pipe rattling and farting, she leaned closer to Chink's ear, inhaling again that feral odour of his hair, placing her lips against the smooth skin behind his jaw, touching her tongue there.

'It's okay, for just another Atlas Mountain,' she whispered.

'Yeah, right,' he said. 'Right, it's really not bad . . . in fact it's terrific! Can you dig the eternal snow? The Sahara's just over there! Rightoh Kate . . . you ski down to the desert, then east a bit, then south across the burning sands. Day after day, "brackish water", manna from heaven. And then . . . one day . . . there it is! Ah, you say, another mirage. So you go on putting one foot in front of the other, trying to unstick your tongue from the roof of your mouth. You rub your eyes. It's still there: Lake Chad! Trees, monkeys . . . and lotus flowers in the lake. Cool jade water . . . egrets and flamingoes. You come over the top of a dune, there it is! That's an amazing mirage! Look! It's got buffaloes splashing about in the water . . . it's got a canoe with a fisherman . . . it's got a little jetty with a store and a sign advertising beer from Strasbourg . . . and you're actually walking into the mirage, you've stumbled along the jetty, you've pulled off your stinking clothes, you've toppled into the cool water, and now you're sitting on the end of the jetty at a little table, in the evening breeze, watching the sun set over Lake Chad, drinking Alsacian beer and eating a smoked-beef sandwich with slices of gherkin, running your finger through the frost outside your glass!' Chink's voice rose towards a scream. 'And you're thinking, "This isn't real! This is a mirage, man, but with mirages like this who needs the facts?" Lemme tell you, I'm gonna stay in this mirage. It's mine! Bring me another beer, also some fruit.' Chink mimed wiping juice off his chin, then he threw rinds into the lake. 'I like it here!'

'Far out,' said Andrew.

'Phew,' said Chink. 'What d'you say, Kate . . . are you coming this time?'

They stopped at De Brett's hot springs. The small pool was greenish with sulphur and so hot Kate felt the blood pressing out against her skull, a pulse like the one in a baby's fontanelle. Her legs were stockings filled with sand.

'Well lookit that, that's a *real* Californian dick, "man". . . .' Chink held out his own for inspection, free hand raised in mock salutation.

The main pool was cooler. Chink's heavy torso slid through the water, the lights around the pool catching the muscles of his back. Kate was wearing his T-shirt. The man who came out of the ticket booth with a whistle had a greedy expression. When she smacked her lips and waggled her tongue at him he went red and began shouting.

'Drop dead,' said Andrew.

'What a country,' the American kept saying as they climbed back up the hill. 'Oh wow, what a country, can you believe it?'

'We should kill him now, he's so heavy he'd sink,' Chink whispered.

'What about cutting off his Diners Club Seal of Recommendation?'

'Now, you're just the bitch for the job. . . .'

They bought fish and chips and drove on. She couldn't eat. Chink had done a lot of Andrew's speed and was now yakking to him about the Doors. '. . . Jim Morrison's grave in the *Cimetière Père Lachaise* in Paris has more flowers on it than any other in the graveyard. Can you imagine little girls in white dresses with ribbons in their hair coming with bouquets, day after day? They let go of their mothers' hands and run to the graveside. Under the turf's this big dumb vulgar cock . . .'

It was as though his voice was drawn away from her by an invisible tendon. It seemed to lope off, ahead of her, into distance and darkness. It was as though she was going to sleep not after one day, but three. It was as though she was going to sleep for the first time in her life. It was peaceful and foreign, like a graveyard in Paris. *Père Lachaise*, the name of a wise confessor.

'. . . they don't know what's happened to them,' said Chink's voice as it disappeared. 'The mothers don't know . . .'

They veer in the dark, rise and fall. Then the headlights dragging them up a slope rising before them. They seem to be pivoting about his dark heavy head. She can't see his face, his back's turned to her, shoulders drawn up, turning with the heavy vehicle. Andrew has crawled into the back, is curled up with his knees under his chin. The American's asleep in the front next to Chink. 'I'm not dependable.' The way he has to hold his arms and shoulders to drive, is so solid and quiet. That's a strange thought, 'quiet'. Yet it is quiet and peaceful. In *Père Lachaise* they let go of their mothers' hands and run to the graveside. One of his shoulders lifts, his huge head rests on it, he's grappling across himself. Then he shakes a cigarette out of the packet: flare of a match, the American's mouth gaping where he leans against the opposite side of the cab. Chink opens the window to fling the match out. The wind blows his hair about, the sound of the engine enters. Who'll carry her inside? The bed will be there, she won't have to do anything, head lolling against . . .

'Home James and don't spare the horses.'

'Shhh. . . .' Legs and arms like stockings filled with sand. Someone's feet on the gravel driveway. . . .

'Open the door will you.' They let go of their mothers' hands and run to the graveside. A snake comes out of his flies, flat-headed, bloated with heat. It sinks its fangs into her, its tongue flickers to swab her skin, a flood of slow honey, she jerks and shudders. *This is the end, Beautiful Friend, the end*. . . . Not Dave, the smell of pickled frogs. What a joke!

Little Janie is very happy now, we all get on well over here. I don't think things would ever have worked out as they were. Now at least we're both free. I feel I've done that much for you. . . . *Ah, fuck off, shut up! That for comfort. There's none. The other for King Snake. The other for Chink.*

His head hangs there above his shoulders. Being driven, being carried in. The darkness is motionless. They rock and rise in it, they turn and turn about his head.

. . . write c/o the Biology Dept Australian National University, if you want to. . . .

That, formaldehyde.

'Look at her, will you? Ah. . . .'

'Home James. . . .'

9 *Killing the Fish*

CHINK: Once I went fishing in a small river south of Te Kūiti. There were good pools. It was getting towards sunset. Everything was right, beautiful . . . the day, the place, how I felt, and there were fish rising everywhere. But I wasn't catching anything. So I reeled in. I watched the sun sinking, and I just sat and thought. It was so quiet! I sat very still, and I really went down . . . you know how you can. I watched the sun hit the top of the clay bluff at the other side of the gully, and I thought.

Yeah . . .

The sun got behind the bluff. I was still sitting there. There was nothing but a red line at the top of the bluff: 'the gap between the worlds', remember? that you can go through, if you have the guts.

Then I got up and chucked the line in, without looking, just flopped the fly on to the surface. And I hooked the biggest fish of my life. It was enormous, man, a monster! I played it and played it, running about a hundred yards down the bank, dodging through the mānuka and the gorse, jumping over rocks, Jesus! 'You beautiful big fucker! Come on darling, come on come on!'—stuff like that. I could feel its life in the line, its strength, its fear, everything; it was like I was plugged into it, it was so close it was part of me.

And then I fucking killed it. Of course. I landed it and killed it!

Ah. . . .

Chink snaps his fingers, his eyes shut.

That's how it is. You kill the fish every time. You kill a bit of yourself too. Like Einstein sitting in his chair, and then: 'Hey, everything's powerful!' Oh ho. Yes, right. But he killed the fish . . . he *had* to. Like Newton seeing that the sun was the Philosopher's Stone: 'Ow. Oh, I see. . . .' He killed the fish. He blew it. You can say the truth's *in* this thing . . . in its flaw . . . but the thing itself's a dead fish. Soon it will stink. Because you've stopped the motion. If it was right, then you'd never know . . . you'd never see it . . . because it's continuous. So you kill the fish every time. You never know . . . you never *will* know. . . .

But listen, what matters is being in the place, the fish rising, sunset, and your own head like a deep pool. Then standing up and casting like you didn't even think about it. You gotta take these risks, otherwise where are you? It's a price you pay.

Up till then it's beautiful, it's amazing. . . . Up to and including that cast: beautiful, phew. . . .

Chink flops back in his chair.

He said he'd suddenly thought, 'Yeah, I could be a musician!' That was before he went fishing that day.

'In the light of present material,' letting the phrase drift into silence. You never arrive. You never leave. There's no centre.

And yet you had a purpose: you came to fish. And so . . .

'Yeah, I could be a musician!'

Well, why aren't you, sonny boy?

'Who could hang on for long with that kind of tension?' This is what she's thinking, now.

I have had to learn the simplest . . .

'Who are these people! It's you . . .'

. . . sometimes she's conscious of remembering with so

much care that the love the care comes from must seem like an insult. There are problems she's always been on the outside of. Her mother used to talk about them. But Kate never imagined they'd matter much to her. How much should she tell? (How much does she remember?)

The movement, the *transport*, of the care with which she wanted to be with Chink faltered when he told her too much. It was as though he was putting her down.

'Let's do it by numbers, lady. . . .' When he was angry his face was blank. It often seemed to her that he *had* to win arguments, and that she had to let him. The process was as automatic as: *My cup runneth over*: waste, dilution: killing the fish. But not happiness, simple sufficiency, Chink smiling: his face an invitation.

What did reveal something about him was his father's shadow falling on the white palings in front of him, through which he slowly wiped the cloth, with a dull sense of the significance of what he was doing. The significance gained form as he grew up with the memory of this moment. The form was passed to her in what Chink said, reminiscing. It makes no difference how many removes there are between her and what she remembers. She has to follow these circles back, or around. She has to go over it again and again, and then again. She has to invent the whole thing. Turning, as though to look at him again, and finding him watching her with half-closed eyes:

'Let's go, Kate. What d'you say?'

And it comes up out of her, immediately, as though she's dropped to her knees in front of you and sobbed out:

'Listen. I want to talk to you, I want to tell you!'

10 *Yellow*

Today the first cicada then warm rain trickling on ngaio bushes, the blackbirds in them. Yesterday I was happy. I painted the shed doors yellow: a homage to the hills, their gorse, then barberry, then kōwhai, and broom, and now delicate lupin flowers around the sea's edge, and the ragwort just starting: that yellow, yellow! the colour of Hymen, of marriages (I was taught) but I think a sacred colour: spring, piss, and sulphur . . . exorcism of winter. Near Bethells in the north is a place I've been back to where pōhutukawa like old elephants have sunk together to their knees, where in early spring the kōwhai bend with yellow flowers. It was too early for many cicadas when I was there first. Instead tūī and blackbirds and some wood pigeons had gorged themselves all day on kōwhai flowers: dead drunk they gurgled among the branches, above the elephants, above Chink and me in the grass. . . . Too early for cicadas then, but they were there when I went back, and today there was one, here in the south, cracking and vibrating until the rain came. It's not the same. Something has changed, a season, something. . . . In that grove where the elephants lie down their blood will burst out every year. But these hillsides march into the sea. The lupins hang out marriage bunting on the shore, they turn their pods down like thumbs. . . .

11

I feel like some tedious drunk at a party: starting *right* at the beginning. I mean this is the first time I've addressed you 'to your face'. There's some kind of compulsion.

My name's Kate. I'm not yet thirty. I'm tall and big boned. My skin's olive. My hair's black, straight, and cut short. My eyes are blue. I wear glasses to read and at the pictures. I've never been fat but I seem to be getting leaner as time goes on. I'm going to be one of those tall stringy old women who look as though they could survive forever like strips of biltong. My armpits, which Chink used to call 'tartubs', leak dark licks and curls. I shave my legs. My top lip has 'an Italian bloom', Chink used to say, 'like a Blackboy peach'. My mouth's very wide. I have one gold tooth (my father's idea—my practical mother objected). My nose is delicate and straight with pale nostrils. My eyebrows are also fine, though very wide and dark. My forehead, which is usually covered by my fringe of hair, isn't high like Chink's was. My ears aren't delicate but you don't notice them because they're very close to my head. Chink's ears were what's called 'lugs': they had no lobes. My lobes are long, sensitive and downy. Blemishes: a large mole below my navel. Two similar moles, one high on my left cheek and the other just below my left collarbone, might be regarded as assets. I suppose an appendix scar counts as a blemish.

I guess I've described myself in a man's terms, as though through a man's eyes. (Chink's eyes.) Am I real to myself only as Chink saw me? I can't change the way I am. What I might wish to be is simply part of that. *You* think it out.

When I'm up I'm crazy, when I'm down I wish I was dead. But I don't like the grey areas.

Since having Janie I've used a coil but I resent it, it's an intrusion I can't change. I sometimes long for the world to open and suck me in and pour into me at the same time. I mean everything you do has some restraint attached to it. The nearest I ever got to that dream of abandon was having the baby. I loved that. I was reborn. I could feel every nerve and muscle in my body doing something about it and every bit of my head too. I fought against the mask they wanted to put on me at the last minute to help my breathing.

Then back came the restraints: Dave complaining that he thought it was time the baby was weaned. This was at six months. So I weaned her. I could have gone on for another year. I resented that so much I lost sight of the fact that it was my fault: I should have stuck to my intentions. And after that fucking with Dave was often hopeless: it was as though he was doing that according to a manual as well.

This is getting very confidential. But you can see why it was so important when the world stopped that night at Chink's flat.

I'm a young woman, Kate, not yet thirty. It's as though I can start any time. I've got enough energy for most of my friends put together. But I carry on in the same old way. The voice which you can't hear but which I hear calling and calling to the world, or announcing *I'm in Xanadu!* saying *I'm going!* shouting *Let's get it on!* shouting *Kate Kate Kate!*—I fob it off with temporizing promises.

And he's dead.

And yet I do feel as though I could begin now!

Poor Wedding Guest. You're probably feeling the way Chink must have sometimes: *Oh Christ, now what's this. . . .*

I'm the youngest of a large family. I have five brothers. None of them lives in New Zealand. Three are in England, one doctor and two engineers. One is a marine biologist in California. The oldest, James, my favourite, has ended up as a teacher with the British Council in Tehran. He never married. All the rest have kids. We're a large successful scattered middle-class family. My father was a lawyer. He was killed in a car accident when I was fourteen. I didn't really miss him. When I think of him I remember his voice: a commanding bass. But he drank too much. I remember my mother shouting one day that when he died all his ambitions would seem as useful as a painful pee in a rusty bucket, to which he replied that he couldn't be held responsible for the poor quality of the receptacle but, by Christ, he could vouch for the quality of the piss.

I loved my mother. It's her I resemble, in some ways. She was Welsh, a compulsive singer, with a large primitive feeling for family, but given to a brand of sarcasm which only my father could match and beat. Quite often the whole family was caught in the crossfire. We tended, as children, to be mawkishly well behaved, but with secret lives.

I lived with my mother in Dunedin until I left school. I was *dux*. Then she insisted that I go north to university in Auckland. Something had got to me during my last year at school, some kind of boredom, or indifference. I didn't even sit some of the scholarship papers.

'You need to get out now before you're bored with being young,' my mother said with a certain flat inflexion she reserved for such shit-stirring comments. So, with some difficulty, she arranged for me to go north, on a teacher-trainee's bursary. She was right. I perked up. I had a good time. I also missed her. I found her conversation had spoiled me though at home I'd wanted to get out, away from it.

She told me not to come home for the short holidays. When I did come home for the first long summer vacation she pestered me with questions. Naturally I said it was fine.

She'd had it all in letters. I added detail. She was enthusiastic. I couldn't make sense of the tone of her interrogation. Then she told me she was going back to Wales, to her family, a brother, and that she might stay 'for some time'. I noticed that she'd been dyeing her hair and I suddenly imagined it grey. I saw how the skin under her chin had loosened, how the angular lines of her body had become brittle, how her nails chipped easily, how tired and restless her eyes had become, how she coughed over the cigarettes she smoked from early in the morning. I suddenly realized that she'd been lonely since my father died. It had never occurred to me before! Except as a formula, that is.

At the funeral, which had been characteristically matter-of-fact, her tears had embarrassed me. Afterwards she'd launched herself ferociously back into the ordinary business of work and life, sitting smoking at the kitchen table with her markbook and piles of assignments, drinking endless cups of tea, pressing books on me which I didn't want to read—I remember Piaget—and referring always to 'your father' but never calling him by his name, which was James, like my favourite brother. None of *them*, incidentally, had attended the funeral.

When she said that, that she was going back to 'her family', I felt a terrible loneliness open in front of me, like the door of a derelict house. Her choice of phrase was hasty rather than cruel. But it hurt. And in spite of my brash answers to her questions I had no idea what I wanted to do. I'd been answering the way I sensed she wanted me to. I realized I'd be alone: there'd be no other 'family'. But I saw at the same time how she looked, how lonely *she* was. So when my mouth opened to protest, there was a pause like an actor waiting for a cue, and then I said, 'How wonderful', something like that. I think she heard the pause. She began to cry. When I'd finished my training, she said, she'd shout me a trip over to see her in Wales. If she hadn't come home by then. But she died two years later of bronchial pneumonia, when I was in my final year, when I'd just met Dave, when I was pregnant.

Bang. Reality. One of my mother's favourite phrases was 'come down like a ton of bricks'. She used to smack her lips over it, as though she relished something that definite and material. A favourite put-down expression was 'shillyshally'. She made the word limp and whine.

That was our family. We all insisted too much on independence, or had that insistence thrust upon us. How much I really loved my mother I didn't find out until I was in deep trouble. Then I felt her absence as something far worse than the lack of furniture and light in that derelict house of loneliness. I felt it as the loss of a kind of energy which I could have drawn on till I had the power to march into the house, illuminate it, fill it with loud voices and used objects, objects which would have the confidence, the material affection, of those chewed pencils she'd left lying around our place in Dunedin.

The trouble came soon enough. I'll spare you the worst of it, Wedding Guest, though I wouldn't have some weeks ago. If I feel like dedicating this brief reckoning to my mother it's because her power has seemed recently to become available at last. And not too late. That's the wonder of it, that feeling.

And dedicate it also to Chink. Darling Chink. Blessing you also frees me.

Yes, I know: *The Rime of the Ancient Mariner.* The patterns that matter are the ones we're given, not the ones we impose. They emerge, the patterns emerge, that's all.

That's why I say I don't give a fuck whether you believe in Chink or not, or in me. Why do you think the Guest stayed? We all have to talk to ourselves sometimes. My father had the habit of bailing people up at parties. I remember as a child listening to his insistent bass, from the top of the stairs. Among my mother's nicknames for him were 'Mariner' and sometimes 'Marinated'.

Xanadu and the Mariner . . . familiar as my mother's chewed pencils. And then a part of Chink's code. Do you expect me to avoid this?

The doctor said in as many words, 'You're pregnant.' The telegram said in as many words, 'You're motherless.' Somehow neither message was a surprise. The doctor merely put his signature to my certainty. He made it possible for me to think of a future: from a preoccupation with the certainty that I was pregnant, where my imagination was working at close range, I raised my eyes, increased the perspective, and saw a baby. There was a clear moment in which I said to myself, 'It's a girl, she's Jane, she's like me, she's like my mother.' Then I went home. One of my flatmates was waiting. She frogmarched me into the kitchen, sat me down at the kitchen table, and put a cup of tea in front of me. Her earnestness, which I'd misunderstood, made me laugh.

'I'm only pregnant,' I said. 'It's not the end of the world!' Something in me was singing like a power transformer, a high whine of energy, nearly hysteria. I was clinging in my mind to that clear vision of a little girl, called Jane.

It wasn't that, she said. There had been a telegram phoned through from Wales.

But somehow the fact of *that*, though I understood it, was unable to jar my vision of a daughter like me, like my mother. The telegram belonged to a process the major part of which I'd understood and accepted in a flash, and even with joy. Raising my eyes, I'd seen small dark Jane. I could neither lower them again, nor turn back to see my mother where she lay dead.

I'd been taken over. My present contained all the distance I was capable of covering just then. It was as though I thought, 'I'm the mother.' I didn't feel guilty or heartless. It did occur to me that no one stood between *me* and death: that I was next in line. But then I thought of Jane: the positions, their equivalents, seemed unchanged.

It was three years before I mourned my mother. It's taken another three to get me to where I am: the house lighting up, the voices coming back.

All that was in mid-summer. Dave and I got married the first week in March. With friends we rode over on the Devonport ferry across the windy harbour, and got drunk in the Devonport pub. I was only about two months pregnant.

The flat we lived in was half an old house above the Naval Base. The garden had run wild. I used to lie in one hot corner of it, behind some hibiscus bushes, sunning my nipples and belly. In winter I studied hard. I used to catch the ferry over to the city every day. At one stage, I used to spew over the stern. I gained a peverse kind of pleasure from this. I gave up smoking, stopped turning on, had no desire to drink, studied my diet, wanted to fuck a lot, and with Dave went nightly through a comical rigmarole of breathing exercises.

In October when I sat my exams I was nine months pregnant. It suited me. I wore hot yellow, my favourite colour. I wore extravagant trinkets and 'gauds' (a word I favoured then). I enjoyed dressing up this way. During exams, when I felt lousy and uncomfortable, I had to be escorted out frequently to pee. My picture even appeared in the paper: large Byzantine eyes, the blue of them darkened. I was riding really high. The climax was the birth of Jane: like bursting with joy. She was as I'd seen her: long-boned, dark, a girl. She was also overdue. It was as though we'd all been taken in hand.

When I stood at the window of the hospital to watch for

Dave coming to visit, my milk would dribble on to my feet. He, pale with overwork, would gaze at me with a kind of apprehension. His expression seemed to say, 'I've got more than I bargained for.' I didn't like the cigarette stains on his fingers, the smears and dust on his glasses. I was proud of my power, my new-felt beauty, my stature.

Beck despised Dave and went out of his way to bait him. When I was around he ignored him. He loved Jane and would play with her for hours. Finally Dave reported some sour comments Beck had made. I hadn't realized that Beck had been doing this behind my back. When I accused him of it he replied that he saw no reason to apologise for what he did 'outside my house' . . . Dave also lived a large part of his time away from me. He offered this comment blandly but I knew him well enough to guess that he was needling me. So I was angry. For revenge I told Dave about the conversation. So he lost *his* temper. (He seldom did.) We were having breakfast. Jane, who was one year old, was emptying the contents of a kitchen cupboard on the floor. Dave dumped his breakfast in the sink, breaking a plate, kicked the mess on the floor out of the way and left the house. I found myself despising the petulance of his gestures. That day he went to find Beck, had a row, told him not to come near our place again. By this stage I was really angry. Beck was *my* friend. I rang him and told him to come any time he liked. I was sick of an accumulation of proscriptions and irritations in my life. I suppose I was looking for a way back to the sense of stature I'd had when Jane was born. That had frayed, worn thin, become grubby, had been lost or thrown away, and there was no replacement.

One afternoon Beck came round. Janie was asleep but due to wake soon. I was sunbathing in my usual spot, reading. I heard Beck call out from the back steps. 'I'm down here,' I shouted. It was too hot to move. He'd brought some dope for me. We were sampling it when I heard the baby on the porch wake up. I knew she'd play happily for a few minutes. I didn't worry. Then I heard Dave: 'Hey, Kate!' Janie began to wail. Left alone she'd have been fine for a while. I made a point of leaving her for a few minutes before picking her up. Dave came through the bushes. We were turning on. The baby was crying. I didn't have any clothes on. Beck had been told to keep away. Dave stood there taking it in, then he went away and was gone for two days. I found out he'd stayed with a girl who worked in the university library.

When he got back we made up. He'd realized that the ingredients of the situation didn't mean anything. Yet it was at this point that the real crisis occurred. Because I was glad to see him back, because I felt guilty, for lots of confused reasons, I found myself saying, 'Anyway, Beck's a turd burgler, you know that.'

Immediately I looked at my husband with hatred. He'd made me say that. Characteristically he didn't notice this look. He was happy to have the affair sorted out. I doubt if it seemed to him to be a victory: he didn't think like that. But I did. I felt crushed. Before long I was despising the way he'd 'gone to weep on that girl's shoulder', and at the same time grinding my teeth with jealousy of her . . . far worse jealousy than I ever felt over Chink's women, of whom I was even somewhat proud.

How that mill does grind. It's so monotonous, so obvious, and it never stops. You talk yourself into something, you feel guilty about it, that makes you feel resentful, you blame the person you've wronged for getting the whole process started. The bigger the display of self-righteousness, the greater the culpability is likely to be. It's as though we believe that if we keep the mill going it will manufacture truth. We become shrill. We develop techniques of sarcasm and irony. The millstones rumble and squeal, our lies are given back to us, dusty nourishment. This is the bread *no one* can do without. This is our K-ration, our survival kit. When you are starving and there is food within reach, you don't go breaking your teeth on stones. That's it.

We moved south since Dave had to spend some time with the medical school in Dunedin. I bought a car and took a part-time teaching job at Kaikorai Valley High School. Janie was two and a bit. The car and a downpayment on a house had used up the rest of my inheritance money. But I was working. Dave was getting a Master's Bursary. There was family benefit. I had some quick love affairs which made me suffer in the usual ways but which I enjoyed, for the confidence they gave me. I don't really know what Dave thought. His calmness was sometimes like indifference. I suspected his kindness of being secretly spiteful. He said he wanted more children. I said I didn't.

For a time my claustrophobia left me alone. Then, as our routine became familiar again, it returned. I wasn't sleeping. I was often tearful. The psychiatrist my doctor referred me to prescribed mandrax, made wisecracks about behaviour patterns in young married women, quoted James K. Baxter's lines about young delinquent bags, wanted to interview Dave about our sex life (what sex life?) and extracted from me some kind of screwy rave about my mother. What I'd tried to say was that she would have cut through the bullshit. He accused me of saying that I felt I'd failed her. This performance disgusted me. Perhaps he was right: perhaps I'd come to him starving and he'd offered me a stone. I 'snapped out of it', which may have been the shrink's intention for all I know. At the time I thought he was brutal, unsympathetic and cynical. I didn't go back, except to renew my prescription. Quite often I found I was breaking through the mesh of claustrophobia: making gestures I enjoyed, which filled me with hope.

Jane, at two and a half or so, had become difficult to feed. It was mid-winter. To warm up after shopping one freezing Friday evening I'd gone to the pub with some friends. Janie was in the car. We all drank a couple of quick whiskies. Then I went home and made dinner. Dave was exhausted. I felt marvellous. But as soon as we sat down in the kitchen to eat, Janie started whining. 'Leave her alone,' said Dave. 'She'll eat when she's hungry.' He bent his head to his plate. He smelled faintly of formaldehyde. Jane was grizzling away, keeping one eye on me. I couldn't stand it. I picked up her bowl and dumped it on her head. The food splashed all over her face, all over the floor. Then I picked up her glass of milk, *chocolate* milk, and poured that over her head too. We faced each other. She opened her mouth to yell. But the sight of her was so comical that I started laughing loudly. That was miraculous: she also screamed with laughter, licking at the horrible mess as it trickled down her face. It was an inspired gesture, it was *honest*, and we were friends, we understood each other.

Then I saw Dave's weary arms reach in as though from the edge of a frame and scoop Janie up and out of the picture, her mouth frozen upon that wonderful laughter. He was *coping.* He bathed her while I sat there at the table. Then, calmly and without a word, he came back and cleaned up the floor. Ah, for Christ's sake!—what was a little mess for once! Why hadn't he entered into the spirit of the thing? Hadn't he seen what it meant? For *me*? Having broken for a moment through the net I felt as though something was now forcing my head down and back through it and closing the gap. My nose my eyes my throat were clogged with dust, it was dark, I was being crushed. 'Why did you have to spoil it?' But although the question had seemed simple at first, it began to grow, until I could no longer ask it. I couldn't get it out. It was like retching dryly on nothing.

My 'breakdown'. By the year's end we'd separated. I was still under observation. At the end of the summer Dave went to Australia on his scholarship. He took Jane. I didn't argue. There was no point. I couldn't look after her and I couldn't stand the sight of him. I heard that his girl-friend from the library in Auckland had gone to join him. I didn't care.

By the following spring I'd pulled myself together (let's put that in quotation marks: 'pulled myself together') for long enough to get discharged, let the house through the university housing officer, sell my car. (I stopped 'shillyshallying'.) I did this with the grim concentration of someone threading a needle with shaky fingers.

Then I flew up to Auckland to stay with Beck. I had plenty of money for several months, apart from what Dave was sending. So I planned to rest, really rest, have a good time, do nothing. Then I thought I'd 'review the situation'.

Beck threw all my mandies down a storm drain and spent a week abusing me. He took Dave's side. And then he lifted his wings like a bright gaudy little bantam hen, and I scuttled in.

And there was Chink . . . sprawled out . . . his nose running. . . .

A little more yet, Wedding Guest.

I want to ask you a question. That makes you real enough. I mean, I'm expecting an answer.

If I gave you three guesses at what my question is, what would you say? Let *me* guess at those:

1. Do I think my case is so different that it compels you to stay and listen?
2. Do I believe I can expiate (which sounds like spit) by sitting here going through all this?
3. Do I believe it's not too late? or that by starting again I can exclude what's happened?

Give up. For once I'm going to surprise you. *Those* questions stink of formaldehyde. But don't fret, the smell no longer bothers me.

Here's my question. (Here's my stone.)

How do you like my tone?

(Hey, listen to that. It's a song, it's a wee number!)

Yeah, how do you like my song, you *cunt*. Chink would've eaten you alive. Smile, for fuck's sake! It's a wedding not a funeral.

Here I've sat for days, looking out the window at the same 'slice of life', like a section Dave might have mounted on a slide and looked at through a microscope. You can't imagine how familiar it is.

If I'm beginning to get the hang of you, then it follows that I've got a fair idea about myself. If that world-section is familiar to me, then I must be on similar terms with myself. It's got to be reciprocal. Sometimes I've written to your dictation. Sometimes that's made me want to scream.

Who are you, Wedding Guest? We killed Chink, remember? You're Them.

Only that procession there behind you, over your shoulder, is a wedding. When I get up and go out, you'll follow. When your back's no longer turned, Wedding Guest, I too will have joined the procession.

12 *Home James*

The day was grey, a promise of brightness in the south. There he stood, hands shoved into the old pea coat, gritty dockside wind blowing into his eyes.

The others hadn't been able to get a ticket for the kombie. Poor Californian John had said he'd 'come with you . . .'.

'Get fucked,' Chink and John parting on very bad terms.

So that lot drove off to have breakfast at the railway station, and Chink and Kate boarded the ferry and sat in the stern, arms round each other.

'Anyway,' said Chink, 'Andrew's jumping probation.'

Traffic ground past on the multipetal overpasses. It occurred to Kate that these structures would be beautiful without the traffic, which continued non-stop, slewing and backfiring into the ramps leading off to Murphy Street, Aotea Wharf . . . the heads of the truck drivers could just be seen in the cabs of their vehicles above the concrete balustrades . . . the purposeful set of their necks as they turned the trucks on to the ramps reminded Kate of the long night drive.

> They let go of their mothers' hands
> Home James & don't
> Spare the horses

. . . meat, paper, wool, fire extinguishers . . . onions, and there go some 'day old chicks'.

Below the ramps was a rusty confusion of railway lines. A suburban unit went past, dingy splendid crimson. The windy air, whipping around grey cranes and derricks, was harsh with exhaust fumes, diesel, and the penetrating astringency of the harbour: not quite an open sea smell, since it retained something cloacal . . . the air would also clear in the south . . . closing his eyes against the grit, the leaden glare of low mid-morning light, 'Let's get out of here, let's really get out of here!'

The *Acapulco Maru,* Japanese, was unloading immense coils of steel cable: an ugly battered ship held tenderly against the wharf buffers . . . the image has stuck with Kate, the same class of memories as that of Chink's mime at the back beach.

But the blackbacks lined up along the edge of the wharf, the decks of the ferry swarming with children—these must have reminded her of the Devonport Ferry, because she began to tell Chink about the first year with Jane. If he was surprised to hear about this 'other life', he didn't show it. He sat as though expecting one of the *Acapulco Maru's* coils of steel to drop on his head. As she talked he looked out towards the harbour mouth where a wedge of blue sky was slowly splitting the dark cloud that also covered the city. Kate was saying how she'd begun to do weaving that year: something she could stop and start, as the baby allowed her. She found she was good at it. She had a gift for improvisation.

'Crafty,' Chink with a hideous grin. 'The young mother . . .'

At this moment the ferry began to move away from the wharf, towards open sea, the wedge of light: out into the blue. The nasty maverick smile stuck on Chink's face.

'Here we go, lady. . . .' Taking Kate's hand, lifting his chin from the collar of his coat, he stalked to the bows and stood there until the ferry cleared the heads. It was choppy, but the sky was blue, the air clear. . . .

'. . . distance, wow. . . .'

It was the end of the summer holidays, the ferry was packed. Finally he stretched out on a vinyl squab in the cafeteria, surrounded by families getting a late breakfast. Kate leaned over and kissed him.

'Home James, don't spare the horses.'

'Don't spare the horse,' he cracked.

She had breakfast: juice, eggs, bacon, the whole shebang. She sat at the opposite end of the cafeteria from where Chink was sleeping: sat there, sometimes with a fork half way to her mouth, staring at him. '. . . they let go of their mothers' hands . . .'

Then she wandered about the boat. She expected to meet someone she knew. But there was no one else, not even a face which made her turn for a second look.

Later she had a beer in the bar, and read the paper, which was full of disasters. 'What am I crossing to, what am I leaving behind . . . ?' Around her, over the throb of the engines, fragments of talk were tossed to and fro, as though by the pitching of the ship in the open straits. The voices were insisting, insisting. Some of the men looked over at her: a tall dark girl, white-faced, a red bandanna tied around her throat, playing with the cigarettes she lit one after the other.

Then the boat steadied: it had entered the Sounds. Steep scrubby land slid by, and small islands and neat bays blazing with pōhutukawa flowers. Through the window of the crowded cafeteria she could see Chink lying as before, with his old pea coat on, the shabby toes of his boots turned out, his head rolled over sideways, one hand stuck right down in his crutch.

He appeared at her side, his hair wet where he'd splashed his face in the washroom, at the moment the ferry was about to berth at Picton.

Blue sky, breeze, small craft in the Picton Sound: 'Pumpkin weather,' said Chink, pulling off his coat. Yet the air had an alpine clarity, a dry snap to it, *distance*. They ambled down from the terminus towards the esplanade.

'Well lookit that, never seen *that* before. . . .'

In front of them was an immense concrete vulva . . . oh really? When you walked around it, it turned out to be a concrete whale, made into a slide . . . but the children appeared to be slipping down between the labia of a gigantic snatch. Well *that* was worth watching for a while, in the authentic zesty summer holiday air sun and sea breeze. It was hard to know which was worse: a whale flensed and laid open down its backbone, or that puffy quim . . . and zimmm! here comes little Terence with his shorts rucked up . . . Chink: 'Imagine health stamps. . . .'

Chink came up with that word 'flense': turned out he knew something about whaling in the Straits and Sounds, and also about seals along the coast below the Seaward Kaikōuras. He told her about an old man he'd met who at fourteen had first gone out in a chaser, oar and sail against the rip in Tory Channel, had become a harpooneer, now had an elbow blown up like a balloon with old bone splinters. He regretted the rarity of whales 'these days' not for *their* sake but because duck shooting didn't measure up 'as a sport'.

'Did you know Errol Flynn's chauffeur came from Picton? . . . How can you *settle* for less? I mean it's a matter of scale all the time, it's dead simple. . . . Everyone's hooked on some scale . . . give them something too small or too big and they freak out. . . .'

Chink's 'am I serious' routine. . . . Meanwhile Kate imagined the old harpooneer fucking a whale . . . or a yellow Japanese crane in the ocean south of Java . . . astraddle it with a tin hat on and a rivet gun in his hands . . . 'Here it comes, red hot from an old-timer!'

'. . . the word like "flense" for what they do to seals is "flat" . . . they "flat" them . . . bit like running over possums with a logging truck: all that's left is skin and fur. . . .'

He'd never seen that kiddies' slide before, without Kate would never have stepped far enough off the asphalt of the road from the terminus to confront that ambiguous totem, but would have kept on at least as far as Kaikōura.

At about three in the afternoon they checked into a hotel, selected on the merits of its name: Terminus. In the public bar a loud pool school was in action. Through from the bar at the reception desk, Chink helpfully enunciated Kate's name.

'Yes, Mr and Mrs ahem Hemmedin. . . .'

And investigated the room for wallboard. It was high, intact. Potty and Gideon's Bible in a cabinet by the bed.

'Amazing. . . .'

Down the corridor, an immense bath.

'Amazing, amazing. . . .'

They went out: fish and chips, a swim, a couple of jugs in the bar (no game of pool). Upstairs with a huge bag of Bon Chrétien pears and a jar of wine. It was just getting dark. Greenish scalding water thundered into the old-fashioned bath. Then sitting up in bed, eating pears, sipping at the wine, Chink read from the Gideon's:

> . . . I praised the dead which are already dead more than the living which are yet alive.
>
> Yea, better is he than both they, which hath not been, who hath not seen the evil work that is done under the sun.
>
> Again, I considered all travail, and every right work, that for this a man is envied of his neighbour. This is also vanity and vexation of spirit.
>
> The fool foldeth his hands together, and eateth his own flesh.
>
> Better is an handful with quietness, than both hands full with travail and vexation of spirit.

'Phew, dig that. . . .'
And:

> Two are better than one; because they have a good reward for their labour. . . .

Yeah . . . and put the sunny Bon Chrétiens on the floor and lights out. . . .

Easy to imagine that, as time passes, so do the connexions that memories hang on. But it's the memories that atrophy, shrink to fine points of focus, while the connexions, the bonds, get tougher, and longer, and lit by a concentrated dreamlike glare, a scrutinizing light whose purpose seems to be the destruction or at least the weakening of those surreal embraces, but whose actual effect is to temper and reinforce clutchings, spans, couplings, hair-fine parabolic filaments of 'meaning', until the whole intricate structure locks into some kind of equilibrium, and hardens there, until it resembles a gorgeous electronic circuit, in which links matter more than points of stasis, because it's important for the power to *continue,* no matter how it may be modified en route . . . and what you want to be reassured about, is that the juice goes in one end, and comes out at the other. . . .

So that the memory becomes a power-grid: power-links between points of meaninglessness. So long as you don't get in there with a bomb, or don't shoot your way to the Master Switch and throw it to 'off', so long as you keep that whole circuit bathed in that hardening inward glare, then your power's always going to be *present.* Throw the switch, and you're left with an exquisite map of microscopic dots of rubbish: resting places but no travellers . . . towns but no roads . . . you used to know how to crochet (you remember the word 'crochet') . . . you used to know where your sister lived (you remember her name). . . .

Kate has seen them like that: their circuits like tinkling chandeliers which have gone out.

In her ear, like a cicada, is that phrase: 'the meaning of fiction' . . . Julian, white-faced and red-haired, crows' feet at the corners of his young eyes, is her personal demon. But she likes him. She imagines him playing with his child.

Opposite her, in the window, the Wedding Guest looks back. She's no longer worried about motives . . . she's no longer in any particular hurry. . . .

'Well now.'

Kate addresses her, watches her lips whisper, '*Well,* now. . . .'

. . . along the road a trail of Bon Chrétien cores, on verges or chucked over fences into blond paddocks, and later just out of reach of surf, all of them loud with wasps drinking the saliva of Kate or Chink, Kate and Chink, as well as sweet pear juice. And somewhere along the way, the empty wine carafe dumped in a forty-four gallon drum rubbish-bin by some beach. A lot of rides, Chink always asking to be let out again. After dark, a cabin at Kaikōura. . . .

That's what Kate's got. She didn't even see the wasps. That's how it is.

Next day Chink shook her awake, pulled off the pink candlewick bedspread and the rayon sheet.

'These Norfolk Pines are the southernmost Norfolk Pines in the world, a tip for The Guide please, ta.'

His shoulders were straight. He was pointing like a dog. He

promenaded south under the nitty pines, marginally successful transplants only, even in this temperate enclave: he and Kate were getting into different latitudes, where the 'Philip's Planisphere' (showing the Principle Stars visible for Every Hour in the Year) for lats. 30^s–40^s which Kate had bought on a whim a week or so ago in Auckland, was going to be unreadable, unless you knew your way around well enough to make the necessary connexions by guesswork. Anyway, had they been able to see the stars in the morning sky, which had a pearly membrane of high cloud stretched across it, and lower down long streamers across the indigo buttresses of the Seaward Kaikōuras, they'd have noticed Capricorn rising and chasing Scorpio westwards: Chink being a Capricorn and Kate a Scorpio, information they've already traded, as a formality. The morning will be spent under sensual Capricorn, while Scorpio slips down behind the barricades in the west. Capricorn rising . . . by late afternoon Scorpio will be down, Capricorn dropping fast. Come darkness, Kate and Chink will look up at the Pleiades, a tender cluster above the western horizon, and Aldebaran blazing in Taurus. They will leapfrog up the firmament, through Orion to Canis Major, right overhead, just out of range of the scimitar of the Milky Way which, on this night, will sweep in an arc up and through the centre of the sky. . . . Meanwhile the Norfolk Pines stand along the sea marge like burnt-out rockets. At their bases, from desiccated grass, some bright marigolds grow. There's no one else about yet. Towards the western end of the esplanade is an explosion of geraniums. . . . Chink and Kate move on to the beach, a steep ramp of smooth pebbles. The sea bangs the stones around, even though the day is calm and still. Then the beach gives way to rocks. They clamber back up to the road. An oystercatcher, Pinnochio-nose (who's lying?) is fretting down there among the pools, orange beak flashing this way and that against the grey and buff rocks. Other flashes, of light, are breaking through above the cloud streamers against the mountains which Chink and Kate see as they turn to look back across the wide grey bay: there are green pendants on the slopes. A fishing boat is riding at anchor out in the bay. It has a square old-fashioned deck house, high bows. It moves with an odd jerking motion, the bows dipping down the angle of the anchor chain. Ahead of them, past a pale clutter of pumice along the seashore, they can see the sheds and jetty of the fishing company. Even though the high cloud is beginning to break up, the light is still glaring and low, throwing bright fragments into relief: marigolds, geraniums, the beaks and feet of seabirds, the far-off glass port holes of the fishing boat, green gems at the mountains' throats. . . . A sudden ricochet of light off the tin roof of the fishery sends a shatter of reflections among the windows of cars around the buildings. Then the cloudy retina closes again . . . the scene remains as though photographed: foreshortened, clear, birds hung in still air . . . and something has happened to your eyes: having trapped that detonation of light they stare back past white cataracts. . . . In the doorway of Virgo Fisheries Ltd lolls a man with such an eye, nacreous disc at its centre. Behind him fish are slapped on slabs . . . white rubber aprons and smears of blood . . . the quick flicking of knives . . . while a transistor radio emits the squawks of a commercial breakfast programme.

'Gidday.'

'How are ya.'

The man flicks his cigarette butt out on the asphalt and turns back inside.

Gulls fight over fish-heads floating below some concrete steps where the high tide mark shows at a greeny line of slime and weed. There are triangular orange trickles of oxide below iron rings in the concrete pier. Some rowboats have been pulled up on to the dock. Cloudy rainwater and fish-scales wash over the base boards.

The cloud is really lifting now, the membrane getting thinner, tearing here and there. The atmosphere is heavy. There is no sea wind. In the dusty stands of weed along the gravel road where Kate and Chink are walking the insects are starting up: 'Wit wit wit'. Under this is a persistent harsh continuo: the vibrations seem to strike at the *inside* of some deep part of their ears. The sea now resembles molten lead. Two grey herons cast perfect reflections on slick sand. Chink and Kate walk past a fishing boat beached for refitting. It's being painted bright yellow. Lower down are uncompleted brush strokes of red lead. Along the side of the road is a dry waste of thistle and tussock, grey with pumice dust.

They come to a flat moonscape of rock where the road ends. Here the planes and surfaces are smooth and extend on all sides with shallow catchments of water which reflect light. The rock, wrinkled in soft folds like the skin of some great beast, has a silvery patina. Limpets cling to this skin like warts. Chink and Kate walk across it, past bladderweed and kelp embracing smooth white stones. The beast-skin gives way to such stones, these to a clanking volcanic rubble and a dark sea marge where lizards flick and shuffle into shadow. The lizards seem oily, yet they move with dry precision; *flick, flick,* like their tongues. In the dark crannies where the sea is washing the kelp glistens as though oily . . . stirring in the shallows and clefts of rock.

Then the grey is swept away by sunlight. The cloud membrane has torn right across. High puffs of cirrus trot over blue sky. Heat bounces off the rock. Bumblebees stagger by, inept formations of shags make it to shit-splattered rocks where they spread their wings to the sun. Thistle, low thorn bushes and flax begin cracking and popping with heat.

Her eyes have gone nacreous, they're shining blindly with tears like the mother-of-pearl eyes of a watchful guardian, her glass cage of memory is jangling, the Wedding Guest opposite her is shaking her head and whispering, 'Oh fuck, oh fuck . . .'.

That distance! She's really feeling it . . . on that barbaric rind of coast: Chink's scale, the spaces he's hooked on: nothing less than that transparent blue distance, into which the mind pours out, like an estuary into the sea. . . .

'Can I come with you?' She senses some kind of progression from her Badedas bath to that Pacific skyline! Now, there's a weird one! So all at once she's laughing and laughing. She's *free*. . . .

At this point Chink has stopped. A deep sound comes from low in his chest.

'What is it?' Like a child deep into some game, she's ready to believe anything.

He's staring ahead, past a pagoda-shaped rock formation on the edge of a stagnant inlet. Beyond this murky water is a small hillock. It's chalky, shaped like a shoulder blade, a dry scuff of tussock at its base, its upper edge scalloped sharp by wind. Beyond it the coast, precipitous and darkened with cloud above the ranges, recedes into the heat haze, a bare escarpment shining here and there where sunlight breaks through. Above the cloudy ranges the sky is a bleached-out blue, and below, where the deeper colours of the sea show among brown and white ribs and snags of rock, there's a flickering show of light, like thousands of jostling candles in some temple or procession.

'Hey, what is it?'

They skirt around the shoulder blade. Once their ears have got used to the sound of the waves and have dismissed it, the silence is trance-like. Not even birds.

'What is it, where are we going?'

She inhales a hot waft of something rank and feral, so sudden it shocks her, like a loud clap of noise by her ear. Birds scream upwards from the jagged rock formations ahead: terns and blackbacks, red insides of gaping beaks.

'Ah the darlings, the darlings!' Chink has stopped again, his face broken by a helpless grin of such release as she's only seen when he's making love. . . . Thinking he means the birds she looks up but he seizes her head and jerks it down, pointing her gaze at the gnarled confusion of rocks ahead.

And there they are: the seals, at ease on the jagged rocks: lithe plump flanks . . . eyes large and dark and lovely, long lashed, tranquil pools . . . yawning with satisfaction, a flipper scratching at buff pelt . . . tender muzzles. Kate can see them everywhere, lolling on their stomachs or sides, or else propped up, small heads in the air, catching the sun and the breeze.

Some of those near-at-hand heave themselves in fright to the sea, and slide in. At once their grace is miraculous: shrugging off gravity like water over their shoulders, they turn to look back, sleek heads snouting up, huffing sea from their nostrils, and then dive away again, unthreatened, corkscrewing sideways with flippers slapping the surface of the water, browsing through dark kelp and bladderweed along the sides of the rocks, through the surge and backsuck of the swell, across rip-currents at the mouths of deep clefts, and from time to time driving on their tails up out of the water for long enough to shake a spray of sea from their pelts.

Kate and Chink sit for a couple of hours. After a while the seals ignore them.

'That,' jerking his thumb at the shoulder blade hill, 'is like a totem for me . . . the face of it that looks north . . . it marks a place. . . .'

He stops to watch a seal levering itself up on to the rock. Its slick pelt dries quickly to a light matt brown. It yawns and scratches, closing its eyes. Around it is a filthy litter of dry weed, rocks stained brown, urinous pools. Chink laughs, a sound like a seal bark. They go back the way they've come. They eat oranges, chocolate, cheese in the grass under the escarpment . . . Capricorn rising. . . .

. . . it's all beginning to fade into the coast: somewhere along the maze of her memory the whole morning has slipped back into those dark clefts, their flashes of pink, and flicks of lizards, and glossy seals. It's as though Chink has a pelt, a lubricious sheen. Her sense of the importance of it all is fluent, moving with grace under language. Then it has to get up, like the seal that interrupted Chink: up into the light, among the slovenly wrack. . . .

In the distance people are pygmies: a thin clank of voices. They stumble painfully over the rocks. In our own element we're inept.

Chink and Kate are swimming. The cavalcade passes by, aware that these swimmers are naked. The voices fade around the point. Chink dives, shaking his white arse in the air. Brown fingers of rock stretch into the sea. A diver appears around one of them, comes ashore and flaps up the beach in black wetsuit and flippers, with a creaking bag of crayfish. They hadn't seen his stash near their clothes. Wordlessly he re-enters. Fins of Beast brush her legs . . . Chink in greeny water floats on his back. . . .

Then they're on the clifftop in dry tussock, under the noon sun. They've sucked all the oranges, their skin is dry with salt. Through her eyelids she sees red.

'Close my ears.'

Her long thighs comply, his voice speaks in her belly.

'This is Dick Seddon's Great Dive: he stayed under 5 mins. A record!' Lizards under rocks, dark weed in sea crannies, pinkish hydras and polyps. He's telling her a story. 'In the palace of the King of the Sea . . . the changes are either incredibly fast or else so slow you don't know about them. Some creatures metabolize oxygen, others have learned to slow their heartbeats down to one or two pulses an hour. Others have developed alternative systems . . . tubes reaching to the surface . . . portable survival kits. . . . But elegance is common to all . . . even the immense cocoons and sealed suits of armour favoured by some denizens have grace. It's something . . . to do with movement which is slowed down until no superfluity is possible. . . . But the loveliest are the butterfly fish which flutter in slow motion through the halls . . . awakening reckless thoughts of laughter. . . .'

. . . shoulders off the ground, clutching his head, his ears uncovered and her cries pouring into them, gulls flipping on hot convections up past the cliff edge. Then he's come up, seal smell on his breath. Bam. That's it. Wow. . . . Looking sideways through the noon sunlight she sees a sheep looking back, its jaws grinding patiently sideways. It's too much. . . .

'You're cheap 'n' nasty,' she says. 'You're trash, you're . . .'

The socks he pulls on over his white knobbly feet are full of holes. As they're walking back around the coast he says, out of the blue, 'Remember Te Waiorongo?'

She does now: 'the tranquil and peaceful waters'. She remembers Californian John black with rain on the Ngāruawāhia bridge, the darkness over the desert road. *Home James.* . . . She has the impression, lost in the glass maze of her memory with its Bon Chrétien cores yellow with wasps, its voyeur sheep, its sensual rind of coast, that the whole of that journey was a movement out into space and light: out into Chink's scale of things, driving behind that blue wedge of sky beyond the Wellington heads, on to pumpkin sunshine, beyond that again to the Kaikōura Bay, noon light and heat, the horizon from that clifftop, on and out. . . .

They hitched on south. Late in the afternoon they were dropped at Cheviot where a show was in progress. Voices on the p.a. system: 'Now in the ring Mark Pate on . . .'

Chink: Did you hear *Willie-th-Pimp?*

'. . . (on Winnie-the-Pooh) . . . would all those who have fleeces veges ecksetra in the shed please remove them . . . would all Lions serving as stewards at the cocktail party . . . Winnie-the-Pooh has been scratched . . .'

. . . smell of ripe horseshit, horses farting and flapping their leathery nostrils, *prphapahgh,* and those young country women standing fist on hip, with small children in white shirts and jodhpurs, and all of them with such *confidence:* they stood by their landrovers, putting empty beer bottles back into chilly bins.

The showground was in a bowl cradled by hills. Chink found it hard to separate land shapes from the shapes of women and horses: the way sleek light struck the blond hillsides. . . . He moved as though followed by a spotlight through the twitching brilliance in the leaves of trees, among these people who looked at him with something like scorn. The evening sunshine gathered like a cloying mist through which he appeared to wade, a smile slipping in and out of his expression: an identification card he flashed on demand.

'Isn't this unbelievable, Kate?'

Tomato sauce from a hotdog ran over his chin. The quartered-orange sections of a garish merry-go-round canopy whirled. They drank beer at a bar set up where men sat around on haybales. Chink's face was red from the day's sun, the grin was opening his head.

But the sun was on the blond rim of hills. They went back to the road to get a ride. They were dropped a few miles further on, by the Hurunui River. The sun had set. They had pears, chocolate. There was water in the river. The sky was clear, the stars bright. They climbed a fence, scrambled down through dark willows. Above them, as they lay dizzily on the grass, the stars whirled. As this motion ceased, as the light poured down to them, as they began to hear the night sounds of the river and of sheep on the other side of it, it was as though that impenetrable indigo thickly sown with stars backed off, slewed out and away from them, leaving the stars hanging in a void, leaving Kate and Chink hanging there . . . 'the splendour of the heavens': the Temple of Rangiātea. . . .

'What a trip.

. . . falling asleep among the stars. . . .

She stops. Opposite her the Wedding Guest's mouth is open. She's got this far. She's followed that movement out. She's remembered how space opened in front of them.

But something slams down. Along the circuitry of her memory, in its glass halls, she finds herself baulking at a figure, the face of a man. She imagines, in rapid succession, a coil of dark steel dropping from the *Acapulco Maru*'s sling, bright water turning leaden, windscreen wipers clearing spaces on streaming glass, the figure of a man, the figure of a man driving. . . .

He was a worker for the Tussock Board. The inside of his battered Ford, which he drove at breakneck speed towards Christchurch, had a low stink of solitariness: muttonfat, boots, tobacco. In the back seat, chucked into one corner, was a stained tartan rug and an N.A.C. flight-bag with a tie hanging out where the zip was broken. Here Kate sat, wincing as he cornered. Chink sat in front. From time to time the man turned to Chink and made some comment. He spoke unemphatically.

His voice was dry and carried effortlessly over the noise of the car and the rain. The third of his profile which Kate could see from behind had an ironic repose. He leaned into the corner against the car's door, his casualness concealing the skill with which he drove. His eyes were slightly hooded, sardonic, his nose hawkish. He was dark with sun and wind. The large hand with which he steered seemed hardly to grip the wheel. It rested there, vibrating, a cigarette held at the base of index and middle fingers.

The only thing she can remember him saying was, 'It's not a bad life.' As he said this, half-turning towards Chink who was looking straight ahead through the windscreen, the eye that Kate could see from the back seat wrinkled up at the corner, his mouth tightened with a dry smile. The car slewed through a ramp of gravel on to the long straights of the plains approaching Christchurch, the man's cigarette flew in a shower of sparks down the side of the car, a spray of rain landed on her cheek before he wound the window up again with a crude wrenching motion of his right arm. He and Chink were of a size, their shoulders similarly broad and hunched. As she dozed for the rest of the trip Kate often confused them, imagining that Chink was driving again . . . 'Home James. . . .'

She remembers nothing more about the journey south.

'I mean, *what changes*?'

It goes on, in the old familiar way. In a sense it's beautiful.

Here she was today thinking and looking out her window, her world-section waving its gentle edges out there where the ragwort in the hill paddocks is waving its yellow banners for the end of summer . . . she's changing, the procession is passing, she's entering upon the rigours of another season . . .

everything is waving to her. . . .

She was thinking about Kaikōura. She was dying for a long fuck in the sunshine. She was thinking that Ingrid's okay and the baby's lovely but Curtis is a drag—oh, he's kind, he's terrific, but he's a pissoff!

'Chink, you were never unctuous, thank god for that, nor was dear Beck.'

And she was thinking, 'When I've finished this I'll get a relief teaching job and save some money and go and see Janie in Canberra. She's nearly six!'

'If I could only see *you* again Chink. You poor old bastard.'

Then in came Curtis. When their eyes met she must've had fuck written all over her face. He'd brought her a cup of tea. There he stood with it. It dawned on her that he'd been dying to make it with her for weeks. He was obviously right there now. She stood up before he could put the tea on the table, went past him out the door.

'Must go to the grot.'

She sat for some minutes, shaking.

Because that leap's dumped her without her will and without her having thought of it, down, just less than three years after that trip through Kaikōura.

It was winter, the last of Chink's life, and the worst. He'd been away for months. She was living in Dunedin. She had a barmaid's job at the Gardens. She'd made up her mind that Chink had gone for good this time. No one had heard of him since he'd left. The job was lousy, it was cold. She was on the verge of pissing off north to the Bay of Islands.

Then Chink came back. This time he had a car and plenty of money. He'd changed. His face was pudgy, he'd turned into a real lush, and he had a collection of fancy gear: some O-tincture, some coke all got up in caps, likewise smack, prescription ritalin . . . and three *cases* of Ribena black currant concentrate. The car was a second-hand '69 Jaguar. It had a cassette player in it.

She was behind the lounge bar thinking, 'Fuck this, I'll go tomorrow, I'll *fly*.' She bent down to take some glasses out of the rack. When she looked up Chink was sitting at the bar in front of her.

'I'll have a helicopter. . . .' The old hardness of his eyes was dimmed by the plumpness surrounding them, the violet lush's bags. Some humour had gone too.

She left that night. But after a day or two it wasn't much use. Sometimes Chink didn't even stay with her. He was getting around with a neat character called Stu, a photographer. They egged each other on. Chink was drunk half the time and blocked out of his mind the rest. Kate felt as though she were tagging along. She didn't know what was the matter. When she suggested going north, Chink was silent. One night he fucked her as though it was an assault, groaning words which she couldn't understand. Afterwards he wept, secretly, blundering out of the room. Her nose was bleeding, the knuckle of one finger had turned blue and puffy by morning. Once or twice in town she saw him avoid her in the street.

Stu said he wanted to photograph her. That night as the three of them were walking home, Chink, with a long swing of his arm, flung a half-full tequila bottle through one of the second-storey windows of the university science block. Someone shouted. They all ran. When she got home neither Chink nor Stu was there. The sound of them coming in late in the morning woke her. She heard them go into the living-room down the passage. It was the day for the photographs. She had a shower then went down to where they were.

They were standing in the centre of the room, facing each

other, in the act of passing a whisky bottle: Dimple Haig, Chink's favourite. They both had a hand on the bottle as she came in: it was as though they were in the process of sealing some pact. It was dark in the room, a yawn of space, away from the low winter sun which by early afternoon was off the house altogether. From habit she switched on the light which hung directly above them. It increased the impression of a set piece. Then Stu tipped the bottle up and took a big swallow.

'Take a hit,' he said. 'It's gonna be cold as hell.'

The whisky dried her mouth, burned her stomach, but tasted bland. Chink pulled a wool hat on. Beneath it his white face was heavy and sullen. A stipple of flush beneath his eyes told her he was drunk. Stu shoved the bottle into a bag with the camera gear. Then he followed Chink out.

A queue of anonymous days, as dim as the claustrophobic winter spaces of the house, leaned into her from behind as she approached the daylight. Turning back against this pressure to switch off the light she imagined she saw, like a television ghost, the outlines of the two men with a hand each on the whisky bottle, as though each drank to himself in a mirror: a drunk in a derelict house. Their last sentence, which she hadn't heard, hung there. Had it concerned her? Chink's silence told her yes. Then she switched off the light and turned with the tide and walked outside to Stu's car.

He and Chink were in the front seat. The camera bag was in the back. Kate climbed in next to it. She hadn't had breakfast. Chink sat motionless, the wool hat pushed low on his brow, his hands stuck into the pockets of his old blue pea coat, his shoulders drawn up to his ears, staring ahead through the windscreen with the bored expression of a sailor surveying the bleak dockside of some coastal port. It was like a second-rate impersonation.

'. . . and now you . . .' She'd remembered the phrase.

After they'd driven some way along the Port Chalmers road Chink said, 'Pass the bottle.' He took a swallow and sat with the bottle between his knees. The stink of the tannery at Sawyer's Bay entered the car as they passed.

'Look up there!' Between Mount Cargill and the misty continuing range a ragged frond of blue sky was waving in from the valley to the north. 'It'll be fine over the hill,' Stu said. 'For fuck's sake cheer up.'

The shabby main street of Port was cold and deserted. While Stu went into a milkbar to buy cigarettes Chink and Kate sat silently in the car. Some proscription hung between them. Even if she'd wanted to she couldn't have reached forward, a gesture made familiar by repetition and travel, to touch his head or neck, breathe his tender hair smell.

'What about the Atlas Mountains?' She was going to say it, 'Wha' . . . wha' . . . wha' . . .', sadness shaking her lips until she whimpered. But an unloaded timber truck gunned past on its way up from the wharf. Then Stu got back into the car with chocolate fish. Chink shook his head. Kate pushed hers into her mouth, swallowed her words. The cheap mush seemed no more tasteless than the whisky.

Looking back as they wound up the hill west of the port she could see a motionless line of nappies hung out along the back of Curtis's place. Then they turned up into low freezing cloud, to cross the range.

On the other side it was clear and dazzling. In the distance the foothills beyond Palmerston showed sharp with snow. There was a dirty mush of snow along the side of the road where the sun had reached, and where it hadn't the hoar still lay brightly. The sea below was brilliantly faceted, blue and silver.

'Yeah, look at it!' Even Chink sat up straighter and tipped

the bottle again, in salutation.

There was ice in the shaded corners. As Stu crept down the steep incline towards the coast, the back of the car seemed to lift off the road and shake and then slide sickeningly away from them. Vomit rose in her throat.

'Please stop, I feel sick.'

'We're almost there,' said Chink, and wound his window down. The icy air struck her violently. She cried out and retched, grabbing for a handkerchief. Stu skidded to the side of the road. She spewed out the door. Through a blur of tears she saw Chink sitting without turning. He tipped the bottle, looked out at the shining panorama. Stu stood some way off. When she'd finished he came around the car with a clean handkerchief. Chink lit a cigarette and sat waiting.

How she feared and hated the dragon-patience with which he guarded his hoard of torments. She didn't even know what they were: he'd never been straight about them.

When you go to someone for help, what happens? Ah, admit it. There it is: the shit on your shoes, the wound in your hide, the tear in your eye. You say, 'Help me.' The reply you get is, 'No, *you* help *me*.' Then begins a bargaining over who needs help the most, over whose puncture is more serious. That's what happens. Yet it works, as often as not: a resistance, a reef on which the leaking hull of your pain can break up and sink at last, as Kate's might have, or Chink's, that day . . . gone down as though beneath the dazzling tinsel and azure meniscus of the sea, the glaring horizon.

Ice had set in the Pūrākanui inlet. There were no birds in the estuary, but crowds of them were wheeling above the long spit dividing the estuary and lagoon from the sea.

'I've seen them crashing into that stuff, that slush, sometimes it kills even big birds,' said Stu.

The ruts in the road were frozen solid. The cold in the sand of the track struck through Kate's boots. Here, in the overgrown path where the sun never came in winter, the frost crystals were so large and distinct they might have been the elaborate constructs of a science of cold: they were unreal, like models, and yet so perfect that they alone, out of the entire surrounding jumble of weed and branch and rock, seemed not to be superfluous.

From the cliff to the left of the track hung ragged rows of icicles. The excavation of the small old quarry was filled with thick ice: when Stu jumped on it it cracked like a gunshot, a twenty-foot greenish fracture whipped out through the surface. The sand at the beach was also frozen: it was possible to cut it to a hard edge. This Chink did, using the large Green River butcher's knife he'd brought in his mussel kit.

Kate's boots were rubber so she walked out into the water and bent to scoop sea into her mouth. It was too shallow to be clear but she welcomed the grit and harshness of it.

Stu had walked on towards the bluff at the western side of the beach, over which was the other small beach he'd decided to use.

They were all spaced out widely in the cold brassy air: Stu, bent under his camera bag, about to disappear behind some rocks below the clay bluff, Chink carving sullenly in the frozen sand just beyond the opening of the path through the bare lupin and elderberry, and Kate pacing eastwards along the waterline, clutching under her coat the hand numbed by the water. There was no sound except sea. Even the wheeling gulls in the distance above the sandspit were silent, or else what small breeze there was blew their cries away.

She walked on for a hundred yards. Turning to look back she could see Chink, crouched in the sand at the western end of the beach. He could have been a child playing by itself, and so used to solitude that it's peopled its world for itself, and can talk all afternoon with these allies.

As she walked back he grew. She abandoned the image which had entered her mind: of picking up and hugging a solitary child, no bigger than Janie aged six, covering her serious face with kisses. . . .

He didn't look up as she walked past him towards the bluff. The frozen sand around him was carved into an intricate maze of sharp-edged rectangular walls and boxes. Pressing with rapt concentration on the back of the blade, he began to cut an extension, pausing for a moment to flick his tortoiseshell bracelet up out of the way.

On the other side Stu had collected a pile of driftwood and made an enormous fire. He stood panting by it, the bottle of Dimple cradled in his arms. He was squinting at the rock face. The low shadows of the early afternoon sun struck into it.

'It's perfect!'

'Phew, pick up on David Bailey.' She had a drink and stood by the fire. In the distance, out to sea beyond Warrington, tiny fishing boats could be seen in the clear focus of the air. They too were unreal, like a child's toys. As she looked out towards them across the crystalline glare of the water her eyes seemed to yaw on that surface, as the car had done on the dark ice of the hill. Stu was standing in silence, fiddling with his wristwatch. She sensed the mute presence of the sentence she'd missed: some pact, some kind of desolate mirror image. She felt sick again. There was a thin high whine of silence in her ears, a sound like cicadas. For a moment she hesitated, her nostrils tightening against that odour, suddenly hot with more than the heat of the fire, with some stifling nauseous access of energy which rose under her ribs, pressing her throat. She was about to raise her hand to shatter that shrill screen of silence like a pane of glass whose insistent faults blur any vision. The day's clarity, the piercing focus of the cold air, seemed themselves to be that desperate filter obscuring what was near-at-hand. Though the light might lead out to infinity and so back again, that too was an illusion. It all was. *Break it.* She raised her hand, raised the sentence, a heavy instrument, to break the pane: 'What did Chink say . . . ?'

She didn't say it. She stepped out of the heat of the fire, taking the scarf from her head with her raised hand, feeling the blood drop like mercury in her heart. The sweat was cold on her top lip, her forehead.

'Let's get it on.'

Real despair is impersonal. It seems finally to have no object. Chink, carving his labyrinth in icy sand, was as distant as the fishing boats being offered on their burnished tray, where her eyes slewed towards the bulge of the horizon.

But the energy which had fed her sickness had gone. She watched as Stu checked his gear. Then she took her clothes off and posed or walked or bent as he directed, feeling no cold, but getting into her overcoat from time to time and standing by the fire, sipping from the bottle. Soon she was drunk, dazed with heat and cold. Stu moved quickly and surely following some instinct. She stood with one leg propped high on a rock, the other knee turned outward, her head and torso bent as far back as she could get them. Stu was photographing from just beyond her foot, shooting along the length of her leg.

'Hey this is getting a bit tawdry.'

'Hang on sweetheart.'

From under her brows she could see the beach beyond, upside down . . . and Chink come over the bluff and walk around the headland with his mussel kit. She turned, pressing her arms to the weathered rocks, hearing the shutter click and click beside her. She huddled by the fire in the overcoat, one breast and one leg carefully exposed.

Then it was enough. He passed the bottle over. She was shaking, the tears were running down her cheeks. She stood facing the headland where Chink had gone. Stu's cold hand pushed the coat aside and touched her breast.

'Why don't you dump Chink, the bastard's driving you mad.'

That was it. She saw them again in the centre of the room, in a formal attitude of agreement. In the derelict house. When she looked at Stu his face was doggish with desire. Passed over, passed on, like some used item. She pushed his hand aside and gathering the flapping overcoat around herself ran down the beach. The blurred pane broke. The near-at-hand rushed towards her, her feet struck against the shell-studded rocks of the headland. Slipping and clutching she got around. There was Chink, standing at the end of the outcrop, staring at some point far across the bay. At his feet brown sluggish kelp, green water. The mussel kit lay full beside him. She couldn't get a word out. When she was close he heard her and turned slowly, as though out of a vision. Then he ran forward and gathered her up, like a child, pulling her coat shut, pulling her against him.

'You fucking bastard . . . oh Chink, oh Chink. . . .'

Then he took his wool hat off and pulled it over her ears and led her to shelter by the cliff.

'Shush . . . hey, little one. . . .'

When she could speak properly she asked for a cigarette. He lit it and she got it, shaking, up to her mouth. The pain in her feet was agonizing. His eyes, for the first time since she'd known him, were openly overflowing with tears. He talked on and on.

'It's almost spring, we're past the solstice.'

'Can I come,' she kept saying. 'Can I come?'

. . . while his big hands, purple with cold, rubbed clumsily at her arms and shoulders, touched her cut feet, while he stared with those lidless tearful eyes into her face.

She was thinking, 'Perhaps this time he won't go away.' And looking out through eyes closing like a lover's, at the tiny fishing boats on their sea of brass: Beck's frail gorgeous galleons of faith.

13

If I get to know 'the material' well enough, I've kept thinking, then some sort of order will emerge. But that's been a kind of half lie.

I know it so well already that it's all present. Sometimes I can't remember the sequence in which things happened. I keep looking for something outside it all: a bad habit my mother taught me. But her endless supply of quotations would fizz like hard metal dropped in acid. Mine are downers: I grind them between my teeth and feel my sad blood thicken and relax. . . .

1. '. . . what I give to all I withold from each' (Reb Bunam)
2. 'You come from' etc. (You know the one)
3. 'O sightless tides / What blossom blows to you from spring hillsides?' (Curnow)
4. (Wait for it:) 'This fabulous shadow only the sea keeps' (Crane)

What a dreary little anthology. For a while sentences used to jump out of books at me. It was like I was seeing 'evidence' or 'clues' or 'material' everywhere. I picked up a book of Crane's poems, I saw that line, I shut the book, I began to cry.

It's like that little bastard Julian that Beck picked up so long ago: 'A pregnant woman discovers the meaning of fiction' . . . *that* shot straight through the filter and lodged like some shrill implant just by my ear.

In fact I don't know how to get into this. I feel like writing at the top of a fresh page: SUICIDE! I mean, this is a serious matter. But I sit looking out the window at the ngaio, and listening to the cicadas, and how do I remember Chink? With love . . . that is what's risen to the surface.

'You selfcentred heartless bitch.' Say it, then.

When I cry these days it's no longer for myself. It's as though it's because there's sunlight among the kāpuka and the ngaio, or rain . . . blackbirds, or a cicada. I don't understand it. But the moment leads me out.

I always thought there were three kinds of suicide: suicide committed out of complete despair; suicide committed to regain love; and suicide committed with reason not feeling. The first kind, I thought, was meant to succeed but often didn't. The second kind, the saddest, wasn't meant to succeed. The last kind was meant to succeed and usually did.

That's bullshit. It doesn't work, there's no place for Chink in it. For him to have a place in it, he'd have to permit it to fit him from the outside. But Chink's death emerged from within, as far as the unseen side of the skin of the whole of his body, and if we have auras then as far as the limits of his aura, and if we have astral bodies then as far as his astral body travelled from the body that held me in its arms at night. It didn't describe him, it created him.

It's impossible for me to imagine Chink's death without also imagining landscape and music. Yet neither exist. The landscape isn't a setting: his death creates it, as he moves towards that moment when death will complete its creation of him. After that moment of his death, the landscape ceases to exist. If I was to go back to Bethells now, right down to the bit called O'Neill's, as I couldn't such a short time ago, it wouldn't be the place where he died. It would just be Bethells Beach.

And the music isn't an accompaniment to his death, but has gone forever, though when I imagine it it's close to the pitch of 'killing the fish'.

So those of you who doubt that Chink committed suicide are only playing with stencils, colouring-in-by-numbers, identikit. Your doubts are irrelevant. Even if Chink did not, in your terms, decide to do away with himself (let's drag all the stencils out of the cupboard), even if he did go out to Bethells (alone?) and drown 'accidentally' having dropped a tab (alone?), it makes no difference. It was the shape he was taking. And how can you surrender to something which by-passes or subsumes the will just as surely as love can subsume reason? (Why didn't I dump Chink?) You stop the clock. You say, 'At *this* moment it happened. Its meaning is *here*.' You describe what you've stopped: a dead fish: Chink, on a trip, caught in the black surf. Meanwhile the 'truth' continues, breaking and reforming like the lines of phosphorescence in those dark breakers that dumped your only evidence into some fissure in the rocks.

What if you'd been able to make out a big smile on your evidence? Yeah, that would have been 'open to interpretation' too:

'What a way to go!'

That's obscene, not my light heart. You'll learn nothing from the black sand and rips of Bethells, no matter how long you spend walking up and down the tide line.

'Look at that undertow . . . that's how it would happen.'

So what? It *did* happen. That's it.

And you won't learn anything from your memory of Chink picking out a twelve bar blues in the clump of nīkau palms at the bottom of the section of Beck's bach. Go and have a holiday there and see how much time you spend thinking of Chink, and how much your surroundings remind you of him. You'll get stoned, you'll trip, you'll swim, you'll eat mussels and rock cod, you'll sleep, fuck, laugh, talk. You won't drown. Your 'description' won't *mean* anything. Every so often the conversation will reach out, touch Chink: 'Do you remember . . . ?' It will be very gentle. You'll feel guilty because this touching disgusts you. The subject is cold and heavy. You'll feel guilty because you're thinking of him so little. Well, don't feel guilty. Don't let it spoil your holiday.

How can I explain it? I don't mean to absolve myself. An order has emerged, that's all, and it's happened in spite of my struggle to work to a design.

I suppose the design was *I am to blame.* I suppose it was a kind of vanity. But what's emerged isn't like that at all. I began to realize it a while back.

It's all moving. I'm beginning to move with it. I don't understand, but I accept it. And so here I sit, your 'selfcentred heartless bitch', looking out through the open window at the broadleaf and the ngaio . . . clear late summer sunshine, and a cicada, yeah! . . . a cicada playing the blues!

'Listen Supercock I'm gonna give you a definition.' (Beck letting Chink have it, back up in Auckland again, the spring before his last, yellow kōwhai weather, blue distance weather.) '. . . now listen: your trouble is Darwinian paranoia, a paranoia of biological necessity, a paranoia of practical genetics: the idea is that one cock can get around numerous women for purposes of procreation and so most men are, practically speaking, in terms of the survival of our species, redundant, unless we regard them as drones, suicide-soldiers, slaves. It's the women we can't cut down on, right Kate? . . . huh . . . all right, but this is the origin of what Kate calls 'male chauvinism' though I bet she's never thought about it. First: deep down most men know they're irrelevant unless they can prove themselves to be good studs and all that. Second: so they come on *machismo* but it's a sad sham and it destroys them as people. Third: they struggle to retain the power they know they don't deserve, they use this power in sexist programmes, phew, listen to *me*, they emphasize the symbols of maleness rather than its functions, since function and symbol are usually contradictory. Result: like, here's Chink with cock written all over him, yards of it, but he's got no children and all his other kinds of vital energies are directed inwards, not outwards into the species to educate it or reproduce it or protect it. Analysis: he's really a human dildo, a eunuch with a strapon, he's impotent, he's a self fucker. . . . Listen, all supercocks are really at an infantile stage of development, they wanna get back into the amniotic fluids, they wanna drown in their own come, they wanna be absorbed back into the process they can only guess at when they're fucking. Meanwhile the lady looks on patiently, and gets her kicks, or more likely gets hurt, and sometimes wonders why the stupid bastard has to go through all those changes, why he goes limp like a wee macaroni the moment she suggests he's letting her down, or not getting her up . . . what a merry-go-round, Jesus! So if you wanna get off the merry-go-round you go gay: it's practical and sensible apart from anything else like fun, not that I could tell *you* that. Well, what are you, señor Prick, Chink suh, B'wana, do you have brains in your balls, are you a dildo, or are you a *kamikaze* fucker, dying to die, to get back, to be started over again . . . ?'

Of course Beck was putting Chink on. On this occasion Chink slowly unzipped his fly, took his cock out and held it across the palm of his hand.

'You're probably quite right, Auntie.' He was grinning straight into Beck's face. Then he tickled it 'under the chin' until it began jerkily to stand up.

'Stand up when Teacher comes into the room.'

But she's also thinking, 'Old Beck had a hunch . . .'

They were walking from Waitakere station over the hill to Bethells Beach (not Beck, he'd gone on in a car with friends to the bach he shared down by the river), just Chink and Kate, ambling through dust while minahs chopped in and out from the sides of the road in front of them, flicking white wedge tails. Chink was singing:

Some folks built like this
Some folks built like that
But the way I'm built
Don't you call me fat
Because I'm built for comfort

I ain't built for speed
But I got every thing
Oh that a good girl need

Somewhere, over towards cleared ground, the magpies sounded like grand pianos with squeaky castors being wheeled around the hills . . . a concert was in preparation, some kind of spectacular, something vulgar to remember it all by. . . .

From Eden Park the Waitākere ranges had been visible, purple in the distance. They'd been at cricket with Beck. He'd shouted, 'Stick it right uppim!' *Nok:* a cap had flown in the air, the ball had bumped under the grandstand. Beck: 'You beauty!'

'Stick it right up him,' she said, as they walked along. 'I don't want to spend the whole time out there listening to you two eating each other's hearts, doing your routines. I've been through that.'

'Right.'

Because I'm built for comfort
I ain't built for speed

he sang, down in the sunny ponga grove below Beck's bach. Everything was terrific. The cicadas were beginning to twang and scrape away.

'Bring us a few really shapely shells,' she said one day as he was off for a walk.

He brought some empty ice-cream tubs.

'It's all that's left.'

His smile was sunny, malicious: 'Woo-hoo-oo': Wolf howlin'.

*

One day they walked back along the valley and turned up the hill by the chicken farm. It's the light she remembers again, and the lizards in the dry toetoe debris by the roadside. Coming over the crest of the hill, they see a dry vista of mānuka and yellowish clearings, bright flashes of old bush in the gullies. Then the valley opens out south-west to the roar of the sea, to a sky sandwich: to chow on a sky sandwich, to get cloud sauce on your chin, to share a slice with a friend . . . they like that kind of appetite, smacking their lips over space . . . they like to think that if blue is distance and yellow is where they're drunk with being, then they might live in a green space. . . .

Wait, what's this. . . .

She's tracking some bright filament. She follows herself and Chink into an old grove of pōhutukawa. Orchids grow in the deep cusps and bowls of these trees which she thinks resemble elephants. There's a gaudy play of light in the stiff leaves of baby nikaus, down there among the old trunks: points of yellow and green fire. The trunks are grey and wrinkled. The light soaks into this, but blazes in new leaves. They climb through mānuka, delicate black filigree above their heads, scurf of lichen and dry bark on the boles. A bird seems to say 'Chink, Chiii—iiink': his head turns that way. Wind in the branches sounds like the sea: they're underwater, held in the flickering light of a wave. Bellbirds and tui among kōwhai flowers sound like ships' bells filtered by sea and distance. *The light, the light* . . . she's been here before, it's as familiar as anything she knows about him. From the crest of the hill, jutting like the bows of an immense galleon out into the valley, preparing to launch itself across the plug of ironsand in the valley's mouth, they look west at blue, at space, at sky sandwich, at the sea's thin white line of foam. Behind them, below them, the birds gong and warble among yellow, the small nikau burn with yellow fire . . . above their heads the minute black latticework of dry mānuka twigs . . . above that the blue northern sky. . . .

'*That's it,* that blue!'

It's raining. In the window her reflection watches her lips move. She says, 'I'm going crazy!' There's the Wedding Guest telling her she's going crazy. 'Hey, stop it!' (Hey, stop it!)

But she can't laugh. Her face has gone stiff. She's got something. She opens her eyes and writes:

1. he's green, he's got blue, it's distance, to approach her he's got to subtract blue from himself, he's got to change what he has into what he's diminished by, his power's reversed, he gets the Tasman instead of the Pacific.
2. she's yellow, she hasn't got blue distance, to approach him she's got to add blue to herself, she's got to change what she lacks into what she's augmented by, her impotence is diminished, but she reduces his scale.

'She gets a fucking Badedas bath . . . !'

Yeah: she's increased, he's diminished. She's alive, he's dead.

How neat.

'I'm crazy.'

The door bangs open where she runs out and through the house to Ingrid and the baby playing with empty preserving jars in the yard. The yellow shed doors are open in the sunlight. Yellow ragwort is glaring on the hillside opposite.

Comforting Kate as she cries in her arms, Ingrid watches the baby at the same time to see if she's frightened, and tries to understand what Kate's repeating, over and over: 'I'm yellow, I'm yellow, I'm crazy . . .'. She doesn't understand it, how could she? And Kate's been so much better. . . .

*

From the grove they walk downhill through shadow, in a primeval agglomeration of trunks, leafmould, the haphazard bright regeneration of pongas. In the raupo swamp at the bottom of the valley there's a simmer of wind in flax, toitoi, bulrush. The bulrushes resemble bees' legs laden with pollen.

Beyond the immense dam, the plug of ironsand in the valley's mouth, there's a lake, Lake Wainamu.

Chink: 'Lake Chad . . .'

Grass stalks blown from their fixed points in circles and arcs on the dark sand make delicate relief lithographs, maps of mazes, of ways into the interior. The sand burns like glass.

Chink: 'Follow me.'

A white butterfly flickers above the sand in the distance, like a loose white robe, a burnouse.

The Guide: '. . .'.

The water is green and cool. Ducks clap and panic. Then it's quiet again.

They've made it. They've got there. They're drinking beer, eating smoked beef sandwiches. Their feet dabble through the dream surface of the lake.

They all play the following game except Beck who says he fdoesn't dig the symbolism.

Down towards the beach, where the river spreads into the sand, there's a deep cave in the cliff. The game is to get blocked and go there at night. There are ten of them altogether. They draw lots for which one will go right into the cave then turn off the torch. This one has to take up a position anywhere along the floor of the cave, which goes straight back into the hill. The remainder of the players outside draw lots for the order in which they'll run at full speed into the blackness. At any moment they expect to smash into solid rock. Their legs fail. Then those who are in there already pressed against the walls of the cave or lying waiting on the floor, put out their hands. Or they all pounce on the victim.

Everyone becomes hysterical with laughter.

Only three people are able to run very far in. Chink's one of them. He flies through the blackness yelling wildly, grazes himself on the wall he runs into. Where he comes to a stop shouting 'Ow!' is a small ledge with a sick penguin sheltering on it. He says he could smell it when he stopped, something fetid, he could hear its difficult breathing. In torchlight it's revealed, a sad bird, puffed up defensively, one round eye filled with maggots.

When the torch is off and everyone's been quiet for a while, the glow worms light up along the ceiling of the cave, as though the scale of the universe has been reduced until stars press down on your head.

'Te Pō kumea . . .'

Outside, where Beck sits warming himself over a joint, the stars recede again to their proper perspective.

In daylight the river is sluggish. There's an oily sheen on the water from the swamp, orange tongues of iron oxide by the stream, bright mica in the sand. . . . The universe is tipped up. You grind stars under your feet. Space is solid, it shifts and sucks just enough to slow you down. Running into distance (chasing a frisbee), your feet bog, you expect to smash your face into rock, to be crushed.

Lifting your eyes to the horizon, you experience salvation. You are poured out. You sense how that 'barrier' recedes forever.

You're not moving. But *it* is.

*

The north end of Bethells Beach, the part called O'Neill's, has pōhutukawa with white trunks hugging the slopes behind the dunes. Standing in the sea are crude bulwarks and dragons' teeth of composite rock: fiercely dense firings of scoria, clay, iron, shell. In stormy weather gobs of yellow foam whirl inland. The sea boils in jagged fissures. In fine weather a haze of salt spray hangs in the air. Ripcurrents drive crooked lines of waves against the rocks. You can see what might happen.

'Chink, who's this Stranger?'

Chink's wet head jerked towards her. There was a patch of black sand on one cheek, like a contusion.

'Sorry,' she said. 'It's just that you've mentioned him or her once or twice as though I should know.'

He rubbed at the sand on his face. Then he rolled over. His belly was black with it. He scratched at it with one finger then lifted more and lazily dumped it on his belly and thighs.

'It's not important,' he said. He sat up and looked down the beach. 'It's just a fancy of mine. Or it could be like that guy over there on the rocks. Could be anyone. It depends.'

'The fisherman there?'

'Yeah, the fisherman, why not . . . ?'

At the far end of the beach (they were all at O'Neill's) a man was fishing from the rocks with an enormous rod, standing motionless and patient above the water which crashed below him. Kate hadn't noticed him before. Through the thin haze of spray and heat he appeared unreal, and with that hypnotic immobility of all patient fishermen. But she couldn't see why Chink should have singled him out, unless it was because the man singled himself out by being the only person with purpose on the beach.

But Chink appeared to be satisfied with his explanation. Or else the question didn't interest him. He stood up and sauntered into the water and when he was deep enough plunged under a breaker, reappearing seconds later with a shake of his head. Then he swam out some yards with his strong easy stroke, ducking the waves, and bodysurfed back in. He did this several times. Then he walked back. The solitary fisherman was also coming towards them along the tidemark. He and Chink met in front of her and dipped their heads in greeting: that familiar all-purpose male greeting.

'You want to watch it,' said the fisherman courteously. 'The tide's going out.'

'Yeah,' said Chink. 'Not much good for fishing either.'

The fisherman walked on, a short sun-darkened middle-aged man, with a wet sugar-bag over one shoulder, wearing white plastic sandals. As he got further away all that could be clearly seen of him through the haze was the dogged tread of the white sandals.

'So the Stranger's a chartered accountant who in retirement follows a lone romantic streak.'

Chink grinned, licking salt off his chin. 'That'd do,' he said. '"I was a chartered accountant until I discovered my romantic streak."'

'"I was a romantic until I was discovered by a chartered accountant."'

They went lazily through a few more changes in the little word game. But Chink's eyes followed the distant tread of the fisherman's sandals as he walked away from them with that solitary patient purpose through the heat haze, stopping once or twice to shift the big rod case to the other hand, the dark sugar-bag to the other shoulder.

15 *Dynamite*

The most he could do anymore was hold a match to her cigarette. The cigarette was shaking so much because her hand was shaking that much. He had to follow the cigarette with the match like a turret gunner in a war movie taking a bead on the enemy. He kept getting metaphors like that: avoiding the issue? the 'saving grace of humour'? So, laugh.

There seemed to be a tremor just behind her eyes. It spread to her hand, to the jumping cigarette. His match jumped after it, soundlessly. Its movement said 'Duh duh duh duh duh', a children's matinée. One moment her eyes filled with tears which the tremor shook out on to her cheeks. Then the eyes closed. Then she laughed, she couldn't stop laughing. She shook with laughter. They were completely smashed a lot of the time. At least he was finally quit of his ferocious vanity (he invented the term himself). Dynamite! But was left with a bankrupt compassion (that was his too).

She walked along one side of the street. It wasn't raining, it had snowed and thawed, the air was clear, sunlight tinkled on to the rinsed pavements, small funicular gondolas of water drops hung along telephone lines. She could barely raise her eyes from the asphalt. He observed her from the other side of the street. He thought: 'If I call out she'll step out under a car.' Later it occurred to him that he could have crossed to her. (At that stage his vanity still had him by the throat.) He went into a newsagent's and bought a newspaper then went and had coffee. The Stockholm Conference on the environment was equivocating grandly. Banality. Dynamite! It seemed like a good day to be in the country up Central, but he couldn't imagine what he'd do there by himself. Park the car and drink, look at the Old Man Range, do some snow, ha ha. He wondered where she was going when he saw her on the other side of the road.

He felt very gentle. It seemed to him he felt great compassion. Only later did he realize it was vanity. When his pride and assurance were destroyed his compassion shrank, or at least his ability to articulate it did. Hah! Who are these people. She was always on about her fucking mother these days and it made her talk *like that.* She knelt in front of the heater, taking off her clothes. He pressed his lips to the crown of her head, her dark crown. She seemed so vulnerable! How our compassion flatters us. He made love to her gently and slowly, not wanting her to be alone that night, single that night, or ever, not wanting to leave her body. She trembled, turning her head from side to side on the pillow. He could see her teeth in the darkness. With despair he felt his prick shrinking. He held her, motionless, close to him. He shrank and left her. She slept huddled against him, breathing on his neck. He lay awake most of the night. In the morning he kissed her forehead and talked to her.

Whenever he sat in a room alone, or with her, which was now seldom, or even with a crowd, the Stranger entered. He was mostly quiet these days. He simply leaned in a corner and watched, with an expression of mild amusement, as she moved her cigarette towards his match. Sooner or later the Stranger would sigh: 'You see? Why pretend? You can't win. Look at her. Look at you. Look at the record. Try and imagine the future. Why not be honest? Compassion's a kind of vanity. It makes you feel good. It's an excuse for manipulating others. Don't you feel a shit when you know you've done that? Look at your record, brother. Your own need's the dragon that traps the princess that calls for the knight that kills you that has a need that becomes a dragon that traps the princess. . . . Why not get out? There's no future in that system, only repetition. You don't need it. It doesn't need you. What I have to offer isn't even terrifying.'

Dynamite!

Another time he bent her hand back and butted her in the face with his forehead. He wanted to hear something resist and break. Everything was so fucking passive! It was like being smothered.

But at least he was finally quit of his 'ferocious vanity'.

And with it, of a good part of his ability to 'articulate compassion'.

Those were the words he thought. Their stupid formality made him furious. But he persisted in the same vein. It was like a language she'd taught him. Along with a lot of other stuff. Now that he had, to a large extent, 'lost all interest in self', the most he could do anymore was hold a match to her cigarette. O yeah! In a corner of the room, paring his fingernails, the Stranger smiled his patient lopsided salesman's smile and raised one shoulder: 'Now you look like an intelligent fellow. Take my advice, brother.'

He bought a Fender Telecaster guitar: '. . . plugged into his Twin Reverb amp and very gently thumbed his machine. It responded like a crack of thunder . . .'. That was the advertisement. He couldn't get one beautiful lick out of it.

He'd thought, 'I could be a musician. . . .'

Uh uh. No.

It was the clearest day for weeks: blue and sharp, cold, the sun bright, the far horizon where sea and sky met milky with brightness, the near horizon where pinewood and sky met bristling and hard-edged with black pine tops. In places where the sun hadn't reached the road, grass, leaves, was a thick hoar of frost. The upright crystals jostled each other on the surface of a leaf, like nerve endings, he imagined, somehow erogenous, frozen, a second's tastelessness on the tongue.

She leaned against weatherbeaten rocks having her photograph taken while he knelt in the sun at the end of the outcrop tearing clusters of mussels from the rough stone and stuffing them into a kit. He was going to cook them in beer and butter. He was pissed. He had no appetite. He tugged mechanically at the blue shells. The icy sea rushed in and out below his fingers. In summer the kelp would be chrome yellow. Now its thick fronds and broad muscled limbs were a dark brown, like seals.

Further offshore a few fishing boats were spaced haphazardly between sea and sky. Killing the fish. He imagined fish crowding into their nets, the soundless panic and agony, the net filled with scales resembling a dragon. Reality is a lattice, a net. It's the spaces that count. It's the spaces that trap you. There's no escape. Or . . .

'That's right, brother,' said the Stranger. 'That would be the natural way. How you envied the seals! You could get back there. Just think of it: in your element at last! And the Pacific: peace, brother, peace. . . .'

'Do you have a cigarette?' she whispered.

He gave her one and lit it. Duh duh duh duh duh. What a day! Clear light! *The favourite lost by a neck.* In the net, strangling. Dynamite, dynamite!

'Listen,' he said, 'it's gonna be okay so don't *you* worry. What a day! We're almost past the solstice. It's almost spring! Look at the horizon, all the way to South America, the Pacific, Kate, the Pacific. . . .'

'Can I come?'

16

Leaving Dunedin early, a blur of long roads, driving in and out of rain. Then it began to clear. Imperceptibly his muscles began to relax. But he had to keep driving. He kept the cassette going. Gradually he sank back against the seat, began to look around himself as he drove. He slowed up.

'What a boring road,' he said aloud. He'd travelled it more times than he could remember. The banality of his thought was a comfort.

'Still, it's spring,' he said. That was another one. He laughed for a while. He tried a few more: 'Look at the lambs!' 'I much prefer hilly country.' 'We're averaging about forty.'

And out of Christchurch. His time had these big gaps in it. He took a swallow of Dimple, dropped a dexie down after it. Yes, it *was* spring, getting into it. Something inside him was pushing like a green spear of narcissus or common daffodil under the cold clod of his confusion. He could feel a gap opening up, and a perfume rising through him and passing from his nostrils to envelop him: clarity, softness. . . .

Happiness?

In any case, Waikuku, a name, a bearing, evidence that he was moving. The sense of motion. It had become rare. He began to prepare his brief.

On the banks of Saltwater Creek the willows were tipped with ochre and yellow feathers of growth. And on.

On the western side of the road were stands of old gaunt gums, skin hanging in tatters. The swampy flats seemed almost to extend to the foothills, these to the mountains, hinted at but real, promising more: green, brown, blue, white: the receding colours were like a code: the message left him dazed.

And on: lupin, gorse, the heaps and gnawed corrugations of old dunes. He ticked off Kōwhai Stream. West: a solitary cherry tree in blossom. East: a familiar scramble of lupin. The speeding leisurely car divided the universe up its spine. East and west fell away, marking exact divisions.

Amberley, another bearing: wide green empty verges, 'Arthur Burke' used cars, 'Bell Farm Machinery Ltd', a stunning orange sign with navy blue lettering. And on.

He looked west, where the sun tended, and saw an old calm derelict house but with a clothes line propped up with mānuka poles in the paddock and a solitary pink shirt hanging on it.

Also west the railway line and on that a solitary man in blue dungarees with a shovel on a jigger, gradually falling back behind the speeding car, looking neither to left nor right, neither east nor west. Chink acknowledged his presence with a long glance in the rear vision mirror.

Then to the west was the old Amberley Lime Company's wooden building drying and grey without paint by the railway line, leaning its chute over.

On the roadsigns, magpies. Against the green before the brown, blue, white—against that spring extravagance glossy black Angus yearlings strolled. This was west.

And on. The Hurunui River. Yes. . . .

And then before Cheviot, west: the first hit of the snow white Seaward Kaikōuras, those mountains! whose purity froze and woke him, a vivid rush of sensation to the head.

Then the Jed River. Then Cheviot.

The light was losing out. Five forty-five in the evening when the gap opened up, the 'gap between the worlds', a bright space between the firmament and the mountain tops, and lower down, wedges of light in the foothills, like steps, leading up to that slowly closing doorway. Chink averted his eyes. He looked at the lambs. And then east, at the oriental cosmetic of the gashed and worn hills, the sexual shadow.

'I'm sorry Kate.'

His sadness wasn't painful. He'd have said that he was happy. The green flower had broken through his heart. But still he said to himself, 'I'm sorry Kate.'

And on. The Waiau River, Parnassus! no less! The familiar jokes were okay. Soon it was dark.

He woke cramped in Picton the next morning, and looked east. On the hillside above where he'd parked was a rich yeasty frenzy of yellow wattle flowers. Kate's favourite colour. He got out of the back seat stretching and pissed carelessly by the car. Kate's favourite colour again. It was a beautiful morning. He was as good as there. That speeding cleavage of the universe had been sutured. Deep down he remembered. Deep down he felt how that division (west: the glaring threshold—east: the sexual shadow) had passed through him and through his confusion: how the spring flower had pushed out.

He breathed deeply. The air was sweet: blossom and sea.

'Shit, lookit that wattle!' he said aloud.

His brief was complete.

So: early in spring he'd gone north, alone, in the car. Later he'd knelt in the black sand, in the warm night surf of Bethells. There had been no horizon out from O'Neill's. The stars had been twittering like birds or cicadas: 'Chiii—iiink . . .'.

'Te Au kumea . . .'

Moments before the wave had taken him it had occurred to him that he was in the wrong ocean! The fucking Tasman!

The backyard ocean! A Badedas Bath! He'd opened his mouth to laugh and the wave had poured into him like nothing, like a great rift, like a great space, one he could pass through. . . .

This is how *she* sees it.

She's packing . . . just enough to carry . . . room for presents for her dark daughter on the other side of the Tasman.

Curtis drives her to the airport. He's sweating, close to tears. She kisses him because she's grateful, because he's good. There's no time to care how he interprets the warmth of her lips. Her aircraft tosses itself up into the blue.

II

The Beacon

Everybody loves a parade. He joined the queue at the ticket window. Pick up on the tawdry bangle brigade. Hey, Alaska, whydja need the charms? the little elephants and roosters? Look into the liquorice eyes, lay your fingers on the pale skin. This lady's had a big one, right to the heart, she's laughing, she's having fun and trouble straightening the words out.

Here's Mandy Dandy with cigarette burns on his jacket. Here's Wisdom. Here's Knowledge. Lights at the end of a long funnel. Lookit this one, the faggot with eyes in the back of his head: 'Who's here, who's here?'

Who's here?

Ah, everybody's here. Youth Hope and Beauty are here. And Time, crushing the flowers against his mouth . . . delirious, 'Smell these!' . . . laughing and laughing. . . .

At night the light from the beacon came dimly through the window and fell with a monotonous rhythm on the bedroom wall he faced as he lay unable to sleep, shaking sometimes with silent laughter, watching the parade of the day's events pass before his mind's eye. At other times, especially when the weather was calm and clear, he simply listened to the sound of the sea coming in by the same window as the beacon's light.

The house was quite high up a steep hillside, above a small stony beach, on a long turbulent arm of the harbour. It was high enough to look down in daytime at a gannet as it rose in the gusty updraughts then folded itself and plunged, impacting here or there in the small bay. The moment at which the bird paused in the air before its dive took his breath away. He'd feel a lurch of vertigo lift his stomach as the gannet folded and then fell. He breathed again when he saw the small splash of its impact. The bird would fish back and forth across the bay. He never counted the number of times it dived. It was as though he was afraid the number wouldn't be as amazing as the bird's persistence throughout a morning . . . the thick skull plate smashing again and again through the surface of a wave, the folded torpedo body fizzing downward through the water in a tube of bubbles, the fish transfixed, trailing a speeding dilution of pink . . . then the bird surfacing, heaving itself back into the air, rising on the spirals of wind bent upward by the cliff, hanging again above the water, looking down from that bone helmet at the fishes under the surface of the bay, the targets . . . pausing, folding. . . .

Of course the gannet only succeeded one time in ten. He told himself this statistic which he'd read somewhere. Nevertheless the bird seemed merciless as well as patient and beautiful. He told himself that it was a ridiculous development, that a poor creature should be permitted some less hideous, less enslaving and less brutal and less inefficient method of feeding itself. But at the same time he knew the bird's mastery. Watching the gannet fold and dive, he held his breath, felt his stomach lurch . . . and also felt the hair stir on the back of his neck, and resisted at times an instinct to turn and look up and back, behind himself.

At night he listened to the waves. The beacon flashed on the bedroom wall. Starlight and breeze and the scent of flowers also entered the window. He lay and watched the motion of the beacon's light on the wall. With himself he began to enter into some sort of account of the day's events. The beacon was like a mnemonic. He watched an event as it approached a threshold of pain or ugliness.

Then the tension broke, the scene became comical, he shook with silent laughter.

Flash, and the next. And the next. Flash. Flash. He lay laughing at the show while sleep began to lift him high above the scent of flowers, the sound of waves down there in the bay.

Snake

Goin' down the Necropolis, Res-tau-rant,
See Miss Visual, Can-dy–
She gonna make me feel, aw-rite,
She gonna. . . .

. . . you can't finish a little set like that, what's the matter? could it be the way the endings keep coming closer and closer to you, until the first word you write makes you flinch because you expect the next one to be The End: KAA-THONNGGG! your consciousness spread very thin now, like a roadside bloodstain that's been rained on, coprophagous beetles rolling shit across this pink plateau and down among the cool grass stalks and under the close-weave canopies of penny-royal by the stock-gate: 'What was *that*?' 'Blood, don't touch, it's dirty.' And no one will ever hear the music you had in you, no one will ever look at your songs and think: Kurt Weill and Bertolt Brecht, and now Herman Flag and . . . see, you haven't even got a partner yet, and you're worried about Eternity?

Or could it just be that these bright openings always have a friend in tow, someone you want to be kind to, who siphons off all the jitter your nerves are sending out, and you end up watching a documentary on television and then sliding into an exhausted early sleep brought on by that dull opiate, reality—is that what it is? When what you really wanted was to be out screwing like a rattlesnake (why 'like a rattlesnake'?) *or better still* writing just one song that never faltered, you had it all to yourself, it was aimed by Fate straight for the labouring heart of the American Top Forty, all the way from Wellington New Zealand, and people are singing your songs? it's Jackson Browne all over again, you're so big you can write kindly about roadies?

Nah that's not it. You just want that rush of knowing you could do it. The rest, fame, money, all that, that's shit, that's just the evidence, that's the litter thrown out the window of your Karmabile, that's for the thousands of fans you don't even know, to fight over: your cigarette packets that can cure cancer, up in the class of The Alacoque who could not resist licking up the vomit of a sick patient, or St John of the Cross who got his tongue down to the sores of lepers, now *there*'s commitment . . . used chewing gum blobs that braze fractured souls tighter than brass and zinc bands about the faithful coachman's heart, snot-balls wrapped in tissue which the addicts will trade, deal, murder, and chisel for ever since a wonderful night in the thrillingly intimate surroundings of Beefsteak Charlie's, was it? when they first saw how your most forward part, your nose, was lit so clean in the spotlight, each perfect pore pouting out a small blob of perspiration or shining oil through the film of Number Five Basic and the dusting of Antishine . . . well, call it a *habit* if you like, but they'll say there's nothing to compare with one of those dark boogers unpicked from its tissue, impaled on a twirling needlepoint and heated over a low flame then popped into that rather special nosepipe and sucked right back, phhhuuummm—*aaaagghhh*, and here come the dreams: Rubbing Noses With Flag (he's from New Zealand, right?) . . . Lending Flag Your Hankie . . . Lending Flag Your Nasal Spray . . . and even, if the hit was good enough and the surroundings are right: The Big One . . . Having A Loan Of

Flag's Own Nasal Spray! . . . turning aside in dreaming slow motion and shoving the plastic phallus with its few darkening encrustations right into one nostril and then just keeping on with it until with a crunch of breaking cartilege and a slow flood through ruptured sinus walls, the nasal spray enters your brain and you let go with the biggest squeeze left in your nerveless fist, and its the Hit within the hit, the Dream within the dream . . . and they're so far out by this time they don't even notice when the rockademic in the Bill Blass pinstripes and sneakers autographed by Mick Jagger way back in 1970 and now worn only On The Job comes *haiiiyah*! in through the window from the alley where he's just finished researching the contents of the dustbins for *Rolling Stone*, and pistol-whips the dreaming booger-fiend to one side with a silver-plated handbag piece that leaves on the addict's face a mark not like a skull but like a stylus cartridge . . . indeed, it's Doctor Schlock, the man who brings you Rock Roots on your radio, and what's this? Goodness, sounds like an item about One Of Our Own, that sooper-dooper songwriter Flag who made it with a big hit record in the American Top Forty!

Yes, Doctor Schlock has been doing some sleuth work on him and is definitely of the opinion that Flag is a Solid Feature in the geomorphology of rock, 'Though,' with this *wry* laugh, 'Flag seems to have picked up a, uh, odd sort of following in some quarters, you heard anything? Who knows, this's one of his the first big one it's called. . . .', Schlock's amphetamine DJ impersonation drowned out here as the technician brings up the sound of:

> Goin' down the Necropolis, Res-tau-rant,
> See Miss Visual, Can-dy

. . . drowning out also the rattle of the pill against Schlock's dry teeth as he slumps back to sit on fingers that won't keep still, thinking *How can anyone ever keep up*. . . .

Here come the radio waves across the dark waters of Oriental Bay, passing through a variety of ghosts who like to hover out there at a discreet distance from this, the Beirut of the South Pacific: Korean or Japanese squid-fishermen with their foundation smell of scrotum bowlegging it down to the Royal Oak Bistro Bar, 'Haere-mai' from Juicy Fruit and her sisters, on whose forearms and ankles are the tracks that resemble those left by melancholy poets treading the tidelines of Aotearoa . . . Honda Civics squeezing out chartered accountants in Courtenay Place to see a *macho* movie (this week): *Convoy* or *The Deerhunter* or something, the sort of flick that even with irony added still has them roaring like ten-pointers down in the deserted flooding glades of their libido (next week a disaster movie: it's all a subtle process of checks and balances) . . . 'Reality: how to see it, and how to feel it, more and more, every daaaaay!' And over here on the Oriental Parade side: it's pink, there are a few light-bulbs around its cornices, an appetising aroma drifts across the road from it as people park and cross . . . it's . . . but wait. What are these mid-distance ghosts saying as Rock Roots passes through them? Remember, everything has slowed down for them, these radio waves have peaks as slow as the rhythm Noah felt when there was no shore, no lee, no dangerous smell of seaweed to enter the fo'c'sle at night. . . .

James Heberley (in a monotone): I was born in 1809 in Weymouth, at eleven I went as an apprentice on board a Fishing Smack, my master was a tyrant I ran away, some years later my Master found me out, he beat me with a dog-fish tail, my mother died I asked to go to her funeral, he took a piece of rope and gave me a thrashing, I ran away and shipped to St van le mar in Jamaica, the cane plantations are full of venomous snakes they call fer de lance, after some years of adventuring I shipped from Sydney on board the Waterloo Schooner, belonging to John Guard, bound for Queen Charlotte Sound New Zealand, Guard told me there were plenty of houses in Te Awaiti and Native Women, and that we had nothing to do but to go in our boats and catch Fish, we sailed on the first of April being what is commonly termed April fool day, on the fourteenth of April I found he had made a fool of me, there was no houses there, I got a Tomahawk and went in the Bush and cut some timber to build one, I saw a great many dead bodies, I told an Irishman of the name of Logan he laughed at me, and told me there was plenty in the next bay, so I went, I suppose there was about fifty or sixty on the ground besides Heads Arms and Joints, some of the joints had been cooked, there was like a young child stuck upon a stick before a fire that had been lighted, I settled there and married a wife and fought with her people in their wars, in 1843 my wife's grandfather and uncle gave me Worser's Bay, I was pilot at the Wellington Heads, then I started fishing and in the whaling season I went to the sound whaling, that was in June 1843 just after the Wairau Massacre. . . . (The waves go by and don't bother the old captain one bit, certainly the latest Eurodisco funk-slop concept tracks do not sock themselves into 'the spaces that were his ears', unquote ((sort of)), though his 'voice' does rise a little as he nears his punchline ((excitement? fervour? in *that* world?)) which finally goes something like this:)

. . . and, but, and what I think is, what I thought was, I realized, after everything, *there are no snakes here in New Zealand*, there are no snakes in the bush, they got none, that makes it different. . . .

Dicky Barrett: Only venom ever got me was the arrack rum. . . .

(Let's call him) '*Takiji Kobayashi*': Thassa ri' . . . thereah, no-snake, in New Zealan'. . . .

(Poor 'Takiji', week after week squidding, night work, the company superintendent 'Asakawa' badeyeing him and just inviting him to step off among the sharks cleaning up offal astern, don't slip now and especially not with only me here to catch you, and he had to go and get staggering drunk on Royal Oak draught beer and the prospect of one of Juicy Fruit's lemons (pucker when you fuck): he finds himself standing next to 'Asakawa' splashing the stinking tiles of the Bistro urinal and the super says, turning his stream on to 'Takiji's' cheap shoe, 'What a crusted arsehole of a country this is,' and 'Takiji', looking down at his shoe replies that after that last southern stretch, Manila on, this is paradise, what's more the girl's told him there are no snakes here, and 'Asakawa', 'You jerkoff, she was talking about your pants, har har!' And so it went, until 'Takiji', for defending the snakeless status of his new-found paradise, found himself sinking down in the night harbour through lights cast by the Star Boating Club and the Container Terminus, with no breath or blood passing any further than the hole in his neck, his hands tied to a plastic kleensack of dangerously corroded tins of whalemeat . . .).

. . . through the oblivious ghosts, across the evening waters, past the Freyberg Pool with its reek of an atmosphere too fresh to be real, past the marina where halyards rattle like teeth in the skulls of mariners whose bodies sinking into some groper and ling hole beyond Cape Palliser have been emptied from their woollen slops bought in the Company store at five times Hobart prices . . . in they come, the radio waves, to the decaying pink facade of, it's Pierre's Chophouse! In through the door and past the fake tarred ropes and the fishing floats, out back where plump Pierre is uncorking yet another cold bottle of Bernkeisler riesling for the pissed Swiss demimonde in the corner booth, and where Andre the second cook has just finished blowing his nose into the potato salad of an order that came back with a complaint that the Rahmschnitzel tasted of fish, 'Take it back the fucking peasants won't know the difference,' adding, 'Where's that Herman leck-mich-am-Arsch Flag?' the salad hand don't you know, well where's a young man to get his pourboire these days with the rock lyric market so hard to crack? He's away for now from the cassette of yodelling the Swiss put on an hour ago, away from those *elements* in the clientele, 'I'll eat anything that's edible,' lipstick on her teeth, putting her arm around the other woman's plump shoulder, or the one who complained, 'This . . . fork. . . .' . . . 'Whassa matter, those cabbage shreds've been boiled at two hundred and eighty degrees Fahrenheit in a three thousand dollar dishwasher with detergent that makes holes in aluminium pots, whaddaya want?' . . . Away with Miss Visual Candy in the alley . . . 'You want to?' . . . 'Okay,' one foot up on a dustbin and the other seeking purchase among crayfish legs cucumber rinds and slicks of putrefying sauce tartare . . . this passion beneath the stars, it could break your heart, and here are those waves, they hit just as Flag yells, 'Paradise is with us!' and comes all over Visual Candy's waitress pinny, as usual the dream of central-heated success steps back at the last minute, 'What did you do that for?' in a trembling voice, 'Come off it Flag, get that in me I'd have smelled like a sardine tin in half an hour, there's still two hours till closing, I got servings waiting. . . .' . . . 'Where's Flag . . . you out there Flag?' 'Just coming Andre (ha ha)!' . . . Oh yes, in Pierre's Chophouse the steaks are pretty low (ha ha), and inside it's chaos, 'Listen Pierre, Visual here was upset, if I hadn't got her out and quietened her down she'd have smashed that Rotarian's dinner on his head, bad for business Pierre.' 'It's you that's bad for business Flag, I don't pay you for counselling, out, out!' 'Now wait Pierre, don't do anything you'll regret. . . .' 'I don't regret, *you* regret, out, get your pay tomorrow!' 'Fuck your money you fat cook!', Herman Flag back into the kitchen where Andre and the dishwasher stand with mouths open as he dumps sauerkraut on his head and runs screaming into the restaurant with a tomato sauce squeezer, phut! there's some for the one he spotted an hour ago and graded as a type'll order well-done T-bone with two eggs double french-fries and a side order of greasy onions then eat everything but the lettuce and the coleslaw and leave the eggwhites too, *gouge* the yolks out, and phut! that's for Pierre's blond mistress getting icecream from the cooler by the door, as Flag exits screaming, 'Don't touch it, there's salmonella and the dishwasher picks his nose I seen him!' phut! for the plateglass window fronting on the harbour, and inside he can hear the chairs going over and the scramble of feet as they come after him and he ducks back into the alley over dustbins and in through the side door to the now empty kitchen, grab a plastic sack of fillet steak, and back out up the steps on to the coolhouse roof over the wall drop then through this yard and across to Hay Street and up into the Green Belt, Christ if they call the cops there'll be dogs, drop a couple of steaks to slow them down, finally via Grafton and Maidavale Steps down to Balaena Bay and into the water to lose the scent, leave shoes and pants and wash off that sauerkraut, then wet and half naked, little late swimming heh heh, through deserted paths home, drop the sack on the kitchen floor, 'Anyway they all eat shit there,' he says to nobody but himself, what price rock fame, what now?

You'd like that wouldn't you Flag.

He's got instant replay on his fantasies. But this one just diminuendoes peculiarly as he empties his little grab-bag of real pilfer on the kitchen table: one terrific porterhouse, one crayfish, one salami, two hundred and fifty grams of coffee, one recorked bottle of Nobilo's Cabernet. Take a staggering-pissed melancholy pre-shower glass now with an unwanted cigarette at two a.m. under the light with night outside the windows and a real job-secure day off tomorrow, a still unfinished song creeping back to haunt him with a sensation of uncertainty and fear, 'Whass happening?' as he drops a mandie into the hole in his head and reaches for the bedside light to turn himself off into unconsciousness, hearing a sad voice very like his own say 'Paradise is with us,' with lots of echo, as the finally uncomplicated dark pours into him.

Goodnight, Herman Flag.

Waking early as usual on this his midweek day off, Flag found himself lying in sunlight with a good appetite unspoiled by nausea, yet he felt unsure about how the previous evening's labour had gone: had he been very drunk? *that* drunk? He was told nothing new by his twitching early morning erection and the thought of Visual Candy that twisted his bowels briefly into a cruel knot. Two hundred and fifty grams of fresh coffee on the kitchen table, however, told him not to worry: his life had not changed, yet . . . or, not to hope: he was still on the same Circle Line; allow a few more areas of doubt like the present one to fog his vision and he might just finish by steering the little engine of his Being up his own arsehole into the void within, *woo-hoo* . . . 'Can't you hear that lonesome whistle blow . . .' One thing at least he could be sure about, *that song*. . . . Happening to think of it in the same instant the porterhouse steak hit the pan, Flag felt his appetite shrink just as his hardon had when the coffee told him nothing had changed in his life: if appetite is the enemy of annihilation then let me beat my brains out soon upon the greasy walls of Pierre's Chophouse, because I can't stand it anymore, unquote (sort of).

Sunlight struck him as he sat again at the kitchen table hearing the tap water spit in the hot pan where it lay now in the sink, and the two cats growling with astonished rage over the huge steak that had just dropped upon them from the kitchen window, or was it heaven?

Moments later Flag tore round the corner of the house and booted them half way into the neighbouring section. Of course that left him with more guilt to handle later, but for now the voice within which had told him not to be such a fuckin' idiot had saved him, and he the steak, which had had only its edges nibbled while the cats fought over it.

Sitting in sunlight, forking tender pink porterhouse to his mouth and swallowing fresh coffee, Flag thought about salvation, eternity, and music: salvation is when you are prevented from sharing everything, even down to the air you breathe . . . eternity: now, that's all the time you waste deciding to sink your teeth in . . . while music is a lyre strung between what you have and what you long for, between salvation and eternity, and its strings are stirred to song by the trembling fingers of human passions . . . a materialist analysis. Outside the cats set up a miserable yowling where they had returned to find their paradise an illusion, and the bits of gristle and fat tossed over the sill by Flag can hardly have made things any clearer for them. Was that meat really there? (Was I in the alley with Visual Candy?) Did we get to taste it? (Did I hear that song complete and perfect?) Why didn't we just grab the meat and eat it? (Why didn't I fuck her?) (Why didn't I write the song down?)

Some whorls of grease on the plate in front of him had hardened. No sound, while his lips pouted a little as though to kiss, and then dropped, a little, a little, and then stretched back across his face a little, as though to make a smile, and a sensation of cool air passing over the exposed lower teeth, a sensation of them drying, something that could turn into pain, and then the warm lubricating return of the lower lip and the whole thing repeating itself again: 'Why?'

With fear now Flag became aware of himself sitting at the table where, with a good enough appetite, he'd eaten a steak, no that's irrelevant, so I was hungry, so what? . . . sitting here saying Why? over and over. . . . Am I going . . . crazy? O I want her! howls the voice within.

> Goin' down the Necropolis, Res-tau-rant
> See Miss Visual, Can-dy—
> She gonna make me feel, aw-rite,
> She gonna . . .

. . . 'dandy'? 'randy'? Why why why. With an effort Flag musters another thought to think about as his fancy lays him down along Visual Candy's lithe flank, the fierce twists of damp black that escape her armpits, her purple nipples, her tongue shooting out above the stretched cords of its root as her head tips back and her long belly lifts him up and carries him with her into the pungent frantic moments of her ecstasy . . . that was pretty uninspired.

With relief Flag became aware that the fantasy was banal, weak on content anyway, it had failed to take him with it, and he confronted the thought he'd selected, which went in stages like this: I want to survive, I'm a mess, I'm afraid of going nuts, I have these dark moments, is it possible I'm overloading my circuits, it is possible isn't it that it's risky crowding my obsessions into the same corner, music and Visual Candy, though they belong together in some Higher World, in this one they must be separated by the sword of my will, or else I'm fucked and I do not repeat do not want to kiss off the paradise of a sane world, you didn't hear me say comprehensible, or just, you certainly didn't hear me say explicable, sane is what I want it to be, that's all, and it's only ever going to be as sane as I am, paradise is with us so long as. . . .

There was a moment at which the grease on his plate couldn't get any harder. Flag found no clue there as to how much time had passed, nor did the quality of the sunshine tell him much; his legs hadn't gone to sleep, the anonymous roar of traffic on the road below was without meaning, though in his mind's eye he could see the long black limousine hurrying toward the International Terminus while Herman Flag and Visual Candy behind smoky glass in the back seat prepared themselves for altitude, the cocaine scampering on its little cold bare feet across the vestibules of sensation. . . . Why? Why? Why?

When the plate hit the wall just above the utensil cupboard Flag gave himself a bad fright, it was the first sound close-up for how long? and as the pieces fell on the bench and scattered across the kitchen floor he felt how the shock was the result of his own action, this shaking hand threw that plate, the chair he'd been sitting on lay on its back behind him, and he confronted the aseptic thought in which he'd visualized his will as a sword, aware that he was blubbering . . . not hearing the sound of blubbering as though someone else were doing it, but feeling and hearing himself doing it, while watery snot and salt tears poured into his open gasping mouth. He was right though, and in between sobs he was saying Yes, yes, yes, to the thought of his will as a sword to sever the strings that made such sad music between salvation and eternity. When she was his, then he would sing about her. Then he would be able to sing about her. Then the song would have an ending. *Reprise*: Then the song would have an ending. Then it would be finished, and could be sung forever.

In the paradise of the present he was alone in his kitchen, calming down. Herman Flag, salad hand. He went through to his bedroom and made the bed. He ignored the earphones and the racks of records, also the exercise book and the biro. He picked up his watch from the shelf by the bed and strapped it on. Now I am in my personality, and I have put time on. It was ten in the morning. The steak breakfast had taken two hours.

There was a corner of the garden where Flag had thought he would plant beans, moved by disgust at the reiteration of gouged egg-yolks and the plates that were returned to the kitchen of Pierre's Chophouse with cigarettes ground out among the cold smears of gravy. I'll do some gardening, yeah! When I get hot I'll go and have a swim. Then I'll have a sleep. Then I'll go to a movie. Or, I'll go and see who's in the pub. Let the first strokes of the sword be such pleasant gestures as these. Or I might just stay at home tonight and have a read. Robert McNab's *The Old Whaling Days* was on the shelf. Takiji Kobayashi's *The Factory Ship* was there to be read again. The pirated transcript of James Heberley's journal. Eat the crayfish with a salad, finish the Cabernet, smoke a joint in bed, have a long read, sleep late.

Oh, Captain? . . . the pilot's house at Worser Bay still stands (it wasn't yours), one side is corrugated iron now, uphill is the RNZAF female barracks, downhill the Worser Bay Lifesaving Club, my great grandfather was a pilot at the Wellington heads too, from Worser Bay you would have had a spectacular view of the *Wahine* when she foundered, Modern Johnny Warren was a steward that trip, got his ribs crushed between the Seatoun wharf and a ship's boat when he jumped in after a child, he liked the look of the place so much that night (must have been the pethidine) he came back after hospital and found a flat at Breaker Bay to live in while the compo lasted, kept hoping for a shipwreck he could just *watch* and make a killing off with on-the-spot photographs, kept his telephoto on every vessel heading into the Straits past the nasty teeth of Barrett's Reef and out of sight round the sewage outfall at Moa Point . . . and why not, Captain? Who wants to be a fool *every* time April comes around . . . ? None of *us* will ever see the American whalers gunwale by gunwale in John Guard's Kākāpō Bay, but then *you* won't ever be eating a Half-Pounder in McDonald's Fast Foods in Courtenay Place, willya Captain, ay? and it's the same greasy money I can tell you, that corporate expertise started with whaling, learned its fast footwork in armaments, and here it comes back at us in shitfood franchises . . . funny thing, history: makes you wonder where all the cannibals and headhunters are, have a feeling they may be advertising for fresh meat in the NBR these days (you'd have to know the code), not that you'd ever catch one of them with bloodstains on his three hundred dollar mohair-and-wool pinstripes, picking pink fibre from his teeth below Williams's Deathtrap on Plimmer Steps, say. . . . And here ('Plimmer Steps? Meet Lambton Quay . . .') Barrett's Hotel still stands! Who would have thought, Dicky, that the waterside pub you opened in 1840 would have come to be a clearing house for salacious gossip about leading politicos, whom they were screwing, which one at the top was a chronic premature ejaculator? But then you don't know whom to believe, or trust, these days, and with all that encoded history sitting on the small of his back, can you blame The Man for not taking his time? And there's sake advertised in Japanese in the bottlestore window, that's sharp trading here in paradise Takiji Kobayashi; but don't forget the several poor bastards from Hakodate in icy Hokkaido who've ended up knocking their white bowed legbones together at the bottom of the harbour basin off Aotea Quay, cases that will never find space in Sergeant Looney ('I'm warning you') Tunes (probably Lieutenant Looney Tunes by now) of the CIB's criminology degree, not that you'd want him to think any more inclusively than he already does. . . .

Flag's voiceless communing with his favourite ghosts fills the no-man's land he's laid out between Visual Candy and music, where he leans upon the garden fork, looking at the line of dark earth he's turned over, imagining the beans that will hang in clusters where their brilliant flowers have withered, thinking: Ah, vegetable life! to grow in your soil, in your season, to return to it as shit and have the acephalous suck of worms reduce you to the nourishment of the vine that bore you, so that you return and return: the food, the root, the vine, the flower, the fruit . . . to have no head!

Flag felt slightly sick, this vista that had opened up on a Politics for Paradise made him giddy, or was it the lack of sleep, the emotion, the mental swordsmanship? *En garde*: no progress, but process, *whack*! growth, not ambition, *clang*! and a swipe that lops the head clean off: no impossible dreams, but only the sun, the light into which you climb!

With one boot Flag drove the tines of the fork into the dark earth and leant his wet forehead on the handle, the sun was stretching the skin tight across his shoulders, sweat that ran into the corner of his eye made him flinch, and just over there where a battered flax bush hung its long slick leaves over its dark interior his smarting eye returned blinking to a darker shadow that seemed to have some kind of mass, some kind of bas-relief upon the mottled shade. His mind followed his eye there, he turned his head, he looked at the superimposition of shadow that seemed to suggest a coiled shape; and then he felt all the hair on his neck rise with a sensation of chill, his whole skin crawled and puckered, as the snake put out its head and flickered its tongue in the dim small cave of the flax bush's interior. When horror had invaded his whole body he found himself paralysed, staring into the flax bush no more than three feet away. It wasn't a hallucination. He could see clearly that the snake had a lance-shaped head. As it uncoiled slowly and moved itself into the light he realized that it would be at least five feet long. It raised itself and he could see the yellow chin. Its body was dark grey with a pattern of black-edged diamonds. In the pinkish interior of its mouth Flag could see long fangs. The name *fer de lance* was sucked into his mind by a kind of implosion, as though the venom had taken its brand-name with it into his brain, which was filled with a strange roar of information, for example that the fer de lance's young are born alive and deadly in litters of eighty and more.

The roar filled his ears with painful pressure. His vision was reduced to a series of tarnished scintillations on a black ground; and then he didn't faint, he saw the snake go by him and disappear through the dappled silvery litter of dead leaves beneath a pōhutukawa tree at the far end of the fifteen foot line of freshly turned earth, it hadn't bitten him. And now a spasmodic reflex made him wrench the deeply bedded tines of the fork free, and he hurled it into the shadow under the tree where it clanged against an old sheet of roofing iron that formed part of a broken-down fence between his garden and the next, and even that familiar untidy comforting corner of wreckage had become horrifying. The dirt he stood on filled him with terror. When a cool flax frond touched his leg he yelled, turned and ran still yelling up the steps and around the corner and in at the kitchen door. But even that was no good, the darkness under the sink was swarming with movement. He ran to his bedroom and leapt on to the bed, dragging the covers around his legs, and sat, with his knees under his chin, watching the doorway.

He *had* seen it, as he grew calmer Flag realized that his doubts about that wouldn't make any difference, he would doubt it for the rest of his life and so he wouldn't tell anyone. But in his heart, where his unfinished songs seemed to absorb the venom and grow cold, Flag knew that the snakes were here, they had come at last, and nothing was ever going to be the same again, if it ever had been what we thought. Every day was going to be April the first, from now on in and back.

In Clover

They were wrangling as they walked through the paddock at the back of the house. There were certain practical considerations: isolation, money. She listened with only half an ear to what he was saying: '. . . until next summer . . .' Something, something.

She was thinking that there is the place we live in, and there are the places we return to. It's the places we return to that we love most. They can never be the place we live in. If we return to them, again and again, then we must be away from them, very often, for long periods of time. . . .

'Oh my god,' he said. 'Look!' He began to run back towards the house. The baby was swinging gently in a canvas sling suspended from the porch. She could see that the roof of the porch had come loose from the house. One of the uprights at the centre of the porch had broken off at roof height. The roof was folding slowly inwards at the centre. He was running at full speed across the clover of the paddock behind the house. He had just flung himself over the gate when the porch roof collapsed with a crack. The whole structure came down leaving one corner of rusty iron attached at the right-hand side, bent downward like a broken wing or like a viaduct disaster. He was running across the yard. She could hear him shouting, a high-pitched succession of formless words. The baby was out of sight. She had fallen in her sling and the broken porch roof had come down on top of her. She saw him straining at the wreckage on the ground. There was no sound now. Then with a crash he flung the reddish iron back against the porch, and bent again. She could see that he was looking at the baby, where she lay. Then he straightened up, the baby in his arms. His head was bent over so she couldn't see his face or the baby. He was walking slowly back towards her, his head bent. She could see his head shaking from side to side. All at once the events caught up with her. She screamed and ran, in her turn. He was standing by the gate, his head still bent, shaking it from side to side. When she got there he looked up. 'Wasn't that the funniest thing you've ever seen?' he said. He was overcome with laughter and relief. She looked at the baby with her mouth open. She was smiling a crooked smile. The only mark on her was a smear of powdery old roof paint across her forehead. The tears were pouring down his cheeks. 'Oh my god,' he said, 'wasn't that just, wasn't that just, oh god, wasn't that just the funniest thing you. . . .'

So for once he took some time off and spent the rest of the day fixing the porch. There wasn't much to it. He hammered and sawed cheerfully. By late afternoon it was together again. He climbed up and began scraping at the iron with a stiff brush, saying that he might as well paint it now that he had begun. She found that she didn't really care, though she had often reminded him that the porch needed fixing, that a gale might bring it down.

That evening a friend of his, a journalist, came round just as they were beginning to eat a late meal. He told the story to the journalist, spinning it out, embellishing it. He said for example that he had caught his trousers on the gate and was struggling to unsnag them at the precise moment the whole roof finally came down and the baby with it, the baby making not a sound. He also said that she had become hysterical. She didn't correct him. It was a habit of his, to make a good story of something, and she had got used to it.

The baby was now asleep in another room. They all went in to look at her. He drew with his finger the place where the smear of dry paint had been. The journalist said the baby was lucky not to have lost an eye. This remark, uttered because he could think of nothing better to say—nodding his head stupidly over this infant most of whom was invisible—nonetheless reminded them of how nearly the comedy had been a disaster. They went back and finished eating, drinking some wine the journalist had brought. The journalist was rather earnest and the meal-time passed quietly while he expounded his theory that real comedy was only possible where disaster was barely averted. He illustrated his thesis by quoting from Shakespeare, describing scenes of mayhem from Laurel and Hardy movies, and by telling a number of sick jokes about Ugandan Asians. Meanwhile he seemed to be avoiding her eyes. She found him banal and a bore but her husband enjoyed drinking with him. They would spend long nights drunk, while she listened from the bedroom where she was going to sleep to the level drone of their voices as they went over, yet again, what she imagined to be familiar ground.

She cleared away the plates, washed them, and left them to drain. A mumble of voices came from the next room. She went out on to the porch, to a smell of galvanising primer. She'd thought this over-fastidious—all that had been needed was a coat of ordinary roof paint. By contrast a saw and some other tools were lying where he'd dropped them on the floor at one end. It was a clear warm night. Moonlight lit the level expanse of the small paddock and the slope of the hill behind. The cabbage tree rustled, a dry sound like large insects. There was a cane chair which usually stood on the porch. He had left it in the yard. She dragged it back and sat down. She thought of going in to get a glass of wine from the journalist's flagon; but though she didn't really care about such things, it seemed it might be rude for her to be sitting by herself, drinking his wine. Not a bad reason to do it, given his manner. But she got up and walked down to the gate. When she looked back towards the house she could see the profiles of her husband and the journalist, crouched towards each other over opposite sides of the table, and the flagon between them, in the single lit window of the house. Light came dimly through the kitchen door on to the porch and on to the trunk of the cabbage tree. It would be better to hang the baby's sling from that, from the tree, she thought. She didn't really care that the porch was fixed but, more than that, she didn't really believe her husband could have fixed it all that well. A large moth fumbled at her neck. She shook it off in disgust and moved further into the dark. In the gulley below the paddock a morepork was telling its own melancholy name, over and over, insisting on it. The moon was still rising. She tipped her head back to look up at the sky. In spite of the moonlight the stars were very bright. She found the Southern Cross, took an arc, and had due south. Then, out of habit, or for practice, she found Orion and waving her arms and taking up the points had the Celestial Equator. It was six thousand miles to Peking, six thousand miles to Santiago. Or so. Then she counted twenty paces back to the house.

There she met her husband and the journalist coming out. They were going to get flounder. That explained the journalist's foxy air. He'd anticipated her resentment. But it's late, she said. On the contrary, they insisted, the tide was now perfect and the moon was high. They went briskly around the house and up to the road. The journalist's big flashlight clacked against the jar of wine he was carrying in the same hand. She heard her husband laughing, and fumbling in the hedge at the front where he hid his flounder spear for fear visiting children would get hold of it. She sat on the porch with a cigarette. Soon the baby would wake up and she would feed her. She wished the smell of primer wasn't in the porch. She would have liked to smell the warm breeze blowing across the gulley and the paddock. She would have liked to sip at another glass of wine. A joint would have been pleasant. In the distance she saw the lights of the journalist's fast car winding across and up the hill towards the estuary on the other side.

The next day also, to her surprise, he didn't work. He cooked two flounder for their breakfast, then went off by himself for a long walk. He came back, attached the baby's sling to the porch again, and sat with a bottle of beer in the sun, occasionally giving the sling a push. Then, abruptly, he set off up the road with a sack of flounder towards the pub at the crossroads.

He came back about four o'clock in a cheerful mood. He had sold most of the fish in the pub and, he said, had told the story of the collapsing porch. He hadn't paid for a single drink. The money from the flounder he'd given to the grocer, towards settlement of the account, with a couple of fish thrown in for extra placation.

But his good mood soon wore off. When at dinner time he saw another flounder on his plate, he went out in disgust into the dark and gave it to the sleeping hens. Then he sat reading, picking at a packet of dates.

About ten o'clock, having not said a word, he went to his room. She was feeding the baby. She would not do the dishes. Why should she, when he sat so morosely, having barely spoken to her all day. She heard him tapping at his typewriter. She put the sleeping baby in her cot and went to sit on the porch. The smell of paint was fainter now. It was another warm night. The moon was moving past its third quarter. As it had the previous night, the wind blew across the gulley and the paddock, combining the earthy redolence of bush-humus and wet leaf-mould and the freshness of deep clover. Or so she fancied. No matter how she happened to be feeling in herself, that wind was a constant pleasure, a Zephyr as she thought, 'firing gauche Chloris with passion'—though not when it blew a gale, as it did from time to time, wrecking the young plants in the vegetable garden, making her irritable and despondent, sapping her zest. But such a caressing breeze she imagined could exist anywhere. It was in itself quite neutral, universal, a pure traveller. It was only by placing smells in its way for it to take on as cargo that you attached it momentarily to a particular locale. The 'same' wind could quite conceivably bring her the smell of jasmine, or of Dutch herrings, if such things were in its path . . . but that would place her there also, in that path, and what she was smelling now was wet bush-humus and deep clover, which was where she was. O which was where she was, yes, 'in clover'. . . . Watching her husband, once, scything along the fence at the end of the yard, she had realized the meaning of that phrase. Having struggled through coarse patches of weeds and paspalum, wiry cushions of twitchgrass, he came, after pausing constantly to whet the scythe, to a stretch of lush clover. How simply, then, the severed green lay down across the blade.

Going inside, she met him coming through the kitchen. 'It was so funny then,' he said, 'why does it have to be so fucking dismal now? I want to write it, just as it was, but I can't.' She found his petulance irritating. 'You could have got on to it sooner,' she replied. 'And if you can't write, why don't you do the dishes or something, instead of moping about?' 'Didn't I fix the porch?' he shouted. 'Didn't I put off the grocer?' 'They were only necessary,' she replied, 'you could hardly have left either of them for long.' He went outside cursing.

That night she had a dream in which the porch collapsed and sprang upright again, endlessly, in rapid succession. The baby's face kept reappearing, with a comical crooked grin. Then she saw the porch with jasmine trailing across it, a delicate confusion of bloom and perfume. Her husband was up in the cabbage tree with his flounder spear, keeping a lookout, shouting something like Placate! Placate! She woke up laughing. He was not in the bed. She closed her eyes again, trying to will herself back into the dream. It had been so refreshing.

She must have gone deeply and instantly asleep, because it seemed to be only seconds later that the baby woke her with her crying. It was early morning, just after six o'clock. Through the bedroom window she could see that the hedge was being lashed by a gale. The sky above the hedge was grey and low in the dawn light. Going towards the kitchen to put the kettle on, she found the living-room lights burning, and her husband asleep, lolling uneasily over the side of an armchair. She stepped outside to look. The cane chair had been blown to the far side of the yard. Gusts of rain were being driven untidily into the porch. The hill beyond the paddock was half-covered by a grey mantle of cloud and rain. The wind was from the south, cold and foreign, too cold and fast to have any smell, any place, loaded on to it, and too violent to be a messenger, a 'harbinger', a soft sell. Too brutal to awaken.

Inside it was also cold. She went through to her husband and woke him up. 'Welcome back, fishface,' she said. O his drama, his embellishments! He looked at her with tired eyes, suspiciously, to gauge her mood. 'Go to bed you silly arse,' she said, adding, 'It wouldn't work anyway.' 'What wouldn't?' he said with a start. 'Hanging the baby's sling from the cabbage tree,' she replied. 'There are no decent branches on a cabbage tree.' He was looking at her in astonishment. At the other end of the house the baby was by now yelling at the top of her voice. 'Anyway,' she said, 'it looks as though you've fixed the porch all right. Now go to bed. I'll shut the baby up. You won't get any work done if you don't have a proper sleep. Then we'll be here for ever.' She kissed him. 'I love you,' she said, 'god knows why, you're such an idiot.'

Paradise

It was winter. The wind blasted from the south-west, straight off the pack ice, he imagined. The rain, with a rattle of hail in it, had soaked through his parka to his skin. Water was roaring in the storm drains. The fingers with which he held the mail felt like parsnips. He kept his head down and thought of double whiskies and saunas. The addresses on the envelopes blurred and ran with wet. His trousers were plastered to his legs. He turned corners and shoved letters into boxes by memory and instinct, pausing from time to time to pick up rocks in anticipation of certain dogs: just let any mutt try him today. Wait till they think they've got you then let them have it, yiiii yi yi.

The corgi was worrying at his trousers and had got a few nips into his ankle as well. He marched up the garden path with the dog hanging on and snarling. Dingaling, knock knock. Blast of warm as the door opens. Is this your dog madam? Yes. . . . He let poochie have the rock then booted the animal into the shrubbery. Let's call it quits now lady, I won't claim for the trousers. Back up the path, shreds of pant leg flapping. That made it even colder. Fuck them. Why all the mail, it wasn't Mother's Day. Half was Tisco Television Repairs accounts, the rest was Reader's Digest bullshit. The energy chocolate was so hard with cold he almost broke his teeth. Below him the city was invisible. Because he was so wet the walking no longer kept him warm. Sickie time tomorrow. It would take at least two days to thaw. Have a steam bath, lie in bed dreaming Gauguin, move the TV in, smoke dope.

He turned a corner watching for Honey, a killer Alsatian who hunted silently. The top letter in his bundle was for Taimaile, ha ha . . . the envelope plastered with gorgeous Samoan stamps, *tropique sensuel*: fish, butterflies, lagoons, all that. Handsful of hail struck him in the face and froze on to the surface of his parka. Fuck, *oneone, one . . . one . . . oneone. . . .* The litany had a certain rhythm to it. Homage to J. J. Rousseau. He flapped on. Then it began to snow. Dear Oates, we miss you.

Peeking out at six the next morning before deciding whether to ring the post office, he saw the stars burning with cold fire in the firmament. The air was as still as ice. Moonlight lit snowy pine trees on the far side of the valley. Frost had set on the surface of snow in the yard. The crystals glittered in light from the kitchen door. His breath smoked out through the crack. Wow. Shut the door, turn on the heater, make coffee. He drank it listening to silly patter on the pre-breakfast programme, then slewed and crawled in the car to town. Along the roadside were abandoned vehicles 'of various denominations'. He pondered this phrase which had come so glibly to mind. From the left hand window of the car he could see the empty harbour, very still and moonlit, with channel beacons flashing green and red. Navigational aids for Li Po. Beyond the fluorescent pallor of the water was the peninsula wrapped in snow. It looked to him like an immense old samurai lizard crouched in patience until dinosaurs should once again rule the world, when man with his silly services would have bred himself out of survival. Gone out, and been some time, and not been missed. With avalanches of loose shale the ridges and peninsulas would rise on short legs, open ancient eyes, and taste the foul air with forked tongues.

Or, he now thought, as the car minced across icy satin, the

peninsula was like a lady's thigh, very white. Next he saw a lizard crouched on a lady's thigh. Then *he* was there. Lady, lady, fold your thighs upon my ears. The water turns like a limb and the dry land rustles its claws. I'm ascetic at heart. Near town they'd dumped grit on the road. The car gripped and sped. Reality equals velocity as a function of direction. Inspiration: whatever comes out eventually and needs to be purified again. Why so luxurious then. Easy: the true voluptuary needs to be able to draw a clear bead on the target. There has to be a bare firepath. The metaphor's formally not factually violent. Oh darling you're killing me. Summer pleasures are blurry and fun but their peaks lack piquancy.

Next question.

If survival's not enough, what is?

Oates, can you hear me?

What an immense relief to get out of the mailroom after sorting. He slipped on his dark glasses. The cold air poured down his throat. The light had a musical quality: it rang like burnished metal. The dark latticework of twigs of the Chinese poplars was in perfect focus. He felt extra sharp. There was a nice power in selection and discrimination: a buoyancy. Cleaning the teeth of your senses, keeping them brighteyed. Then wallow and don't miss a thing. Oboy!

To Taimaile he delivered letters smeared with *fauve* extravagance. It left him cold. He was digging the Pacific horizon from his high vantage point. Cortez: 'So that's what it's called.' Here and there the snow had melted, but mostly it was still thick with a frosted crust. Schools were closed. The dogs were playing with kids and mostly ignored him. He whistled and slid. The Four Square grocer gave him a cup of tea. The Catholic Bishop's sister gave him a whisky and a slice of plumcake. He accepted a chocolate fish from a little boy, and a free packet of chips from the fish and chip shop. Everyone felt magnanimous and cheerful. Everywhere people were playing in the snow. A few businessmen with pissedoff expressions trudged to work. So their Ford Falcons wouldn't start. Let them hike off their flatulence, their greasy breakfasts.

Oh yes he was 'in a crowing temper', to borrow the phrase from a dear friend who'd recently used it with some bitterness. A few weeks ago he'd been toe-springing up the hill under crisp autumn skies when she'd whizzed past in her little car. He'd seen her hand make a brief vicious signal at the window. It had spoiled his day. He'd realized that his limber pleasure was solitary. Putting letters in boxes. Her car had disappeared downhill taking his joy with it like a little fluttering trophy.

But today sparrows scuffled shrilly where horse turds unfroze in sunlight. Below him the city glittered under a thin veil of coppery fumes. He was satisfied.

But he needed a leak . . . fortunately his route reached the limits of the city's outer suburbs. For some of it he actually walked beside fields of cows. The children in this fringe neighbourhood kept ponies. There was a long lane, petering out into an unsealed track, which ran steeply up a hillside among stands of large oak trees. He had to go some distance up this to serve a house situated back from the road in a spacious well-planted garden. With relief and pleasure he stood staling loudly into a frosty patch of snow, attempting to write his initials, or 'Oates': this obsession. . . . Above the small port where he lived was a monument to Scott of the Antarctic. The expedition had sailed from there. Well, you needed signals like that. He was going to be a poet. That was *his* raise on survival. There was this soft whine as though some bowel was about to barf loudly. He was just nine years old. He found himself thinking of Scott of the Antarctic of whom his dad had been telling him and of brave Oates. He imagined Oates going out and taking his pants down. It all came out in riming couplets like someone was making his finger crawl like Oates over white. How long does it take to take a shit in Antarctica, how long to write riming couplets at nine? Oh Oates was dead, frozen, and he was a boy poet, frozen also, aghast, the feat accomplished. 'Brave Oates' he called it and showed it to his dad who beat him with the back of a hairbrush. It was necessary to survive, he decided, remembering the lines that had been destroyed, tracks leading out somewhere he would return from soon. It was a fiction he clung to. Meanwhile steam rose through the crisp air to the branches of the oaks above which he could see the faultless blue of the winter sky. Everything was fresh and lovely after the rain and the gales. He whistled between his teeth, craning his neck to look up through the branches.

'Aie!'

Today's bringdown.

She was standing by the gate with a hand to her mouth, a Chinese lady in her late thirties.

Chinese?

Someone had moved and he hadn't even noticed. The last lady hadn't been Chinese, what's more she'd never come to the gate.

'What you-do, what you-do!'

'Excuse me,' turning away and swinging his stream with him. Behind him he heard the gritting of gravel under her heels. Reality. Looking back he saw that she was still there, in fact she'd moved closer. The last of his steam drifted away into the cerulean. The air, calm and cold, was filled with birdsong. There they stood. Between them the immaculate surface of the snow was spoiled by strafings of sour yellow. She pointed at this, mutely aghast, stamping forward on small feet, her body held rigid as though in formal preparation for some martial ballet. She was right, of course (he sensed that her outrage was aesthetic rather than scatalogical): he *had* ruined it, a crude barbarian squirting urine around the immaculate interior of this winter morning. He noticed how the blood had risen under the clear surface of her skin, a kind of emotional haemophilia, passionate vulnerability. Her aristocratic nostrils were pinched whitely together with rage or disgust.

She turned and marched back towards her gate. It was not a retreat. Her back was stiff with the pride of a formal victor.

'I'm sorry,' he said after her. Bugger it, good pissing spots were scarce. This one had been idyllic. Birds in the branches, a paddock on the other side where in summer the ragwort was a sullen blaze of flower heads. Worth the steep fifty yards grunt to the single letter box there, to stand pissing in sunlight as John Clare might have done in 1860 in Epping Forest

> I found the poems in the fields
> And only wrote them down

or Li Po in the courtyard of the Empress, leaning a dipsomaniacal elbow against exquisite marble, or more likely splashing his rice wine into the pond housing ornamental carp. These thoughts improved his spirits.

All the same, next day, he approached the lane without joy. The name he was delivering was Ngaei, a doctor. So he'd met Madame Ngaei, the wife of a Chinese doctor. It occurred to him that it was a good name for an acupuncturist:

'Ngaaeeeeiiii!!'

Ha ha. It was another pristine day. Shoving the doctor's drug company handouts into the letterbox he cast a glance up the driveway to the house. There in sunshine he saw Madame

Ngaei standing with the flaccid hose of a vacuum cleaner in one hand. She was singing

> Takem han
> Ahm stlanga in paladeye

It was poignant enough to make him squawk with laughter. The door slammed. He felt ashamed and barbaric. He really liked her. The style and economy with which she'd registered her complaint had been lovely. He admired her sense of form. Also, an admission he suppressed, he was flattered that she'd seen his cock. He trudged down the hill with a sense of failure worrying at his trouser leg, which he longed to lug to her front door and confront her with:

'This your poochie (succubus) lady?'

Bam!

And facing her, his grossness annulled by this immaculate gesture.

He'd recaptured his pissing spot but he wouldn't crow again for a while, no, nor throw his head back! Oh, his self-esteem had been badly punctured! He was in love. What a lousy trade. In return for being allowed (by default) to piss, he was a victim of that 'formal violence' . . . ah fuckwit! . . . his morning monologues were now from the heart, as his car veered on the black asphalt, as he contemplated the moon's pale carpet rolled out upon the water.

Daily he trudged up the steep lane, shoved glossy pharmaceutical advertising material into the letterbox of Doctor Ngaei, and pee'd just down from the gate, sometimes into mud, sometimes into an ochre rivulet which coursed down the slope from a ditch further up the road, sometimes into snow, sometimes on to the loamy surface of the verge.

*

Inspiration! Purify me. . . . Always he experienced a nagging sense of desecration. The muddy rivulet was beautiful before he augmented it. Seeds germinated in the rich loam. Frost crystals on fallen twigs were blasted by his stream. He observed the seasons with uncharacteristic attention. Within the small enclosure of his woody urinal he watched the light grow softer and dimmer as the oaks put out leaves. Along the verge a variety of tiny flowers appeared, minute blue or pink corollas turning their faces upward. With shame and despair he pissed on them. He couldn't help it. The moment he'd put the doctor's garish rubbish in the letterbox, his bladder ached with tension. Soon even spring had passed and the lane was filled with the honeysweet scent of gorseflower. To this he added his own bitter fragrance. Bees and flies buzzed and hummed in the dense growth of the oaks whose leaves broadcast a constant spray of sticky sap. As summer advanced this secretion stopped and the flies turned their attentions to his staling ground. They were transformed from summer musicians into gutter communicators of pestilence. Again and again he imagined the blood rising under her perfect skin. He could no longer distinguish between her real outrage in the face of his barbaric intrusion last winter, and the passion with which, in his imagination, he saw her responding to his presence this summer. His daily desecrations were painfully fraught with hope. Burning flowers with his hot urine, he felt 'love's tender shoot cracking the cold clod of his heart'. Ashamed, he continued to be flattered. His atavistic id continued to regard this daily ritual as a ceremonial of display. He imagined that the exquisite Madame Ngaei watched it from behind the trees.

His daydreams, fed by his own memories of travel, were filled with fantasies of her past life. He saw her as a young secretary with the Esso company in Hong Kong, riding the morning ferry from Kowloon across to Victoria Island, perfect in a cheongsam, turning the heads of clumsy tourists. Sometimes he saw her as a nurse on the floating clinic in the Aberdeen inlet, surrounded by a chaos of sampans . . . or having dinner with a young doctor, probably Swiss, in the Tai Pak restaurant. Stimulated by images of food, his fantasies took on a sexual colouration. He saw her clitoris as a delicate morsel in a bowl of soup.

At night he awoke yelling from a dream of a lizard scrabbling on dry claws up her white thigh.

When, now, he went to piss on the verge just down from her gate, he experienced a painful moment of paralysis before his stream consented to flow.

He trembled at the prospect of having to deliver a registered letter to her door.

He caught glimpses of her. Once she was in the greengrocer's when he delivered mail there. Her perfume was subtle and subdued. His senses culled it from the dying breaths of cabbages and mushrooms. He banged into the door going out.

He asked for, and got, a transfer. It was late summer. The verge was beginning to be covered by a mantle of dry oak leaves. He pissed for the last time. His water splashed where gallons had gone before. He knew this spot more intimately than any on earth. He'd observed how it was never the same from one day to the next. Madame Ngaei had taught him something.

'I may be some time.'

With relief and despair he walked off down the hill, into exile.

From the autumn garden the beautiful Madame Ngaei noted, in due course, his absence. She sighed with regret. It had become an amusement. The clumsy boy had been fetching and arrogant. From time to time she'd imagined his crude embraces. She'd occasionally enjoyed watching him pee. She'd stood in her hiding place in the garden with a hand over her mouth while she giggled. Now she stood in the front door of her house, in the late summer sunshine. She was vacuuming. Under her breath she sang

> Takem han
> Ahm stlanga in paladeye

On the far side of the lane, beyond the oaks which she could once again begin to see through as their leaves fell, the hill paddock was filled with a urinous frenzy of yellow ragwort. How barbaric nature could be. How she longed to be educated in its gross intrusions. How she hated winter which was coming fast.

The River

His thoughts were bitter and confused. Among them were some phrases he continued to linger over, with a kind of sad wonder. The phrases had been spoken by a man reminiscing about his childhood. This man, as he himself had told it, had been one of seventeen children in a poor family. He'd said that the first to get up had always been the best dressed. He'd also said that his father had settled quarrels like this: he'd sent the two contestants over to the shed to slog it out and then had thrashed both of them for fighting.

It seemed to him that this man must have had a happy childhood. He sensed the presence of a strong humorous authority in the ménage, however poor *that* may have been. He guessed it must have been loving.

His own circumstances, of course, could not have been more different.

All the same, though he found it easy to indulge this mood of nostalgic self-pity, he couldn't altogether keep his mind on the man who'd come from the large family, nor on his own solitary childhood.

He found his confused thoughts slipping, with a sour persistence, back and back to one incomprehensible idea. It wound its way darkly through the tangle of his mind. Putting the idea to himself as simply as possible, he moved his lips over this sentence:

'I wish I'd been named after a river.'

'I wish I'd been named after a river.'

'I wish I'd been named after a river.'

This crazy thought repelled him. He struggled in his mind to avoid it. He ground his teeth and shook his head. His clenched fingers were white as though he were clutching sticks or weapons.

But after a while he abandoned himself to the notion. It had the same melancholy effect on him as his memory of the man reminiscing about his childhood. For some reason his own nostalgic self-pity seemed related to his idea about a river. With relief he allowed himself to imagine it flowing through a rain forest. The plant life was so eager and fecund it competed with the river for space. Trees which had fallen and lodged across backwaters or across the rocks of rapids were soon the homes of orchids and a thousand-and-one other splendid symbiotics. They also clung in beautiful festoons to the trees along the riverbank. Light barely reached the river, which flowed out into light and space soon enough, it seemed to him—into the sea at a great estuary, where life was precarious and yet immensely rich, subject to the changes of salt and tide, storm, heat, and all the planets. Inland, where the river flowed in its green embrace through the forest, the stars were always concealed, not only by the high canopy of the great treetops, but even by the intermediate levels of treeferns and orchids and flowers. Very occasionally, where there was a break in the canopy, you could see the stars, even in daytime, because of the dimness below. Night and day had no very discrete significance, one from the other. You could not say that one was benign, the other sinister, nor that one was more secret than the other, nor that one stood for growth and the other for stasis. Concomitant notions, for example as to what might be good and what evil, were likewise shrouded in the same ambiguous gloom. It wasn't that these contrasts didn't exist, it was that they occupied more neighbourly poles. Ideas which beyond the forest struck fire from each other, here produced a comfortable friction. When, from time to time, you could see the stars by day, were you going to worry quite as much about the Infinite? No, it would be the Intimate that would attract your thoughts. The river flowed in a green dimness, where chiaroscuro was blurred by a syrupy quality of light: the light could have been fluid, like the river, which seemed not so much to run through it as to precipitate out of it, and to collect in its meandering bed, and to flow away, greenish and opaque. What's more, the light, the air, had a vegetable quality: density, greenness. Therefore the river did too.

This was what he liked. The distinctions between things were vague, everything resembled everything else. This comforted him, and made him sad. *He* felt so distinct. Nothing around him seemed to touch him. The elements of which he was composed grated against his situation. He'd felt like this since childhood, or so he now imagined, in his mood of nostalgic melancholy. Whereas his friend, the man from a large family, must he thought have been brought up with a comfortable sense of the way in which the limits of his own person touched and overlapped the limits of his brothers and sisters, and now that he was a grown man, of the world.

In his rain forest he flinched at the thought of animals and birds. That was a flaw. It was almost like admitting his misanthropy, which, as a last resort, he was in the habit of calling 'realism', without however deceiving himself. He cringed as the ethnologist's boat came up against the stream. He imagined tradingpost trash, contagions, the scrutiny of those meticulous wakeful eyes. He imagined the violations of his secrets.

Ah . . . it was a fact, a 'reality', if reality could be single . . . she'd gone, she'd fucked off.

This thought jabbed painfully into him, like a beam of bright light into his eyes. He covered them, his face, with his hands.

He was by now pretty drunk, and close to tears. His self-pity seemed to him so justifiable that his bitterness and anger began to take over from his melancholy.

'That bitch!'

His fingers whitened upon their imaginary weapons.

At the same instant his name came to him:

'Orinoco. . . .'

His heart was stopped by the rightness of it. It thrilled for a moment, like a fern coil in the green mansion, like a tense fish in the current of the river. Then it began to thud and pound again, haltingly. He sank forward, with his forearms on the table. He was dizzy. I've drunk too much, he thought. He could hear himself calling his own name: Orinoco! Orinoco! Orinoco!

'Here I am.'

The sound of his actual voice startled him. He sat up. This was getting bad. Perhaps he'd nearly blacked out. Perhaps he really should lay off the lush. Okay, there was a party. He'd go to it, alone, with a new name. Some company would sort him out. He was getting himself into a state. Hello, my name is Orinoco, I live in the green mansion where the stars shine by day or not at all.

Between his forearms lay a copy of a reputable news magazine. He'd been reading a feature about male vasectomy in India. They got transistor radios as a reward for their sterility. It was this that had first made him think about his friend, the man from the large family. Of course he himself had no children.

Now that she'd gone he guessed he never would have any. He'd imagined men walking about in Calcutta with transistor radios pressed to their ears. It had seemed both tragic and funny. Now it made him angry. He imagined them listening to the cheap transistors and suddenly thinking, What . . . !

Well, let's make it to the party. It was getting late. C'mon Orinoco, let's go.

There was a glass of wine he hadn't drunk. He got up and tipped it into the sink. Better clear my head. He swallowed a couple of dexies from his hoard in the kitchen cupboard. Soon they'd be gone and that would be that. His hands began to tremble. He threw his shirt into the laundry basket and got under a hot shower. All over his body were fluttering muscles, butterflies. His hollow stomach heaved and floated, like a smooth swift current. The water drummed on the rock of his poor head. To be a river, to flow easily down like that. He dried himself with a towel smelling of her. Oh god, she was everywhere. There were things of hers abandoned in the laundry basket. Orinoco knelt tumbling this stuff in his hands. Standing, he struck his head agonisingly on the corner of a cupboard, and dropped back to his knees, a black waterfall pouring over his eyes. The steamy air was choking him. To live in a green mansion, to breathe cool chlorophyll, naked scents of flowers. Pressed to his face, the towel seemed like a weight, she herself, pressing him back. He toppled. She lay across him, damp from the bath. He really had keeled over. His head was cut where he'd bashed into the cupboard. He felt it with trembly fingers. A little blood. His hair when dry would cover it. His skull was awash, boulders knocking. He flung her wet towel at the full laundry basket. Let's go. His drawer was empty, there was no clean underwear. In her closet he found a pair of blue panties. They would do, it was almost a kind of, a kind of funny joke. He pulled them up snug. In the mirror he saw his tight blue nates, an austere line of crimson down his temple and jaw. The image was pleasantly minimal and intelligent, a tasteful if academic representation: Twentieth Century Schizoid Man . . . King Crimson. . . . Oh, Orinoco, Orinoco, no! . . . he would be dense, concealed, abandoned, his lush vegetable fringe and his dim reflections of crimson would conceal piranhas and those microscopic fish made to climb the urine streams of intruders pissing in the river, fang their urethras . . . ah, venereal tropic! He was grinding his teeth again, speeding in the tight corners, shooting rapids, whirling through the precious forest towards the brown salty dangerous bright estuary . . . stop! He couldn't. He shot out into that glaring space.

In the mirror his image had cringed sideways, his mouth was open. I gotta. . . . The light in the lavatory was broken. He stood in darkness, fumbling. His hands encountered this androgynous sheen of nylon. It had gone, his cock had gone! Transistors buzzed and whistled in his head. For a moment he was lost completely, his belly and groin crawled back into an icy void that was no part of him. Then he managed it, the feminine elastic. He heard the tinkle of his little stream. Then he also began to laugh. The tiny fish swam into him. What was he but an intruder. What, after all. What the hell. Ho ho ho.

Okay 'Orinoco'. The pain in his head had almost gone. He wiped the blood off. He was thinking his name at several removes now. His sense of the joke he'd just played on himself was savage and funny. He was shaking like mad. It would make a good story to tell at the party. He could feel the old familiar gaps opening up. He would really turn it on. He would be a real hit. Oh yeah. He was looking forward to that. The lights in the silent flat were all on. His jaws ached. He dressed alone. He was all right. Mmmmnh huh. He was okay. He would just sit down for a moment. His thoughts were concentrated with glad fury upon the details of his monologue.

Circe and the Animal Trainer

The Man across from her at the garden table wasn't good looking but he was sympathetic. Having worked for some years in Geneva she'd probably have preferred to use the French word *sympatique*, without however being able to explain clearly the different shade of meaning. She'd have said, 'You know what I mean.' Such assumptions were typical of her. She had a queer unconscious knack for flattery. A woman of experience, she assumed others to have been likewise exposed to the more glamorous vicissitudes of life. It wasn't on the whole an assumption that people resented. In fact, as often as not, they'd find themselves thinking, 'Yes, I *do* know what she means.'

She was well above average height, for a woman. He was about as tall as her, which made him unexceptional in this respect as in others. That is, he was about average height, with a squarish 'pleasant' face. His hair was thin and well trimmed. His cheeks and chin were shiny because he'd recently shaved very close. Yet there was nothing cosmetic about him. He was clean and plain. His dress was simple and almost clerical: he was wearing an old pale grey suit, a cream shirt, a dark blue tie with some sort of monogram on it. His hands were large, square, and white. His expression was somehow stern and amused in equal parts. There were no nicotine stains on his fingers, no purplish maze of capillaries in his cheeks. Yet he showed the usual signs of wear and tear: his teeth were poor, his waist somewhat thickened.

As a young woman she'd been strikingly beautiful: dark, tall, slender, brown-eyed, soft-voiced. But what had provided her with an altogether extraordinary charm was the following combination: she was wide-hipped, and she was clever. So that having recovered from the first wounding discovery, that her elegance was by no means austere, you got as it were the second barrel: her intelligence. The combination was lethal. She'd left in her wake an army of vanquished pretenders to her heart. And yet she gave the impression of being quite unaware of this carnage. No doubt she assumed, even then, that her suitors understood 'how things were', and would be able to view their feelings with a certain amount of ironical amusement, not to mention, at a more terminal stage, disdain. It never occurred to anyone for a moment to suggest that her apparent facility with the adroit management of passions, hers and others', might have had little or nothing to do with will or *savoir-faire*, and everything to do with an infantile inability on her part to follow the fragile thread as it wound its way back into the maze of human feelings, at the centre of which, in a dark court paved with bloody flagstones, each man had to reduce the Beast to his own scale—or rather, an inability on her part to offer any such way out, even to realize that some such means of escape was going to be necessary, and that she was going to have to provide it. So that she must often have wondered at the flicker of animal reflex as it drew back, for a moment, the lips and brow of her lover: the bray, the whinny, the growl, the roar, the grunt, the snuffle. 'Can't men be pigs', she'd sometimes say to her friends.

Mind you, there's no reason why you should assume straight off that her apparent *savoir-faire* in fact concealed this failing.

It's just that intelligences with a certain talent for logic often fall down on contingencies. And her intelligence, in the full sense of the word—her *élan-vital*—was faultessly logical.

. . . and it's also that you are, if you're honest, invariably tempted to keep types as types. You're tempted to say, for example, that every man must have his Ariadne before he can have his Circe. That goes by way of definition. The one follows the other, in life if not in myth. She—she must be one or the other. And the lady in question, because of the kinds of affairs she'd had with men—she must be Circe. So you're tempted to say.

At this moment she'd paused in her talk to the friend across from her at the table. She was sitting back in the sunshine, her legs crossed, one foot swinging idly. Her face wore its customary expression of alertness and pleasure. Yet he'd sensed that she was about to tell him something out of the ordinary. Her manner was, as ever, faintly seductive. Now that she was approaching middle age her former elegance tipped over frequently into more ample gestures: smiling, she rocked back in her wrought iron chair, looking at him from beneath the frankly cosmetic perfection of her dark eyebrows. He faced her quietly, his hands clasped together on the white-painted iron table top next to his spectacles case and his empty coffee cup.

She was thinking that her friend was like an animal trainer. Somehow he was able to understand with different senses from most people. She'd said nothing out of the ordinary, yet she realized that he'd anticipated her desire to do so. She found this placed a certain restraint on her. He always made her feel exposed. And yet she was well aware of her usual powers: he'd been in love with her for years. And so, of course, she was instinctively trying to disarm him by these means. But it was all too familiar. It was almost like a parody.

She was thinking that he'd called to her so often he was almost deafened. Then how did he hear her? It was those other senses, those other powers. What did he dream of? She imagined him sleeping, exhausted, deaf with whistling. Outside in the yard his chained loves twitched their dreaming paws.

'What do you dream about?' she asked.

He smiled, unclasped his hands, and spread them.

'I dream,' he said, 'that I might be allowed to cease faring upon the seas and to stay in your palace forever.'

It was a little routine they'd repeated more times than either of them could remember. She found herself wanting something different. Yet she'd started it, this time as others. Of course it was he who'd coined the nickname.

She realized it was now time for her to start talking. He was making no attempt to conceal the fact that he was listening, waiting.

'Listen, John,' she said. 'I want to tell you something but I don't know where to begin. . . .'

'. . . *at the beginning*,' they said together. If they'd in fact been sharing their lives all these years they couldn't have had the patter off any more glibly.

'At the beginning,' she repeated. 'But listen, I don't know where that is. I know, John, that you're going to think this is pre-menopausal melancholy, but it's not. I don't know how to tell you what I want to without producing a wretched string of clichés. I just can't think it out. I'm really very unhappy.'

'Well, you must have had *something* specific to tell me, or you wouldn't have called me. And I wouldn't have come. You see, I do keep hoping.'

She smiled, for form's sake. But her manner had changed.

'I trust you to understand more than most people do or can. I want you to explain to me what I'm saying. I suddenly remembered something the other day. It upset me very much. I don't know why.'

She lit herself a cigarette and looked away from him down the garden. In all the years he'd known her she'd never quite dropped her guard like this. There had always been ways of coping: little games, little routines:

'Knock knock.'

'Who's there?'

Now that she was off-guard, her former elegance seemed to have returned. It was as though, of late, her conscious attempts to retain her grace had become effortful, almost clumsy. Now he found his heart swelling again at the sight of her, as much with a fresh access of affection as with pity. Her expression, as she considered how to start, was thoughtful, almost serene. Yet her fingers trembled where she held the cigarette. 'You are a lovely, lovely woman,' he thought. 'You were wasted in this role.'

He reached over and put his hand on her arm. She continued to look away across the garden. She'd had a successful career. The garden was large and well planted, with nothing fussy about it: the kind of garden which looked after itself, with the chief exception of the grass, which she cut herself, energetically, using an old push mower. The shrubs had grown up and tangled together since she'd been there. Some of the trees had even had to be taken out to allow space for the others. The lawn was speckled with the first fallen leaves of autumn, yet, at the far end of the garden, a mandarin bush was just coming into its blaze of symmetrical fruit. There was a small dark gazebo overgrown with a choko vine whose fruit hung in pale green heavy bunches. And there were ginger plants still in flower, the garden filled with their cloying fragrance.

'No hurry,' he said. 'Today I don't have to be there till the afternoon.'

'What I suddenly remembered was this,' she said, still looking away towards the blazing mandarin bush. 'When I was a little girl we lived here, in Auckland, in Epsom. Medicine's always been in the family. Both my brothers are doctors. I'm a doctor. So were my father and grandfather. My father was an ambitious man. As children we were always given this sense of solidity and permanence in our situation. We were aware, from early on, that there was a tradition in our family for hardnosed dedication to a demanding profession. As I remember it, life was very full and active for us children: we always went somewhere for the holidays, we kept lots of pets, there were endless excursions. There was always something to do. Idleness, in play as in work, wasn't really tolerated in our family. We were encouraged to speak our minds, to be direct, to be clear, to be curious. This is the background, you see. . . . We were confident that things were where they were. We were confident children.'

He knew all this already. He'd often listened to her reminisce, with affection and gusto, about her childhood. It had become a formula for him to say he envied her, although at his age he no longer had any particular feelings about his own very different childhood.

She was still looking away from him, seeming to squint slightly at the bright end-of-morning sunshine which fell in shafts through her trees on to the mandarin bush, and on to the dark overgrown gazebo where he'd once, long ago, had to do battle with the Beast and then find his own way back. Since then he'd worked, married late, been happy and—the word made him grin—successful.

'We're both so *successful*,' he said. 'What are we doing sitting here clutching each other like children who've lost the way?'

'Oh John.'

She had in fact brought her other hand round to hold his where it lay on her arm. Now she turned to look at him. He saw that her eyes were full of tears, her lips quivering. A wee dewlap by her chin was trembling also.

'My dear,' he said. 'I'm sorry. Please go on.'

She said, after pausing to push the tears away with the back of her hand, 'Remember how I've told you about our pets? Oh, we used to have everything. We used to put guinea pigs on the table at opposite ends of a long piece of grass and see what happened when they met in the middle. Daddy used to buy day-old roosters and tell us they'd escaped just before Christmas. We had endless Scotties. They were so smelly and mangy. I loved them. And then there were the Paradise Ducks . . .'

She'd managed a laugh of sorts, smiling through her tears. He knew the story about the Paradise Ducks. Though he rarely smoked, and never in the mornings, he reached across and helped himself to one of her cigarettes. Against his will he was beginning to feel irritated.

'John, I'm waffling on,' she said. 'You've heard all this a million times. But the point is, it's as though I've always left something out. You know,' she continued, after pausing to put on a pair of dark glasses, 'a moment ago I thought of you as an animal trainer. I thought of your tamed creatures running in their dreams. We all leave something out, John. Because I haven't got your gifts I can only guess at your secrets. But you can look into my eyes. You can see right through me. That's why I trust you to listen to what I'm telling you. That's why I'm asking you, John, not to pretend you don't know what I'm talking about when I get to the point.'

'All right,' he said. He was thinking, 'What do you know about compromise?' He was also thinking, 'In that case why have you put on your dark glasses?' He clasped his hands again on the white table top.

'The other day,' she said, 'I suddenly remembered how our street in Epsom had plane trees in it. It was actually an avenue. I don't know why I've never remembered this before. I've told you everything else. . . .'

'Go on,' he said.

'Well, I got lost once. I was very tiny. Perhaps I'd just been to primary school—one of the first times I was allowed to go by myself. I'd always known our street by the plane trees. This day I couldn't find them. I couldn't find it. I couldn't find the trees. I don't remember how I finally got home. I guess someone must have found me crying. What had happened was this: while I'd been away at school or wherever, the Council had been around pruning the trees. They'd cut them right back to the trunk, you know how they do with plane trees. Pollarding. There were no lovely shady trees left in the street. Only these ugly rows of huge knotty clubs. That's what I wanted to tell you about, John. . . .'

She stopped abruptly. Behind the modish dark glasses her face was white. In telling the story to him she'd understood herself what it meant. Throughout her entire busy successful confident life, all those things which had come to seem familiar and solid had, at a certain moment, been changed. Everything, everybody, one person and one thing after another. She'd been lost again and again. Only *he* had somehow never changed, or been changed. He was the same John.

'Oh John, my dear John,' she said. 'You know what I'm asking you, don't you?'

He got up from his chair and stood by the table opposite

her. He looked as though he was about to deliver one of his lectures at the university: his square fingertips resting lightly on the table top next to the spectacles case and the empty coffee cup.

'I've understood your story,' he said. 'I've known you for a very long time, and I think I've always known that about you, though I've always wondered whether *you* knew it.' He was looking straight at her, speaking very deliberately. Then he sighed loudly and sat down again. 'You know,' he went on, 'how I've always liked to mix my myths—how I've even done that for my students.' He smiled slightly. 'You see, you've even got into my professional life. I've always said that Theseus and Ulysses and the rest of them stand for aspects of the one man, and that Ariadne, Circe and Penelope stand for stages of initiation. Silly, trite stuff. And yet year after year I've told my students this, and thought of you. You see, the most distant point of Ulysses' journey home was in Ithaca. Home may not be where you are, but it's certainly where you're going. It's where you're always going. How can I come here when I'm here already? And when I'm always going somewhere else?'

He stood up and walked around the table to where she sat motionless staring down the length of the luxuriant early-autumn garden at the dark gazebo and the blazing mandarins. She hadn't looked at him once since he'd begun to talk. She was sitting like a gauche schoolgirl. There was nothing he needed to say. But he went on, anyway, standing behind her chair, looking in the same direction as she was.

'My dear friend,' he said, placing his hands on her shoulders. 'It's much much too late for you to offer to be my Ariadne and show me a way out of the maze. And I already have a Penelope.' He leaned down to speak close to her ear. 'All I ever wanted,' he said, squeezing her shoulders gently, inhaling a perfume like gardenias from her neck, 'all I ever wanted was to be changed, to be changed by you, Circe. That's all I've ever wanted. And that's not what you're offering now, is it, my dear?'

'And now,' he said, leaning still closer to kiss her cheek, 'I have to go. I've work to do. Down among the little animals at the university.'

He walked back around the table and picked up his spectacles case.

'I'll ring you later,' he said, 'when I have some time to spare.'

He walked across the patio to the door.

'*Au revoir*,' he said.

'*Au revoir*, John,' she replied, without turning around. '*Au revoir*.'

Of course, it was the expression she'd always used. Of course he knew that.

The Gringos

The Gringos, a former rock and roll band of the nineteen fifties, seldom met these days. When they did it was by accident. Though none of them now played professionally they'd all kept their gear, with the exception of Nigel who'd sold his kit after the band's breakup because he'd felt stupid playing the drums by himself especially when his wife was listening.

But he still had his suit and since his attachment to performing days had increased over the years he'd also guarded those potent accessories: two pairs of blue suede ripple soles, a couple of chunky rings set with huge fake rubies, some velvet Mississippi string ties.

He was pretty sure the other Gringos had hung on to their clobber too. In their heyday they'd had a band suit: a midnight blue threequarter length jacket shot with silver lurex, shoulders padded right out, wide scarlet silk lapels plunging to a single button at navel level, a scarlet Edwardian waistcoat with a rich paisley pattern, pegleg pants with a zipper on the inside of each ankle, blue silk shirts with a foam of blue lace on the front and scarlet piping on the cuffs. The Gringos had been good enough to afford this number and they'd played anywhere there was a hop between Christchurch and Invercargill, though Dunedin was their base and summer at Caroline Bay in Timaru what really took care of the brass.

There they'd got the cops out more than once as local

bodgies and yahoos packed dances to pick fights with kids on holiday at Caroline Bay. Of course The Gringos got the blame, or rock and roll did. But they played four summers anyway. In those days there was no bullshit. The lead guitar's pickup went straight into the amp and the metallic music came straight back out again. The two saxophones blew right in the faces of rock and rolling kids. The Gringos' bass went electric long before that was common but he still marched it up and down, solid and even, that splitsecond ahead of the beat, the notes sliding out from under the guitar's syncopation.

From time to time they used a second guitar but they found it complicated the music too much. Then there was Nigel with his basic kit: snare, foot-bass, hihat, one tomtom to the side, and one cymbal, a pair of seldom-used danceband brushes, and a rack of hickory clubs. The rim of the snare was battered, the paint and chrome flaking off down the side. But he wasn't just a walloper. If Pete had the knack of keeping his marching bass just an eyelid-bat ahead of the beat, Nigel had an equally necessary talent for staying that splitsecond behind: this was what gave the music its truculence: 'shootin' the agate'.

After the old rock and rollers stopped being heard—those endlessly interchangeable pros who blasted away behind Chuck Berry and Bo Diddley and even Elvis Presley—Nigel thought the only rock drummer who got close was Charlie Watts of the Rolling Stones. But he didn't listen to much 'modern' rock music. After the Gringos stopped playing there didn't seem to be much point in listening either. And after about two and a half minutes of any rock track he listened to these days he kept hearing a coda asking to be played, some final chop, a chord that would stamp down like a shoe on a cigarette butt. But the music went on, *nah nah nah,* like jazz. He didn't like jazz, never had. Years back a friend had tried to get him to listen to Charlie Parker.

'That's bullshit mate. The bastard doesn't know shit from clay.'

It was Chuck Berry from the start and it was still Chuck Berry as far as he was concerned when the band broke up. A few years later he'd listened in disbelief as a new English group called The Beatles sang 'Roll Over Beethoven'. The music had been ironed out a bit, he could hear how the equipment had changed, but it was the old Chuck Berry number all right.

Only it wasn't the same. Why he felt like this he didn't know. When he thought about it he decided it was because he wasn't playing anymore. When he talked to the band they said the same. Also Lorraine didn't like rock and roll anymore. She said it was all right when you were a kid, but. . . .

But *he* could remember her dancing back then in 1959.

It had occurred to him that the Gringos lasted only a short professional time: '56 to '59. It was a thought whose meaning he couldn't catch. The *real* time was more than four years. Here he was in '73, he had one kid who'd be leaving school soon, and two more as well, he had a house up Brockville and an okay job with Cooke Howlison, it was fifteen years since the Gringos had played 'Maybellene', the last song they played as a band, Chuck Berry's first hit, their homage to Chuck. But *then* was still the most important time in his life.

'It was okay when we were kids,' said Lorraine.

And his son, who was fourteen, said he liked the old records but it made him laugh to think of his dad playing in a rock and roll band at Caroline Bay in Timaru.

'I can't imagine it.' Ha ha.

All the same the boy would skite to his friends. Sometimes a bunch of them would turn up, look at Nigel, and listen to some of his collection: 'Maybellene', 'Johnny B. Goode', 'Sweet Little Sixteen', 'Memphis'. Then he'd play them Little Richard,

Screaming Lord Sutch, Elvis, and even Muddy Waters. The records were scratchy and worn. Down in the basement rumpus room of his house he longed to put on his gear and show them what it had been like. They stood around, amused, *listening.* He played his collector's item, a recording of Chuck Berry from the film *Jazz on a Summer's Day* at the 1958 Newport Jazz Festival, a performance of 'Sweet Little Sixteen' with Jack Teagarden's trombone blasting in behind. It made him sweat. He wanted to say, 'It took over, see?' They jigged awkwardly, shifting their feet. Then he'd play 'Rock and Roll Music' or 'Roll Over Beethoven', knowing what was going to happen, and sure enough one of the kids would always say, 'But that's a Beatles' song . . .'

When he went back upstairs with his records carefully under his arm they'd put on Osibisa or the Moody Blues or Grand Funk Railroad or for fucksake Simon and Garwhatsit. It was rubbish. He'd hear the *clak* of pool balls on the miniature table and from time to time the fizz of aerosol freshair as they doused their cigarette smoke with Pine Fragrance.

At fifteen he'd been a chippy's apprentice and smoking a packet of cigarettes a day. He couldn't afford it. But like everything else it had to be done with style. You spent hours practising, letting the smoke dribble from your lips and back again up your nostrils. You practised lighting matches inside the open half of a matchbox. Kidstuff. . . .

It was no coincidence that the Gringos all had similar jobs. Nigel was a warehouseman. So were two of the others. The other two were clerks. They were all married. They all lived in suburbs near Dunedin. So it was natural that they all got home on a certain day and saw a photograph of Chuck Berry on the front page of the evening paper, and all reached to ring each other up for the first time in months or in some cases years.

It took a while before any of them was able to get through the scramble of lines. And then, as if by telepathy, there was nothing to say.

'D'ja. . . .'

'Yeah it's. . . .'

'When I got home. . . .'

No sooner had Nigel hung up, heart thumping, than the phone rang again.

'Hey, d'ja see. . . .'

'Yeah Chuck. . . .'

'Inna paper. . . .'

'Fuck me dead. . . .'

They met in the pub. What had happened? Where had the time gone? They went over a half forgotten litany of names and dates and places. They remembered songs. They swallowed tears.

The day before the concert Nigel gave in to a nagging temptation. In the bedroom he took a large box down from the top of the wardrobe and from it he carefully lifted out The Suit. It was wrapped in tissue and then polythene and had been impregnated with thymol crystals. The Shirt was there too. He hadn't got it all out for so long he'd forgotten the texture and feel of the heavy cloth. It was perfectly preserved. He held the jacket up by the shoulders. He felt furtive and exalted. Quickly he buttoned himself into the Shirt with its chemical smell and its frenzy of lace. The neck button wouldn't do up. No matter, he'd. . . .

Sitting on the edge of the bed he undid the inside zips of the trousers and stepped in pointing his toes like a dancer. In spite of their generous forward pleats he couldn't get the trousers past the tops of his thighs. They'd have to be altered.

Spreading his legs to hold the pants up as far as they'd gone, he grunted into the Jacket. Though cut to drape full and free, tapering not to the waist but to a point below his backside, the Jacket crushed his armpits and wouldn't button. Lorraine could let it out for sure.

Keeping his legs spraddled, his arms held out from his trunk by the crushing jacket, he pushed his feet into the Blue Suedes. They fitted.

He shuffled sideways to the wardrobe mirror. There he saw a fat-faced man of forty with a shiteating smile, whose hair, still black, had receded from his temples along the path the comb still took it, straight back. The fat man's hornrim glasses had slipped a little down his nose. He was standing with his trousers half-up like someone caught having a nasty in a bus shelter. Between the straining buttons of a lacey blue shirt came tufts of black chest hair. The man's arms were held out sideways. The bottoms of his trousers were concertina'd against the insteps of blue shoes whose scarlet laces trailed on the floor.

Skip the waistcoat.

'Jesus Christ. . . .'

But he stood outside the town hall with a dry mouth and a pounding happy heart. The other Gringos were there too with their wives. That made ten altogether. They felt like a club. It was a cold spring evening. The rest of the crowd was mostly young. The Gringos felt conspicuous but proud. They exchanged derisive glances as the crowd whooped it up. Some of *them* had got dressed nineteen fifties style: there were kids of nineteen and twenty with makeshift ducksarse hairstyles and there was even one beautiful girl wearing pedal pushers a sweater and a pony tail, and bright red lipstick. Nigel's eyes wandered her way. He wondered if she could rock and roll. It was certainly news to him that Chuck Berry was still appreciated or was being appreciated again. Lots of these kids were only a few years older than his own son! What did they know about the old style?

'The old style . . .': he caught at the phrase as it sidled through his mind. Then they were going in. He was still examining the phrase as they took their seats. The ten of them sat in a row. All around was the racket of a young excited audience. But no dance floor. A *town hall.* Like for concerts, the symphony orchestra.

He was still thinking 'the old style' when the backing group came on: guitar, bass, drums, electric piano. They powered straight into some standards beginning with 'Johnny B. Goode' and going without a pause into Little Richard's 'Awopbopaloobop'. It was deafening. The amps were six feet high. There was wire all over the stage. The bass player kept getting off licks like cracks of thunder which jabbed at Nigel's ears. He could *feel* it in his guts. The guitarist and singer had beanpole legs. He banged his knees together as he sang and played. He appeared to be chewing at the microphone. You couldn't really hear what he said. The audience sat somewhat sullenly.

Then there was a pause. There were groups chanting 'Chuck Chuck Chuck!' It just wasn't like rock and roll. The Kiwi backing group came on again and began tuning up. They looked scared. The phrase 'old style' was still whining away in Nigel's ears which he felt had been damaged by the preceding hour of noise. He watched the drummer up there as he straightened out his kit. He had about twice as much gear as Nigel had ever played with. For a start he had two tomtoms mounted on the foot-bass and another to the side as well. Then he had a total of four cymbals including a sizzle and not counting the hihat. What for? You didn't need it. Nigel admitted the joker was quick and fancy. But he couldn't play rock and roll. He was whipping the music along like a jockey taking his nag away in the home straight but what you wanted to get into rock and roll was slouch, you had to shoot the agate. You had to feel the slug of it like the sexy splitsecond between the thud of a girl's heart and the squirm of the artery in her neck, her breath gasping as she swings back under your arm, catching her flying hand as she goes past again, then rocking back in close. Or it was like not letting a fuck accelerate away with you before the lights changed, yeah. . . .

This thought struck him as original. Leaning sideways to confide it to another Gringo he missed Chuck Berry's entry. When he heard the crowd go mad he looked up and saw a lean wolfish black man wearing a check shirt and narrow peglegs grinning back over his shoulder as he slung his guitar and moved across to the electric piano to tune. This he did with such care and absorption, moving from member to member of the backing group, that the audience thought it was a puton and began to howl.

But the Gringos knew better. Nigel was sweating but he sat like a boulder. The wolfish man struck a few elegant licks off his guitar. The sound was simple and familiar. The amps had been turned right down but he waved to turn them down further.

Then he cracked off a couple more licks with a bit more velocity behind them, grinned, rode rubber legs to the front of the stage and all at once was into 'Reelin' and Rockin'' while the Gringos sat petrified in their seats three-quarters of the way back from the stage of the town hall with all around them a howling audience of kids not much older than their own.

At one point as Chuck lolloped into 'Too Pooped to Pop' a group in front of the Gringos struggled out into the aisle with a banner which read 'We love you Chuck'. They ponced round the front of the stage with it and back down the next aisle. Chuck Berry acknowledged this gesture with an ironical double-take.

But the music rode on. He swung his gat arm knocking the steely chords off the instrument as though brushing lint from a coat. He rode one heel across stage, the other leg stretched out in front. He did a pretty good splits and never stopped playing. Lowering the guitar between his legs he shot wads of sound into the audience which was by now dancing wildly in the aisles, not rock and roll, just. . . .

But the Gringos sat without moving, as though turned to stone. They didn't miss a thing. They noted the glances Chuck shot at the electric piano player who couldn't rock the instrument. Nigel noted with satisfaction the looks Chuck sent from time to time in the direction of the drummer who was sweating blood. The bass player had been briefed. He marched it up and down.

And Chuck Berry, lean as a knife, lazy as calm water, mean as a wolf, sang and strutted and rubberlegged and licked away at that guitar whose pickup went straight into the amp while the music came straight back out again, no bullshit, metallic, 'in the old style', as though Chuck could never get old, as though rock and roll could never die, and the Gringos sat there with their wives while their Suits stayed at home with the real *Gringos* folded up inside somehow with the thymol crystals.

Oh Maybellene
Why can't you be true?

sang Chuck Berry. The *Gringos* had been a good rock and roll band for four years and that had been a lifetime. It was fifteen years since they'd played 'Maybellene' for the last time at Caroline Bay in Timaru in the summer of '59, and that had been even longer.

The Shirt Factory

When I sit here on the back porch of my house in the mild autumn sunshine I can always see, below me, the roof and facade of the little shirt factory which employs a number of the local ladies. The same sunlight that warms me enters the windows of the factory and, I like to imagine, brightens the workshop floor for the few minutes that remain before afternoon tea. After this pause which is of course taken for granted and even extended by the length of a garrulous sentence or two, or by a few leisurely final puffs on a cigarette, the ladies go back to work, confident that the remaining hour and a half of their penal rate day will pass quickly enough. Then they'll all come out into the street, into the same sunshine or what remains of it, some of them will stand chatting for a while, but before long the windows of the little shirt factory will be dark, the area in front deserted, the machinery silent, the work-day done with.

By all accounts it's a satisfactory place to work. The hours aren't long, during school holidays the mothers of younger children can come to a special arrangement regarding the 'three-quarter day' system, the machinery, though quite noisy, isn't dirty or dangerous, the workshop's light and warm, and the ladies themselves would give a hard time to anyone who suggested that *they* were to blame for production being down, and they'd most certainly be quick to leap to the defence of any sister who was the object of derogation of any kind.

In short: we've come a long way. The ladies have the confidence of workers who know their rights, who aren't afraid to demand and defend them. In fact they have the confidence of equals: if the factory manager can announce cheerfully that, 'girls', he's off to Southland 'for a bit of duck shooting', then you can be sure 'the girls' feel no compunction, every Friday, about taking the last hour or so off, producing combs and doing each other's hair. This has become an established ritual. At lunch time you see them leave the factory, as usual. After lunch they return with scarves tied over the piled rollers in their hair. At the end of the work-day they emerge, shyly but also somewhat stridently, confident in their fitness to face the weekend, their assorted types of hair waved, primped and permed, each one under the magisterial gaze of the entire female workforce of the factory. Exceptions: one or two younger girls. But by and large it's a job which suits women whose children are more or less off their hands.

Well, here I sit looking down at the factory, and I'm reminded that Friedrich Engels was the son of a Barmen cotton manufacturer, that he settled permanently in England at the age of thirty and worked in the family cotton factory (partners Engels and Ermens) in Manchester for most of his life, incidentally supporting Marx out of his 'allowance', not to mention writing articles for the New York Daily Tribune which were published under Marx's name . . . and I'm reminded of my old friend Otto.

Dear Otto. . . .

And the shirt factory ladies who can let their hair down between afternoon tea and knockoff time . . . 'Workers' Paradise'. . . .

And Engels' letter to Marx from Manchester, 8 September 1851: 'On Friday evening I suddenly received a letter from my old man in which he says that I am spending too much money and must manage on £150 a year . . .' Engels at this date being in his thirties, and already a veteran of European revolutionary movements: the 'Young Hegelians' of Berlin, Hess's Communist agitation in Barmen, the abortive Baden uprising in which he served as Willich's adjutant. . . .

Who's this high minded cynic? you're going to say. But don't get me wrong. I'm not committing myself. After all, there are two ways of looking at what I've described: either you can say that Engels' dependence on his father's firm (and his later partnership in it) for twenty years was a betrayal of his avowed principles, and that Marx, supported by Engels (tally for 1868: £10 to save Marx's property from being distrained for debt, £15 to pay a gas bill, £40 for expenses connected with the wedding of one of Marx's daughters, etc etc), was likewise a hypocrite, not to mention a grasping parasite—either you say this and wash your hands of the whole matter, or else you see Engels' commitment to a job he loathed, in company he despised, to support for more than twenty years a man he believed in, notwithstanding his own considerable talent not to mention ambition—you see this as a moving and remarkable record of devotion to the principles he wrote about and defended so tirelessly all his life. And, if you take this view, you remember also that Marx may have depended on Engels, but he was hardly comfortable for that reason: the 1850s and 1860s were, as Marx's daughter Eleanor (I don't know if it was she who married in 1868 with £40 lent by Engels) later recalled, 'years of horrible poverty'.

And the shirt factory ladies' Friday afternoon ritual: is there more than one way of looking at this?

But I'd better tell you about my friend, before it gets cold out here, before the sun goes off the porch. There can't be too much of it left: look, here come the ladies now, out of the door, into the street.

I may, incidentally, have given you a wrong impression: I'm not a scholar of Marxian philosophy. I've certainly never felt the least desire to plough right through the *Grundrisse*, nor any desire to study Hegelian dialectics, and certainly not the least attraction to the enormous pile of ephemera amassed by such tireless workers as our Mr Engels. However as an educated man, and a liberal one, not to mention as the proprietor of a small factory, I've always, as they say, 'taken an interest'. I've kept an open mind. And I've had as a friend for many years a quite devoted Marxian scholar not to say Marxist *per se*: Otto. So apart from ordinary interest and curiosity, I've been stimulated into probing more recherché corners of the matter by his constant friendly but nonetheless ruthless attacks on my life style, economic interests, etcetera. In addition to this I dare say I've picked up a few crumbs of knowledge in the course of the countless lipsmacking meals he's made of attacks on me and the middle classes in general.

At this stage I feel justified in remarking that there's one ploy which can seriously enrage dear old Otto: that is to point out to him the licence enjoyed by the ladies at the shirt factory.

'So they're allowed to dress their hair,' he screams, 'while you sit up here on the hill drinking Dimple Haig and drooling over your latest expensive bauble, with a paternal smile on your face!'

To point out, subsequent to such an outburst, that he too is drinking Dimple Haig, *my* Dimple Haig, is to risk a diatribe which can sometimes verge on the unpleasant. So I generally content myself with a few familiar jibes about his background: pre-Second World War liberal-bohemian education in what's now known as East Germany, in the house of a moderately successful Bauhaus-influenced socialist-sympathising architect father. Trotting out formulas like that can sometimes save us a lot of time. I also remind Otto that the Communist Manifesto drafted by Engels and Marx is careful to use the terms 'workers and intellectuals': a canny provision which not only permitted Engels and Marx to join their own club, but which also, now, allows Otto the same privilege. These friendly thrusts are too routine to really get Otto going.

I occasionally jot down a bit of verse, for my own amusement you understand: rhyming things, 'doggerel' you might say, limericks and suchlike. Let me tell you a piece I wrote recently. It may help to fill out the rather lean picture I've so far given you of Otto, who, when I showed it to him 'for laughs', flew into a rage, imagining that it was directed at *him*, specifically. What conceit. Here it is. It's called 'The Lament of the Liberal Husband':

My lady's breath is rich and strong,
My lady's tastes are hearty.
She sucks at sweets with scarlet lips
Then wipes them on her nightie.

My lady's frank in everything,
Not delicate in any.
She always says 'I want to piss'
And never 'spend a penny'.

Oh she is big in haunch and thew,
Her breasts resemble bladders.
Her belly's wide, her buttocks broad,
Her hair's a nest of adders.

And when she spreads to take me in
I dream the Pit is gaping.
A pen of sows all in full rut
Could never match her squealing.

For she was weaned on fish and chips
And plates of bread and butter.
She learned her airs not in Genève
But in a council gutter.

And oh I love my lusty slut
For she was born a winner
While I was raised in a liberal house
Where lunch was not called dinner

And where the shelves creaked under books
And the radio played concertos
And my sisters practised ballet steps
Like pubescent flamingoes.

Otto, needless to say, found this offensive in the extreme. I must admit I wasn't without a little friendly malice in making the recitation to him: you see, I was well aware of two quirks, 'hangups' as my son would call them, which afflict Otto who, in other respects, has an admirable sense of humour, a taste for the bizarre and the outrageous which I must say I find refreshing, and an immensely plausible manner, especially as regards members of the opposite sex.

But to return to his 'hangups': bearing in mind his plausible manner, which we'll have a chat about in a moment or two, you need to know that Otto's extremely ugly, and knows it, and resents it. Bearing in mind his plausibility and his ugliness and his resentment, his second 'hangup' will appear as an especially cruel stroke: he has two extraordinarily beautiful sisters, both of whom accompanied him to this country, the younger of whom, Else, is my wife, and the older of whom, Ingrid, is the wife of my older brother, a sheep farmer near Cheviot (Ingrid breeds Welsh Mountain Ponies). Thus, as a result of two unions, both of them entirely bourgeois in all their aspects, Otto finds himself bound 'hand and foot' as he puts it, to a family (ours) which embraces both a capitalist 'industrial baron' (me) and a '*kulak*' (my brother). To make matters much worse, Otto's well aware that the small shirt factory opened by my father prospered during the Second World War as a result of contracts gained from the New Zealand Navy: the factory, operating then as it does now in a small coastal port, was well placed to supply the navy with whatever it may have been the contract required. In spite of the fact that the New Zealand Navy was involved in a struggle against the same forces which caused, or persuaded, Otto's own father, a man of some prescience, to send his family out of the country (the wife and mother died on the way of malaria contracted in Lourenço Marques), Otto still used the term 'war profiteering' to describe the activities of the shirt factory during the war years. In fact I have to admit that the business went extremely well, so that when it was passed on to my brother and myself, my brother, whose interests had never really had a commercial bias, was able to sell out and buy a farm with his share, while I found myself, after quite a short period of time, and given the profitability of the business, in possession of a number of rapidly appreciating properties, capital assets and investments, to the extent that the shirt factory was reduced, in a sense, to a hobby.

Well, we've strayed from Otto's 'hangups', but not far, since there are a couple of related points to be made. One you may have guessed by now: I met Else, and my brother, Ingrid, while they were employed in the shirt factory. Otto was meanwhile confined on Soames Island in Wellington harbour. The mesh of his entanglements, both real and emotional, was by now almost surrealistic. He was confined not so much because he was a German (he was, after all, a refugee from the Nazis and had been admitted to the country on that understanding) as, I suspect, because of his no-doubt well documented anarchist activities as a youth in Germany: at any rate, someone 'somewhere' had decided to wait and see about this Otto until more time could be devoted to him. Meanwhile he staged two unsuccessful but moderately spectacular breakouts from the island, where he resented being cooped up with 'nazis and fascists', and he poured scorn on his sisters in letters which must have confirmed the censors and authorities in their suspicions as to his duplicity or at least confusion: in these letters he attacked the girls for working 'in the war effort'. How did he know about the shirt factory's contracts? No doubt one or the other of his sisters wrote to him describing what they were doing: perhaps the words 'tunic' or 'kitbag' were used.

At this stage the threat of Japanese invasion was real enough. I was on coastal patrol with the New Zealand navy. When I got back on leave, which was in fact quite often, I saw Else. She was the most beautiful girl I'd ever met. My brother, who'd been exempted from active service on account of a heart condition (one of the reasons, incidentally, that he chose to abandon a more or less sedentary commercial life in favour of a more active farming one) was meanwhile being captivated by Ingrid. My father advised us to restrain our attentions until after the war: this made sense both in the wider commercial sphere and in the narrower one of local gossip and feeling. After all, the authorities mightn't have approved of the sons of a government contractee in the war effort becoming involved with a couple of German girls, refugees though they quite plainly were. But they were watched and they did have to report daily to the police. And there was the usual muttering in the community, some of it reaching the 'radio transmitter' extreme, but most of it, I suspected then, prompted by the obvious beauty and accomplishment of the sisters, which left most of the locals for dead.

After the war my brother and I took over the factory and married the sisters: enchantment and security, bliss and prospects, at a stroke! Otto's scorn knew no bounds.

Now for the second point related to Otto's two 'hangups' (the pedant in me always wants to say *hangsup*). But perhaps I should recapitulate briefly. the first 'hangup' I isolated was his resentment of his own ugliness, against which, I suggested, you should measure his plausible manner, especially as regards members of the opposite sex. His second 'hangup', which stands in relation to the first much as a function does to a fixed force, or a profit margin to a fixed asset (for example a shirt factory whose plant's kept up-to-date), I isolated as being his resentment of the unusual beauty of his sisters and related resentment of their familial and class associations (for example me). The first point related to these two 'hangups' I described as being the manner in which my brother and I met and married Otto's sisters, at a time when he considered that they'd betrayed principles (it's not clear which ones), and when he considered himself to have been martyred (the authorities weren't certain as to what cause the martyrdom was for). The second point should now strike you (it does me) as being cruelly simple, not to mention funny: Otto has a son Karl, who is as beautiful a young man as you could wish to see anywhere, whose devotion to bourgeois principles of acquisition hedonism and egoism is as instinctive as was that of his aunts at the time my brother and I first met them, and whose plausibility of manner, especially as regards members of the opposite sex, exceeds even that of his father, the old goat, and *his* reputation believe me might be described as national.

Well, I hope the picture's clear so far. I feel a bit like a scientist stringing molecules together, in some fear as to whether or not he might be weakening the bonds.

At the risk of breaking the bonds, I want to add a couple more molecules to the chain. They stand in relation to the two above much as *they* in their turn stand to the two 'hangups' I ascribed to Otto at the start.

I hope you'll forgive me my synecdochism, my little tropes: as I believe I said earlier, I've always taken an interest, I've kept an open mind, and I could easily, given different circumstances, have become a scientist of some sort—the idea of 'pure' science as opposed to applied science has always appealed to me, and I dare say the extent to which I've come to treat the shirt factory as a hobby is a measure of this interest: that is, my involvement with the factory has tended to slide by degrees from application to research. Of course I like to think that there's a positive feedback into the community as a result of this little interest of mine, though of course Otto would assure me there was not: he would say, in fact he has said, that in the first place I can well afford to indulge my whim, and in the second that licence for female workers to dress their hair on Friday afternoons during working time hardly constitutes a breakthrough in the class war let alone in the continuing dialectic of industrial relations in a capitalist society like New Zealand where, as Otto sees it, working class movements such as trades unions are all too frequently devoting their efforts to the eventual satisfaction of 'retailers and usurers' when they should be 'striking blows' at the 'whole structure of capitalism'; and he adds, for good measure, that my 'paternalistic' attitude to the ladies in the shirt factory really constitutes nothing more than 'bribery' as a result of which they are 'duped' into 'selling their labour more cheaply', thereby 'lubricating the exploitative machinery' as a result of which I 'enrich myself' (wait for it) 'at their expense'.

I do apologise for this long digression. However it's brought me back rather neatly to the point I was about to make which I'd just described as being 'another molecule' I think. . . . Well let's continue anyway. But first I think we should go inside. It's become quite fresh, don't you find?

Pause for just a moment before you come in, and look at that little factory down there. You wouldn't believe how much satisfaction she's brought me, over the years. Oh yes, you may smile: she has indeed brought me comfort too. But does an enterprise on that scale—why, it's almost a cottage industry!—really warrant the kind of rhetoric Otto bestows on it? I must say it seems, in a contradictory sort of way, to be almost a compliment. It's as though Otto's placing me in the same league as Engels and Ermens in Manchester!

Have a drink.

The additional molecules. I've described Otto's beautiful and hedonistic and plausible son. Bearing that in mind, together with the other points I've made, you should now consider the fact that Otto's wife is an ugly woman of working-class origins: the sort, if I may resort to a formula again, whose cardigans have about them that peculiar almost bordello odour of permanent wave fluid. And the second additional molecule is this: persuaded by Else, who was persuaded by Otto's wife (with whom she's on the very best of terms) I some years ago financed Otto in the setting up of a photographic studio the front window of which is now filled with snaps of university graduates, bridal couples, and the like, together with some more 'artistic' representations of fishing boats at Taieri Mouth, corrugated sand dunes on the Pacific coast of the Otago Peninsula, and so forth—evidence, all of them, of the fact that Otto's a competent photographer whose services are in considerable demand. On most Saturdays, for example, he can be seen dressed in a shiny dark suit the obviously worn and careless nature of which gives him a surprisingly rakish air, prancing about in front of a bridal couple by the duck pond in the botanical gardens. And I have to admit he has a talent for making people feel happy: the smiles you see on the faces of the brides and graduates in his studio window are radiant, simple and real. I dare say his 'European manners' and foreign accent lend themselves to his successful formula. He frequently enters prints in photography competitions: these prints are naturally of the fishing boat variety and have never, to my knowledge, rated a second glance by a judge. But his talent with people is unmistakable—particularly, need I say it, with young ladies, with *middle-class* young ladies of the sort that have wedding receptions in full regalia in the botanical gardens or that graduate B.A. from the university, likewise in full regalia.

Well, I think we're now at the point where I can, shall we say, unlock the final casket of the story. The key is Otto's plausible manner. And the contents? A kind of tragic alphabet soup, you might say, atomized fragments of all the points I've made, with a few seasonings. But leaving normal distaste aside, the whole affair isn't without humour. . . .

Have another drink.

Women find Otto irresistible. Why this should be so I can't imagine. He is, as I've said, extremely ugly. So is his wife. She seems to have no objection to Otto's endless amours, in fact she seems to get some kind of obscure pleasure out of them.

My own guess is that Otto's attractiveness has something to do with his mad energy. Of course his foreign accent and all that contribute also. But he's said to be a man of appetite. Not that it's usually put quite like that. His reputation almost depends on it. His hospitality's famous. He loves to cook. In his house some evenings the crush of people's impossible. Flapping his arms, half drunk already, he clears the kitchen and begins to make a stupendous mess. Then, with mocking flourishes, he serves the food. He insists that people eat at table, crammed together if necessary. It's as though he fears the dissipation of intimacy should his congregation take their plates to different parts of the room. He pours wine. His manner becomes bullying, or else drowsily effete. He makes large gestures, as though to embrace the whole table. Or he gazes with moony eyes at a woman. His appetites, his appetites! Rich food, too much of almost everything, a crass celebration which many find endearing. But some in principle only, so they don't come back. There's a latent hysteria in his manner, something beseeching, which is taken to indicate a generous and impatient nature, as are the frequently painful gibes he makes against cautions of various kinds—twisting his goodhumoured weaponry into the guts of this friend who takes life insurance, uttering a contradiction like a belch into the face of that woman whose tastes are delicate and of a mystical hue. The crass, the open, the vulgar, the sentimental: everything, in short, that is customarily 'watered down in the parsimonious stockpots of bourgeois taste'. Such phrases issue emphatically from his smiling lips which seem nonetheless to seize up at moments into a difficult grimace. Good taste and refinement make him cringe. 'Think of the bruised knees of the pitifully hopeful mortals who have dragged themselves and their tragic dreams of immortality up the superb steps of cathedrals.' Such comments he utters almost by rote. We often discuss art. Now, Rubens' portrait of his young wife: that, he'll admit, is superb—the ungainly, lovely, gauche, pampered and fat young woman, painted by an aged husband with obvious simple relish and affection! Indeed Otto seems to long for the unfettered in all things. Like his appetite for company and food (though professing, as he does, infinite scorn for haute cuisine, smacking his lips instead over bean salads and fish, terrines of onion soup with cheese bubbling on the surface, rich stuffed peppers, legs of lamb lashed with rosemary and eaten with quantities of revolting cheap Dalmatian red wine, and so forth)—like his appetite for this sort of thing, his sexual appetite's apparently inexhaustible. Likewise his appetite for action. It's probably this almost unnatural energy that prevents my old friend from becoming as gross physically as he is in his instincts and sympathies. In fact he's malevolently skinny, with glaring blue eyes, a scruffy kind of beard which is largely white these days, and a few strings of long lank blond hair, also laced with grey and white. In fact he looks like one of those proud down-at-heel knights etched by Albrecht Dürer, an artist he professes to admire and, inspired by whom, he's once or twice spoken of assembling a book of photographs, though nothing's ever come of it. He speaks of Dürer's 'social realism' which, he avers, needn't exclude the 'individual imagination', referring no doubt to the allegorical bent of Dürer's genius, rather than of his own. Why he should profess this aesthetic bias, not to mention admiration for Dürer's 'freedom from nationalism', and at the same time continue to take *folklorique* snaps of fishing boats at Taieri Mouth, not to mention of bridal groups and university graduates, is a puzzle, but also a clue. Wouldn't it seem to you that Otto must suffer under the schizophrenic pressures of his work? Don't you think he must feel like a traitor to his tastes and beliefs? Is it possible that his mad energy's compensating for the pain of this contradiction in his life? I offer these suggestions only as such . . . have another drink.

Well, if his plausibility, which I've spent some time describing, is the key to the final casket, I suppose one might say that Otto's failure to follow in Dürer's footsteps (footsteps which seem to me to lead straight to the utterly magnificent and corrupt art of the Italian Renaissance) is the key to what we find in there: the key to the codes of the tragic alphabet soup, as it were.

You see, Otto's savage appetite for women has a peculiar bent to it. I've already intimated something of this. You're familiar with his beliefs, with his 'hangups', with the molecular chain of related points: his beautiful son, ugly wife, artistic failure, and the rest of it. In particular you'll have gathered that Otto's special loathing's reserved entirely for the middle classes, for whatever he sees fit to label as 'bourgeois', and you'll have gathered that this loathing hasn't so much a political basis as a basis in taste: Otto despises the meanness and timidity of middle-class taste—as he sees it, of course. Well, now, in the light of all this, what do you make of the fact that Otto's sexual appetite's aimed without exception at the most exquisite daughters of the middle-classes—is in fact the least dialectical of phenomena, brooks about as much argument as the angry penis of a sailor hurrying from the ship for a one-night-stand! Working-class girls he finds repulsive, without exception. But Otto gets quite beside himself at the races, for example (he takes his camera along), where he may catch sight of an expensive Italian shoe, allow his acetylene eyes to rise the length of a leg, and almost faint at the sudden thought of the scented sweets, subtly laced with irrepressible musk, that must lie within the pantyhose of the poised creature whose Gucci scarf's caressing the jade curve of neck and shoulder . . . it's not hard to imagine, is it? Ha ha. . . . Whereas ordinary girls, like those who might work in the shirt factory, make Otto cringe.

Another drink?

I suppose you'd guess that Otto suffers also under this contradiction in his life, that it's a parallel to his artistic schizophrenia, his failure to emulate Albrecht Dürer. Well, I advanced the possibility as a suggestion only. I'll leave it to you to decide. You see, Otto claims to get an extra 'kick' as he calls it out of the fact that he despises the girls he seduces, and there are, or certainly have been, lots of them. He claims, and I'll quote him, god knows I've heard variations on the wretched phrases often enough, 'there's nothing quite as satisfying as hearing a well-brought-up bourgeois cunt grunt like a sow.'

I'm not wholly convinced by this claim. A certain recent event has, shall we say, disenchanted me even further. It's this event that I've been turning over in my mind . . . you'll excuse me if I help myself without waiting for you. . . . Ha ha, you know I'm reminded of Conrad's story called 'Youth' in which there's the refrain: 'Ah youth . . . pass the bottle. . . .' Yes I must say that sometimes it's as though I've done nothing but loaf about and read and add to my collection and go travelling occasionally, for years now. Bliss and prospects, eh? And in my youth? Well I was no more impetuous then than I am now. I knew what I wanted. I was prepared to wait for it. My tastes haven't really changed, though they have become, I dare say, more refined, a word that drives Otto up the wall.

How's your glass?

Where were we? Yes of course, the 'recent event'.

Listen . . . before we embark on that, I hope you won't object if I indulge in a little fantasy. I think it might put the finishing touches to the background you already have in this whole affair with Otto, which I must say I find myself going into in more detail than I ever intended.

Well, let's 'hop in at the deep end', as sweet Else's therapist once said to her.

I'll just top up.

Now let's try to imagine one of Otto's seductions. Oh my dear fellow, don't look so worried! Put this down to my passion for pure science. A little joke.

Excuse me. Seriously, I can never ignore the fact that Otto's German. An absurd prejudice. He speaks so lightly of his 'fucks' as he calls them, yet I'm convinced that somewhere in the hidden metaphysical depths of his Teutonic heart, he demands some mystical satisfaction from these so-called 'fucks'. Does he get it? He keeps hoping, anyway, dear old Otto . . . aspiring, even. . . .

Rightoh: let's imagine the scene. I see it as having the 'mystical lighting' of German Golden Age cinema. Evening breaks against the western firmament. A lubricious splendour trickles into the streets of the city. She stands, exhaling a peremptory fume of confusion and desire. What is he to do? The odour of her mortality pours into him. 'Tomorrow she could be dead, or I could be.' By this he really means, 'We could be old. We could have missed the beauty.' Inconceivable, impossible, absurd. He senses that her heart, swollen with vacillation, is about to choke her, or her knees are about to give way . . . bending his mouth into her neck. No, she says, no, please, please, my husband, your wife. . . . Breath from his nostril caresses the tender cusp between neck and shoulder. He sees the gooseflesh rise on her pale skin. Her belly moves forward against him, her arms fasten dreamily, convulsively, around his head. With rapt concentration they begin to count together the dark downward steps into a cavern from which issues the distant roar of blood or sea. . . . What is this cavern he descends into? Perhaps it's like the dark brassy interior of her mouth where her tongue shakes like the clapper of a bell.

After this he gets a 'kick' out of despising her. So he says. Something strange about that, seems to me.

I'll just ginger this one up.

So he turned up the other day. He was as crude and abusive as ever. Excuse me. But his hands were shaking. I noticed it because he generally has very good hands. My God, I thought, old Tristan here's getting past it. He told me the following story. He'd got back from his studio the day before he came round to see me. There was a snappy little new Honda at the front of his house. In the back seat was a girl's scarf. He went inside. There were noises from the living room. He didn't have much trouble identifying them. He crouched to look through the keyhole. There was his son with a very beautiful girl. They were naked and 'fucking like dogs' as Otto put it, on the floor. The son's head was thrown back, he was 'barking' and laughing. The girl likewise was playing the game. She was 'whining'. Her tender pale haunches rose into the air. Her forearms were pressed to the carpet. The boy knelt, stabbing. Woof, Woof! Otto knelt by the keyhole. His wife found him there, his eye glued. Normally he'd have thrown the door open and howled with laughter at the embarrassment of the girl. Instead it was his wife's turn to laugh. She called him a 'dirty old bugger'.

That was all Otto told me. He laughed, as usual. But I wasn't convinced. So much laughter. Seemed as though everybody was laughing. But I had a sudden vision of Otto, ugly old Otto the dreamer and enthusiast, whom I, like Friedrich Engels, have really supported all these years, since he's never paid off the loan for the studio—I saw failed old Otto kneeling like a member of the working-classes he loves but finds repulsive, peering through a keyhole into a world of beauty and abandonment, quite out of reach. . . .

Another?

I told him I didn't think he looked well. He said he'd dance on my grave, called me 'a tub of lard'. We sat out there and had a drink. It was a Friday. At knockoff time we watched the ladies come out of the factory. They all had their hair done. Otto was to pick up his wife. We could see her down there, gossiping loudly. She's the forewoman. He left and drove down. From the porch I watched him get out of his car and bow elaborately to the ladies who were standing there. Everyone was laughing, uproariously. Otto was telling jokes. It just wasn't convincing.

Cheers.

Well, what's one to say to Otto? It's the end of the road. I'm really very fond of him. I've treated him more like a son than a brother-in-law. 'You won't give up, will you?' he said to me the other day. 'No more than you,' I replied. Then I just couldn't resist it, I had to add, 'That's historical'. So of course Otto flew into a rage.

One for the road.

'Ah youth . . . pass the bottle,' eh?

It seems to me the time's come to be as straight-forward as possible. Look here, Otto, I'll say, don't despair: after all, we're the same age, you and I, and *I'm* not complaining, not a bit of it.

That's fair enough, wouldn't you agree?

The Letter

Yes, it was for him. He'd guessed it would be. But then he'd guessed that every day for two weeks. He watched his sneakers padding down the long warehouse, shuffling past the old man at the cutting bench, stopping by the telephone. The receiver lay there silent. It was hard to pick it up. He had the impression of acting out a part in a serial.

'There's a letter,' said his wife. The old man was watching him, his scissors gaping like a mouth.

'Where's it from?' he asked, knowing the answer. 'Ah, all right,' he said. 'I'll come home now. Don't open it. I'll kill you. Love. Don't worry. Yes I'm coming now. Just a few more strokes. Ha ha. Okay.'

He took his coat from the cupboard.

'Listen Alfie,' he said to the old man, 'tell Marcus I had to go, will you.'

'Is everything all right,' whispered the old man.

'I don't know,' he said, running out. He was half an hour ahead of time. He leapt past the accountant on the stairs, goosed the security man as he swung out through the front doors of the warehouse, ran past Wesley's green cool churchyard to the Old Street underground. Huh huhuhuh. There was a knot in his stomach. O man. The trains were uncrowded still. He sat with his molars pressed together, smoking a cigarette, in the brassy heat of the carriage. Get Your Happy Now. Fuck it, to be so uptight over such a thing. At the end of the ride he ran up the escalator feeling his bad knee tighten and pop. Coming into the street he was met by the explosions of late summer elms and lindens, by gusts of exhaust, by thick afternoon sunlight. He walked fast through the crowded shopping centre, turned into his street, ran the last few yards. His wife opened the door before he could get his key in. She held the letter in her hands. Her face was pale.

'It went to the neighbours by mistake,' (*O shit*—he held his head in his hands) 'and so didn't get here until this afternoon almost. Are you going to open it?'

'Give it to me.' He looked at the postmark, at the rubber-stamped address on the back. It was the one all right. He shoved the letter into the hip pocket of his jeans. 'I feel I should be dressed for this, I'm gonna get changed,' he said, and went upstairs. He watched himself in the mirror putting on a T-shirt with GREAT BOSTON KITE FESTIVAL 1971 on it, and came back down blowing fanfares through his lips. She put her arms round him.

'Please open it,' she said. 'I've had the thing in the house hours now, I'm going nuts.'

He put his hand on his hip pocket. 'I think I want to be alone.'

'This isn't a joke!' She was very tense. He knew he couldn't open it now, like *this*, domestically, though he wanted to, was sick of the hairy suspense, of the hairy melodrama, of the hairy excuses for whacking out his friends.

'I'm going into the garden,' he said, 'could you leave me alone. Don't worry.' He put the palm of his hand against her face. Her eyes had filled with tears.

'Why such a. . . .' He closed the door on her voice.

*

Outside his small son was engrossed in a game with matchbox trucks at the far end of the narrow overgrown garden. He paused in the game, his face earnest and puzzled, looking at his father home early. He played with the little boy for a few minutes, brrm brrruuummmm, then sent him grumbling inside. He wanted the garden to himself. He pushed into the long grass at the very end, under the blackberry, out of sight of the neighbours. The grass was dusty and hot from the last dry days of summer. Next door some children were playing war, with realistic crumps and burps. He pulled off the T-shirt and lay on his back looking towards the house. Sure enough he heard the kitchen door open, saw his wife come slowly to the corner of the old shed, looking for him. He sat up.

'Go *vek*!' he screeched. 'I've told you already, I wanna be *alone*! Not gonna open this before I'm *alone*!' His stock Lenny Bruce routine. He lit a cigarette and pressed the hot tip against seed pods in the grass. He couldn't feel the letter in his pocket anymore. He decided that he wouldn't open it until his heart had stopped pounding. Strange: the excitement he felt was making him horny. The image of a woman he'd dallied with at a recent party came to him, and he wished vaguely that he was with her now. He felt an obscure need for some kind of ceremony, for something more open-ended than the stifling sense of answers, *solutions*, that the long-awaited letter had brought. Well, here it was, he should be free, they should be free, one way or the other. He turned on his stomach and pulled the envelope out of his pocket. It was already a little crumpled. He held it up by one corner and sniffed it. It smelled faintly of eucalyptus cough drops he'd had in his pocket. The letter inside was typed, he could see that much when he held the envelope up to the light. He could also see that it was brief 'and to the point', no doubt. With each observation he made about the letter it became easier to guess: Dear Sir, We have pleasure/ We regret/ As you may know. Ah, open it, why not open it. He turned on his back and began to flick the letter into the air, batting it like a cat, in the sun. It fell against the long stems of grass, against the blackberry, landing always close to him. Disguised as a Blitzkrieg the children next door were moving in on him. Then he got up and pulled on the T-shirt. He was aware for the first time that summer was passing. Above the shelter of the tangled undergrowth of the garden the early evening was already cooler, the angles of the house were filled with heavy blocks of shadow. He could hear the little boy talking in the kitchen, and his wife's quiet voice. Once or twice they laughed together. He felt suddenly lonely. Only half an hour ago she'd been pale with tension, the little boy had crossly demanded to stay with *him*. He went into the house and minced through the kitchen to the front room, oopeeedoop, hands turned outwards from his hips. His wife followed him.

'What are you doing,' she hissed. 'Do you expect me to go on with these kinds of routines? The child knows there's something up. There'll be a real performance in a moment if you don't open that thing. Why are you so neurotic?'

'Listen,' he said. 'I just can't.'

'Well let me.'

'No no. Look, I just want to get so it doesn't matter before I open it. It's so humiliating to palpitate. Ah, listen, you understand.' He held the letter, somewhat crumpled, against his heart.

'There's no need for all this shit,' she said. He put the letter back in his pocket.

'Yes look, I'm going out for a while,' he said. 'Don't worry,

I'll just have a pint, open it there quietly or something. You two eat, I'll be back soon.'

He doubted it. He knew he wanted to get well away. But he thought to give the pub a try. He was still a stranger there, recognized faces, was seldom spoken to, familiar and foreign. His wife shrugged bitterly, kissed him with an enigmatic sigh. Her lips rested neutrally against his teeth, the expression in her large watchful blue eyes withdrew to a distance where it offered no temptation, no target, no irritant of visible confidence. At least she was more or less used to him. Most other folk didn't believe his comic whims were genuine. He stepped out into a street scored with the long shadows of lamp posts. The sun, growing larger, filled one end of it, burning in the midst of the city's thin halo of gases. He walked away from the sun, after his shadow, the letter pushed into the hip pocket of his jeans, checking his other pockets nervously for cigarettes, matches, money. He passed between the similar disordered facades of rows of houses, sounds of children being fed, murmurs and bursts of music, acetylene flickers of television. He had the impression that the street was longer than before, that he was making no progress. When he found himself by the stale huff of bar air at the corner pub he was surprised for a moment and stood outside on the pavement wondering whether to go in. He realized he hadn't actually intended to. He stepped into the narrow alley at the back of the building. Now, without fuss, zzzt! He took the letter from his pocket and slid his fingernail under the edge of the envelope. He could feel a grin like a dry chap seaming his face.

Then he knew all at once what he wanted to do, getting so it didn't matter, not the woman whose groans had haunted him, memory of the time he'd been freed for an hour, getting so it didn't matter, no not like that but (the line of the song flicking itself through his skull like tickertape) *It's bad . . . That's where Old John / Flogs his daily meat . . . I got messed up around somewhere. . . .* So back on the underground, humming 'He Ain't Give Ya None', smoking another cigarette, feeling better, a decision made, going on a long stifling ride. Get Your Happy Now. I Was An Accountant Until I Discovered Smirnoff. He folded the crumpled letter carefully, put it in his half-empty cigarette packet, put the packet in his T-shirt pocket, and at once forgot about it, the fact of it sailing as cleanly out of his head as he had prayed it would when the time came to go on or turn himself about, when the time came to act upon the letter, when the letter came. He felt suddenly as light as air, and hungry, he who for some weeks now had found anything but bananas nauseating. And so during the interminable ride he smoked one cigarette after the other, shaking them out past the letter but not seeing it. *Don't you ever go down / Down on Curzon Street / It's bad / That's where Old John / Flogs his daily meat. . . .* His reflection in the warped speeding window-glass opposite had a wasted appearance which he found flattering. Singing along.

Hah! He came up out of the ground for the second time that evening, looking around himself with the bright expression of someone expecting to be surprised or welcomed. It was getting dark. Only weeks ago there would still have been two hours of daylight. He was in an untidy roaring part of the city, far from the centre, at a major crossroads where fume-laden gusts of gritty air were whipped up into his face by passing buses and heavy long-distance trucks accelerating through their changing keys of gears into the night and the orange-lit confusion of the motorway ramps. He stopped a moment by a news-stand, getting his bearings. He was cold and wondered why he hadn't brought a jacket. He took out his wallet and checked the money in it: a five pound note and some singles, and more in a fresh pay envelope. Tomorrow was the week-end. Oh well. He turned and went down a wide noisy street past small cafes and junk emporia. At the end of the shopping centre the lights thinned out, the jumble of neon was interspersed with blank house fronts and offices, some of them boarded up and scarred with the tell-tale cosmetic of hand-bills and graffiti: Rod Argent Wedn 11 the Bill Kill the Bill Kill the Bill ent Wednesday 23 July at Bumpers Love Love Love treet Unfit For Children This Street . . . and at the bottom of one such hoarding a Labour Party sticker: You know it makes sense. Certainly, certainly. He padded quickly on. How busy his eyes had become these days.

The last lights in this row belonged to a small fish and chip bar. Fat Jonathan lived above it. He pushed past the cluster of waiting people to the back of the shop, pointing upwards when the Greek owner looked at him. Jonathan took a long time to answer the buzzer, peered through a crack, 'Who is it, whaddaya want, I'm busy man.'

'It's all right, it's me,' he said, butted at the door, went up the dark stairs after Jonathan's immense labouring backside. The flat above the shop was always a surprise to him: kitch velvet drapes, expensive unused leather furniture, potplants, Habitat wall-unit with stereo, tape deck, record and tape racks, television set, and over the windows, rice-paper pasted and painted with pale outlines of women, animals, bits of complicated machinery. Somebody's dream. Jonathan slumped in an armchair four feet from the television screen, the sound as usual off, one arm propped on the edge of the chair so that his hanging fingers reached exactly and without effort into an earthenware cup of chocolate peanuts. His heavy pale hand moved monotonously from the cup to his mouth. His face was blank, bluish with light reflected from the television.

'How are ya man,' said Jonathan. 'Good to see ya, sorry can' help ya jus' now, things is not easy jus' now, I'll ring ya, maybe day aft' tomorrow, got some good shit though.' The fingers dipped and carried.

'Never mind,' he said, looking at Jonathan's hand. The tips of the fingers were moist with milk chocolate. He'd forgotten how Jonathan's voice bugged him. 'I thought I'd come down and talk anyway,' he said, 'or I'd have rung you first.'

'Right,' said Jonathan, blinking at the silent screen. 'That good crystal's hard to get jus' now.'

He took a cigarette from the packet, saw the folded letter. In the flickering silence of the room Jonathan was sucking chocolate.

'Listen,' he said formally, 'would you do me a favour, read this letter for me Jonathan, tell me what it says.' He carefully unfolded the envelope. It was crumpled and had torn down slightly from where he'd begun to open it by the pub. He held it out. 'Do me a favour Jonathan,' he said. He heard the wheedling tone of his voice. His heart was pumping up again. This was so stupid, oh Christ. Jonathan turned his fat neck slowly, reached out, took the letter in chocolate-coated fingers.

'No need for this man,' he said. 'I know ya, lemme have it when you're fixed, I'll ring ya, maybe day aft' tomorrow.' He held the letter back. It was smeared with chocolate.

'No,' he said, trying to hold Jonathan's vague eyes, 'it's a *letter*, I want you to read it Jonathan, open it and read it Jonathan, tell me what it says. Okay?'

'Wha'. . . .' Jonathan's head was like a huge dahlia. It swung back to the bluish screen. 'Nah, look man, I trust ya, I'll ring ya when I score, maybe day aft'. . . .'

He snatched the letter back, stuffed it into his jean's pocket, groped down the stairs in the dark, you pig, you arsehole, ah you fat pig, and out into the lit steam of lard and vinegar, the crowd of thin skinhead girls in short gaberdines, white stockings. One plucked at his T-shirt. 'What does it say?' He turned, her face was pale and vivid, fourteen.

'THE GREAT BOSTON KITE FESTIVAL 1971,' he said.

'You American then?' Her face was framed by others like it. In his pocket his hand grasped the letter. Their faces waited.

'Would you. . . .'

Then he was on the train again. Get Your Happy Now. He jumped to the other side of the compartment. At home his wife was giving the little boy baked beans.

'He wouldn't sleep,' she whispered. 'This is a midnight feast.' He pulled the letter, a crumpled ball, from his pocket. She dropped the spoon.

'You open it,' he said, putting it on the tray of the high chair. The little boy was staring at him with his mouth open, one finger pushing at beans on his tongue. He went into the front room and switched on the television set. He dragged an armchair in front of it and slumped there levering his sneakers off, and lit his last cigarette. *Would you do something* . . . and the girl's childish face freezing with wise anger as he dug in his pocket for the letter, the small galaxy of bright faces around her turning off one by one. A news commentator's face appeared on the screen, mouthing silently beneath immense three-dimensional dollar and sterling symbols. In that animated silence he heard his wife begin to cry in the next room, a wail which skidded up above joy or agony. And as he reached forward and turned up the volume and the television commentator's voice rose suddenly to his working mouth, the little boy wailed too, instinctively, in ignorant sympathy.